Other Books by D

Testimonials

I have read nearly 100 Western novels but I have never read one quite like this before. It is a great story full of suspense, and intrigue. Dan ingeniously takes the five or six subplots and brings them all together into a surprising and shocking conclusion that rivals some of the best Western novels of our time. I also love the creative way Dan mixes fictional characters and a fictional plot with real historical people and places of the Old West. If you enjoy Western novels, this is truly a must read.

  -**Jerry Kachtik**, Consultant to the South Texas Agricultural Industry. Inducted into the Texas Produce Hall of Fame.

Dad grew up in the era of Saturday morning Westerns on T.V. and then he followed his dream and became a rancher and cowboy himself. He took his knowledge of the New Frontier during the 1800's and shaped it into a thrilling and realistic novel that has all the elements you're looking for in a historical fictional Western. Not only will you enjoy the developing plot culminating in a surprising turn of events, but you will also take pleasure in discovering how life really was back in the days of the Old West. A great read!

  -**Dan Burle, Jr.**, Dan Burle Horsemanship Co. and Dan Burle Performance Horses, www.danburle.com

Saddle up and ride. Dan will take you on a historical journey with great characters you can truly believe in. You will really enjoy reading this Western novel.

  -**Mike Menne**, Owner of Electronic Systems Support, Inc.
High Ridge, Missouri
www.essav.com

Three for Hire

Gunslingers on the Santa Fe

Don Burle Jr.
2018

Dan Burle, Sr.

Wasteland Press

www.wastelandpress.net
Shelbyville, KY USA

Three For Hire:
Gunslingers on the Santa Fe
by Dan Burle, Sr.

Second Printing – March 2015
ISBN: 978-1-60047-821-5
Library of Congress Control Number: 2012956394

Printed in the U.S.A.

0   1   2   3   4   5   6   7   8   9   10   11   12   13

Dedication

This book is dedicated to my three wonderful children: Dan, Billy and Lisa. They have brought so much joy to my wife Bernice and me.

Disclaimer

This book is a work of fiction. Names, characters, places and incidents either are the products of the author's imagination or are used fictitiously, and resemblance to actual persons, living or dead, businesses, companies, events or locales is entirely coincidental.

Author's Foreword

When I wrote this Western novel, I wanted to use a combination of real heroes, outlaws and places to portray the legendary American Frontier as it really was. I also wanted it to be an entertaining experience for those who are history buffs and enjoy discovering pieces of information they were never exposed to before.

Even though this book is classified as a Western novel, I would also consider it a historical fiction. Real people, places, and events are combined with fictional characters and a fictional plot to give this novel a realistic feel of what the Old West was all about. This novel portrays the violence of the times that took place out West during the mid-eighteen hundreds when evil ran rampant. However, for every evil deed and person who wandered the Great Plains and the cow towns of Kansas, there were always tenfold the good and righteous who established law, order and decency in the New Frontier which is known today as the Wild West.

Saddle up my friends for a wild ride in the Old West.
Dan Burle, Sr.,
"Keeping the spirit of the Wild West alive"

Fictional Characters

General Schumacher
Colonel Jeffrey
12 U.S. Army soldiers
Mr. Scranton
Billy Daniels
Ray Albers (Scranton's brother-in-law)
Lisa Scranton (Mr. Scranton's wife)

Bret Jackson (engineer)
Timothy Day (asst. engineer)
Shelly, Mandy

Mick Stonehill and his outlaw gang and their family members
Cynthia (Mick's mother)

The Caldwell family from Texas
Father Jose Vasquez
Caldwell's drovers
Doc Flanagan
James Nettle, Johnny Wilson, Bobby Sherwood (all drovers)

The Thomas O'Brien family from Kentucky
Cole and Hank Dempsey
Preacher Walker
The Bannister Family
Dr. Williamson

The Johnson family from Fort Worth, Texas
Todd and Madeline Smith
Martha Shrewsbury
Pops McCarthy
Ed and Joseph, the telegraph operators
Stevie Cain
Patrick Murphy

Note: All other names mentioned in this book are real historical
people.

Table of Contents

PROLOGUE

Unless one experienced it for himself, he could not begin to imagine the realities of life and the struggles for survival on the New Frontier: most accounts painted a *romantic version* of the exploits of the men and women who dared to endeavor to tame what would ultimately become known as the Wild West.

There were a host of reasons that made families pull up their established roots east of the Mississippi River and head west to new settlements and uncivilized perilous territories.

Most came to fulfill their life-long dreams; start up a farm or ranch of their own, to stake out a claim in a gold or silver mining town in order to get rich quick, or to start a new business in one of the many cow towns springing up all around Kansas. Some came just for the experience of the adventure unaware of what they would discover over the next hill, across the grassy terrain of the Great Plains, or the bushy sagebrush fields of the open ranges.

Nobody really knew nor understood the truly unprecedented hardships which they would be facing when they reached their unexplored destinations: such as the scarcity of building supplies to construct their homes, plus shortages of food, water and clothing.

If the settlers weren't struggling with the adverse weather conditions, they were battling Indians who left their reservations, went on the warpath, and raided and killed innocent homesteaders for their food and horses or just because they were "white eyes".

Of course, there were the cattle rustlers, bandits, gunslingers, and the murderers who robbed and killed because evil ran through their veins. They were generally products of broken homes, or Civil War casualties, not so much physically but instead mentally lamed for various unimaginable reasons. Some were even Southern sympathizers and members of secret societies avenging their lost cause. They were all the lowest of the low in the evolution

1

of the new Western society. But even though these outlaws were shamelessly ruthless, there was always an opposing higher level of good ready to take on this lower level scum of the earth. These were the courageous men of the Plains who made it a point to get involved when the cry for help from their neighbors echoed through the towns and prairies of the Old West.

Then there were lawmen ranging from the highest to the lowest on the scale of honest to corrupt. There would be some who would bring the outlaws to justice, and others who would administer justice to the outlaws, on the spot, vigilante style.

Most Easterners were oblivious to all of the trials and tribulations of those who sought out new adventures in the West. The Industrial Revolution was in full swing, housing was far superior to the wood and sod shacks on the prairies and people were moving up the classes with better wages. New technology was being developed everyday which made life more pleasant for the working class. They were more educated, they dressed in the latest styles from Europe, they cultivated the arts and music, and they had more refined tastes than the pioneers of the new territories. Many were desirous of the so called "high society" and for the most part they were law abiding citizens.

In the center of it all were the politicians, many who were generals and high ranking Union officers in the Civil War. Most of them really never experienced combat on the front lines with their brave volunteers who were willing to die for their cause.

Many of the politicians in high offices in Washington, D.C. were true patriots but like most who achieved political power and elite status, they thought they knew what was best for the "common man". They were formal in their conversations and followed the protocol of parliamentary procedures in all political matters.

They also knew how to tame the new western territories and could develop a workable plan to successfully handle absolutely any challenge facing them pertaining to the Wild West.

Or so they mistakenly thought; for it is misjudgment that is often the initiator of disturbing and catastrophic consequences. And so it was in the year of 1879.

CHAPTER ONE:

The Transcontinental Project

On March 5, 1879, President Rutherford B. Hayes (October 4,1822 – January 17, 1893, lived to age 70) (19th President of the United States, 1877 to 1881, and former two-term Governor of Ohio) called a special meeting of five members of his eight-member Cabinet. In attendance were Vice President William A. Wheeler (June 30, 1819 – June 4, 1887, lived to age 67), Secretary of State William M. Evarts (February 6, 1818 – February 28, 1901, lived to age 83), Secretary of Treasury John Sherman (May 10, 1823 – October 22, 1900, lived to age 77), Secretary of War George Washington McCrary (August 29, 1835 – June 23, 1890, lived to age 54), and Secretary of the Interior Carl Schurz (March 2, 1829 – May 14, 1906, lived to age 77).

The agenda of the meeting initially included many subjects, everything from Indian Affairs, foreign policy matters, the economy, to fiscal policies.

Three hours into the meeting, President Hayes commissioned his Secretary of Treasury, John Sherman, whom he had great respect for, to formulate a committee of the persons in the room with the intention of devising a plan to safely ship $1,000,000 of gold bullion in the form of gold bricks from the San Francisco Mint to the Philadelphia Mint. More gold was needed in Philadelphia for coin making and trading to the European countries for goods and services. There were also several countries which had plans to adopt the gold standard and had intentions of procuring their stockpiles from the U.S.

President Hayes knew that his order was to be one of the most challenging assignments John Sherman would ever face in his career because of the potential for dangerous encounters, along the coast to coast route, by the likes of: border raiders, Indians on the warpath, and various notorious outlaw gangs trying to get rich quick. There were even some rumors that Southern sympathizers, even this far removed from the Civil War, were hoarding gold for the future rise of the beliefs of the Southern Confederacy. They were called the Knights of the Golden Circle (KGC). Jesse James (September 5, 1847 – April 3, 1882, lived to age 34) was thought to be a member of this clandestine society. Some believed that this was Jesse's motive for committing so many bank and train robberies.

One thing they all agreed on though was, if they would encounter trouble in-route, it would probably occur west of the

Mississippi River. Because of their naiveté, they also thought that they could outsmart and outthink any one bandit or ruthless gang in the uncivilized West.

John Sherman was President Hayes' most trusted Cabinet member and for good reasons. His devotion to his country was beyond reproach and he was a true patriot. He served in the United States House of Representatives from March 4, 1855 to March 21, 1861. Sherman also served in the U.S. Senate from 1863 to 1877. For the record, after serving as Secretary of Treasury, he returned back to the Senate where he authored The Sherman Anti-Trust Act of 1890 to limit monopolies in the United States. Today it is the oldest of all federal anti-trust laws in the United States. In 1897 President William McKinley appointed Sherman as the Secretary of State.

John Sherman, the son of Justice Charles Robert Sherman (September 26, 1788 – June 24, 1829, lived to age 40) of the Ohio Supreme Court, had two famous older brothers; they were Charles Taylor Sherman (February 3, 1811 – January 1, 1879, lived to age 67), a federal judge in Ohio, and General William Tecumseh Sherman (February 8, 1820 – February 14, 1891, lived to age 71) of both famous and infamous Civil War fame, depending on which side you were on. Some say John resembled his brother, the General, in looks and stature.

There were four United States Mints in the country at this time. The Philadelphia Mint, which was built after the ratification of the Constitution of the United States, was the first. The reason for its location was because at that time Philadelphia was the capital of the United States. The first structure serving as the Mint wasn't much to see but the second building, which began its construction on July 4, 1829 was called the "Grecian Temple" because it was constructed of beautiful white marble with those classic Greek style columns in the front as well as the back of the building. Advanced European style coin making technology was employed in this building.

With the mining of gold during the California Gold Rush (1848 to 1855), the San Francisco Mint was opened in 1854. Because of the volume of gold being mined, a new building was constructed and opened in 1874, which was named "The Granite Lady". It is one of the few buildings, which survived the horrible great San Francisco earthquake of 1906.

This was the U.S. Mint which President Hayes wanted Sherman to ship gold bricks from to Philadelphia.

The other two U.S. Mints used during that time period were:

1) The Denver Mint which opened in 1863 and is now said to be the single largest producer of coins in the world.
2) The Carson City Mint in Carson City, Nevada, which was opened in 1870 to accommodate the silver discovered in the Comstock Lode.

These two U.S. Mints were not relevant to President Hayes' $1,000,000 gold bullion transfer.

When the Cabinet meeting came to an end, President Hayes exited the room. Sherman and the others stayed for another two hours discussing opportunities and challenges regarding their project along with a basic path to an overall plan. Sherman issued assignments to each member present and they set up a date for their next meeting which was to convene at 8:00 a.m. sharp on April 3rd in the Red Room of the White House which was one of the smaller rooms available. It was furnished with a small conference room table which was perfect for their meeting.

By now it was 7:00 p.m. and they agreed as a group to visit the Friar Tuck Steak House for a juicy Texas-cut porterhouse steak and a couple of tankards of ale. Two carriages were waiting outside the White House to carry them three blocks down the street to the well-known steak house. Since they were sworn to secrecy about their new project, they wisely did not discuss it publicly at dinner that evening.

Instead, these Republicans did what most politicians do best, that is to find ways of denouncing and disparaging the opposite party; and so they did, over sizzling hot Texas longhorn steaks, grilled to perfection, and about three mugs each of warm German dark ale imported from Bonn, Germany. From where they sat, they could hear the crackling of the burning hickory logs and feel the warmth from the large stone fireplace, which gratefully took the chill out of the air during this cool March evening. This was a great way to forget about the arduous task awaiting them and just focus on enjoying the camaraderie.

As stated previously, each member of the committee had his assignments and each was to go into great detail about their subject matter at the formal committee meeting. These were the "top-line" tasks as given by Sherman.

Assignments:

Vice President William A. Wheeler
- Identify the railroad lines to use, and then meet with appropriate key railroad executives
- Discuss the train route, stopping points for refueling, related issues, and the exact departure and estimated arrival timetables

Secretary of State William M. Evarts
- Identify diversionary tactics
- Identify workable timetables for each phase of the plan

Secretary of War George Washington McCrary
- Identify in-transit problems that might occur with the Indians, the hostiles as they were often referred to as

Note: The Bureau of Indian Affairs was an agency of the federal government of the United States within the U.S. Department of the Interior. There was a strong movement at that time, supported by General William Tecumseh Sherman, to transfer that agency to the War Department. Secretary of the Interior Carl Schurz opposed that move vehemently. Nevertheless, McCrary was given the assignment regarding Indian interference.

- Identify guards for the gold shipment and who would ultimately be the person in charge of the project on the train

Secretary of the Interior Carl Schurz
- Identify possible outlaw gangs along the designated route who might disrupt the project
- Identify the positives and negatives of hiring the Pinkerton Detective Agency for this project

Secretary of Treasury John Sherman
- Lead the discussion during the April 3rd meeting
- Accumulate the plans from the committee, develop the finished Master Plan and present it to President Hayes for approval

The committee wasted no time. The very next day they all immediately went to work on their individual assignments.

During the weeks between the President's initial meeting and Sherman's first project meeting, a couple of the members met with each other to bounce off "out of the box" ideas. In addition, certain events in-route needed coordination-type planning between members' related responsibilities.

The presidents of three key railroads, whose lines would be part of the route, were immediately summoned to the White House by telegram for a special meeting with the Vice President. (This immediate notification was made possible by the coast-to-coast telegraph, which commenced in October of 1861. The telegraph ended the legendary adventurous 1-1/2 years of the Pony Express.)

The San Francisco and Philadelphia Mints were not notified of the plan as of yet.

The objective at this time was to keep the planning loop small and on a need to know basis. For this event to take place without a hitch, it was imperative that "secrecy" remain the "number one priority".

It took the committee members approximately one month to complete their research for the meeting. It was now April 3rd, a beautiful spring morning in Washington, D.C. The wild plum and cherry trees were in full bloom and wildflowers were showing off their brilliant colors along the countryside.

The chef of the White House and his staff arrived at 5:00 a.m. and began preparing a European style "continental" breakfast for the meeting participants. The roasted Columbian coffee beans were ground and Kolaches (a Bohemian pastry consisting of fillings ranging from fruits to cheeses commonly served at breakfast) were prepared and baked. The aroma of the freshly baked sweet goods and freshly made coffee filled the halls of the White House and seemed to put everyone in a pleasant frame of mind.

The horse carriages transporting the Cabinet members began arriving at 7:00 a.m. First to arrive was John Sherman, followed by the rest of the members. Last to arrive were the three railroad presidents. These three distinguished gentlemen arrived in the same carriage since they were lodging in the same hotel. Vice President Wheeler insisted to Sherman that the railroad presidents attend this meeting since the railroad would play a major role in the planning and execution of the project. Sherman concurred.

At 7:45 a.m. the doors of the Red Room were opened and the members were allowed to enter. The conference room was set up with a rectangular shape table and eight chairs, five for the Cabinet members and three for the railroad presidents. There was a name at each place for assigned seating. Sherman's seat was located at one end of the table and the Vice President's was at the other end. The three cabinet members were designated to sit on the left side of Sherman while the three railroad presidents were to sit on the right side.

There was a small table located by the door inside the room with coffee, hot water for tea, and freshly baked pastries.

Before consuming the pastries and coffee, Vice President Wheeler introduced the three railroad presidents to everyone. Then they sat down in their assigned seats and the White House kitchen staff began serving.

After everyone had finished breakfast, the staff went around the room and collected the dishes and utensils, refilled coffee cups around the table and subsequently exited the room.

Then there was silence.

Sherman quietly stood up, walked over to the double doors, closed and locked them with the sliding bolt lock. At this point, you could hear a proverbial pin drop in the room. Sherman walked back to his seat, sat down, and the meeting commenced.

"Good morning gentlemen and thank you for your prompt attendance this fine April morning. I welcome all of you to this very important meeting. I especially want to thank the railroad presidents for coming to Washington, D.C. and attending today. Vice President Wheeler insisted that your attendance was vital to the planning and success of this project. After great thought, I agreed whole-heartedly.

It is appropriate at this time to inform you that when I met with President Hayes last Thursday, we decided to name this project *Operation Last Spike*; for it was the last golden spike, hammered in on May 10, 1869 at Promontory Summit, Utah which connected the East to the West by rail that has made this transcontinental project possible."

This statement brought smiles to the faces of the railroad presidents and seemed to relieve some of the tensions they were experiencing in this very formal setting. In fact, one of the railroad presidents in the room was actually in attendance on that historical day in Utah and even participated in the ceremony. However, he decided to remain quiet on the subject for personal reasons which he would eventually divulge later that year.

Sherman continued, "Well then gentlemen, let's begin. We all know the task at hand. President Hayes has ordered us to develop a plan, which will successfully transport $1,000,000 of gold bullion in the form of 25-pound bricks from our U.S. Mint in San Francisco to the U.S. Mint in Philadelphia. Our task is to complete this plan today, no matter how long it takes, and then I will present it to President Hayes on the afternoon of May 4th.

Each one of you had your assignments and I have been informed by each of you in private that you have completed them to the fullest extent possible. I thank you for your efforts. However, be that as it may gentlemen, there will most likely be many questions regarding the accumulated facts and proposed suggestions today, along with some friendly arguments on various relevant subject matters as we formulate this unprecedented plan.

In front of you is the meeting agenda. I'll give you a few minutes to look it over."

This was the agenda. It was simple, to the point, and had strict timetables.

8:30 a.m. to 9:30 a.m. Secretary of the Interior Carl Schurz

9:30 a.m. to 10:30 a.m. Secretary of War George Washington McCrary

10:30 a.m. to 10:45 a.m. Break

10:45 a.m. to 11:45 a.m. Vice President William Wheeler

Noon to 1:00 p.m. Lunch

1:00 p.m. to 2:00 p.m. Secretary of State William M. Evarts

2:00 p.m. to 4:30 p.m. Discussions

5:00 p.m. Dinner in the White House Garden

"Are there any questions?"

As Sherman looked around the table, everyone remained silent.

"Very well then, let's begin with Secretary of the Interior Carl Schurz. I chose you to be first on the agenda because we must initially discuss some of the "real" potential challenges we will most likely be facing, on our transcontinental route, which could seriously jeopardize the success of our mission. Your information could possibly identify the essential building blocks for our strategy."

Secretary Carl Schurz began his presentation.

"Thank you Mr. Secretary. Gentlemen, my assignment from Secretary Sherman was two-fold:

1. Identify possible outlaw gangs along the designated route who might disrupt the project and
2. Identify the positives and negatives of hiring the Pinkerton Detective Agency for this project.

I will begin with identifying possible outlaws or outlaw gangs that we might confront along the way. As a former United States Senator from Missouri, I feel I have excellent knowledge about the subject I am about to speak upon.

There is an outlaw whose infamous name has echoed across our great nation from the western shores of California to the eastern banks of South Carolina, and from the Great Plains of Montana to the brush country of southern Texas. Gentlemen, I'm speaking of a man named Jesse James. Just the mere mention of his name "strikes fear" into railroad companies and bank executives across the nation. This man is a ruthless outlaw, the gang leader of one of the most feared gangs in the Midwest, a bank robber, stagecoach robber, a train robber and a cold-blooded killer. He is a Southern sympathizer who was born in Clay County, Missouri, which was known as "Little Dixie" because it was the center of migration from the Upper South. Slaves there constituted 25% of its population.

We know that Jesse's brother Frank rode with Quantrill's Raiders, a pro-Confederate group, and later Jesse and Frank both rode with Bloody Bill Anderson (1839 – October 26, 1864, lived to age 24/25). Some of you may not know much about Bloody Bill

Anderson, a Confederate guerrilla fighter who terrorized the Kansas and Missouri area. You may also be unfamiliar with the Centralia, Missouri Massacre. Allow me to give you a brief history. Bloody Bill Anderson also rode with Quantrill but left the group while in Texas and returned to Missouri as the leader of a group of vicious guerrillas who targeted our Union loyalists and Federal soldiers. In September of 1864 his group captured a train in Centralia, Missouri and killed 22 of our brave Union soldiers who were on that train. Later that same day, his guerrillas killed over 200 of our soldiers in a cowardly ambush."

Schurz, (a former Brigadier General of Union volunteers, and a commander of a division at the Second Battle of Bull Run, Gettysburg and Chattanooga) then stood up, began to raise his voice, while his face turned red in anger as he continued,

"These guerrilla savages killed soldiers who tried to surrender, and they even scalped and dismembered some of the dead. Gentlemen, the Clay County marshal reported that both Frank and Jesse James took part in that massacre. In fact, Frank later stated that it was his brother Jesse who fatally shot Major Johnson who led those Union troops."

As he pounded on the table with his fist, he warned, "Gentlemen, these are the types of killers we could be dealing with."

At this point, Schurz sat down, took a deep breath, calmed himself down, apologized to the group for his uncontrollable outburst and then continued,

"Later, the James brothers joined with the Youngers; Cole, John, Jim and Bob and other Confederates to form the infamous James-Younger Gang. Jesse became the gang's leader.

On July 21, 1873, they committed the first of their many train robberies, derailing; yes I said derailing the Rock Island train in Adair, Iowa. They made off with $3,000."

It was here that Sherman stopped Schurz and said,

"We are all aware that during and after the Civil War, the James-Younger Gang wreaked havoc in Kansas, Missouri and other states robbing both trains and banks. However, didn't I read where Jesse's gang was captured in Northfield, Minnesota in a botched robbery attempt of the First National Bank of Northfield three years ago in September of '76? And if that is true, why would Jesse James be a problem for *Operation Last Spike*?"

"Great question Mr. Secretary," Schurz acknowledged.

"Yes sir, that's partially true. The Youngers were captured but Jesse and Frank escaped.

The James boys went into hiding to regroup after the Northfield Raid. Our intelligence has informed me that Jesse has recently formed a new gang in western Missouri and could be planning to rob trains once again. This gentlemen, is definitely pertinent information to *Operation Last Spike*. Don't you agree?"

Everyone in the room wholeheartedly concurred. The railroad men in the room became very concerned. You could see the worried looks on their faces as they glanced at each other.

Little did the group know that Schurz's acquired intelligence about Jesse's plan was indeed, 100% accurate. On October 8, 1879, Jesse and his gang held up a train in Glendale, Missouri and began another unprecedented crime spree, which included two more train robberies.

For the record, on April 3, 1882, Jesse James was shot in the back of his head by one of his live-in gang members, Bob Ford, in St. Joseph, Missouri. As Jesse was preparing to go on another job of crime, he walked over to a picture hanging on the wall in his house (he was unarmed at the time), to straighten it or dust it off. That's when the cowardly Bob Ford pulled the trigger of his 6-shooter and ended the life of one of the most legendary criminals of the Old West.

Jesse was posing as Thomas Howard at the time but was positively identified as a result of his previous bullet wounds and his partially missing middle finger.

On June 8, 1892, Edward O'Kelly assassinated Bob Ford in a tent saloon, which Ford operated in Creede, Colorado. It is said that O'Kelly walked into the saloon toting a double barrel 10-gauge shotgun and said "Hello, Bob", then pulled the trigger and blasted Ford in the throat with buckshot, killing him instantly.

"Do tell," Wheeler asked, "What became of Bloody Bill Anderson? I hope he is not still around."

"No Mr. Vice President, that psychopathic madman was killed by Union Militia one month after the Centralia Massacre."

"Thank God for that," the Vice President replied.

"Well Schurz, your time is about up. Is there anyone else or any other gang whom we should be concerned about?"

"Sir, there are numerous outlaws who roam the area we will travel but none of the caliber of Jesse James as it relates to holding up trains. However, there is a young teenager in Rock Springs, Wyoming named Robert Leroy Parker, whom my sources say admires Jesse James and is fascinated with trains. He fell in with a horse thief and cattle rustler named Mike Cassidy. In fact, this kid admired Mike Cassidy so much, he changed his own surname to Cassidy and he's acquired a new first name."

"What is it?" inquired Sherman.

"Butch."

"How old did you say this Butch Cassidy is?"

"He's just a young teenager."

"Well then, let's just move on. It sounds like there is nothing to worry about here. Maybe by the time he grows up, he'll go straight."

Everyone sort of chuckled in unison and then went on with the meeting.

Schurz began again,

"My second assignment was to identify and discuss the positives and negatives of getting the Pinkerton Detective Agency involved. For the sake of brevity gentlemen, let me get right to the point. My recommendation is that we keep them out of it completely for several reasons.

1. They botched the investigations and attempted arrests of the James-Younger Gang.
2. Recently, they have had quite a turnover of detectives, which makes me question their effectiveness.
3. Getting them involved could jeopardize the secrecy of our operation.

I highly suggest that we involve our own highly trained federal soldiers to escort our shipment of gold on the train."

"Point duly noted. Can everyone agree on that point?" Sherman asked.

It was an affirmative by everyone in the room.

"So be it. Thank you for your research and contribution to this project Secretary Schurz. You have given us much to consider and you were right on time with your presentation as well. Now let's move on to the Secretary of War George Washington

McCrary. Mr. McCrary, I am sure you have much to present to us in regards to potential Native American issues, so please begin."

"Thank you sir and good morning gentlemen. Last week I talked with Vice President Wheeler after he met with these gentlemen from the railroads. We discussed the possible route which the train would be taking to Philadelphia.

Based on this information, I perceive that there are most likely five states that are in play as it relates to the hostiles. They are Nevada, Idaho, Utah, Wyoming, and Colorado.

First though, at the risk of being misconstrued about my feelings about the hostiles as I proceed through my presentation, I deem it appropriate to quote the great General Philip H. Sheridan.

We took away their country and their means of support, broke up their mode of living, their habits of life, introduced disease and decay among them and it was for this and against this they made war. Could anyone expect less?"

A soberness hung over the room like a thick dark cloud as McCrary paused for a moment to let this quote sink in. McCrary didn't have a bigoted bone in his body but he knew that the facts he intended to present could stir up negative emotions toward the Native Americans.

"Gentlemen," he continued, "I am in the process of accumulating facts about Indian Wars out West for my Annual Report to President Hayes. In it I will conclude that we lost many federal soldiers in Indian battles because we just did not have enough men on the battlefields. I will be requesting more troops to head west. We also lost great leaders like General Canby and Lieutenant Colonel George Armstrong Custer for the same reason."

Later that year he would be adding Major Thomas T. Thornburgh to the list of lost great leaders in his Annual Report, which was published in the New York Times on November 24, 1879.

McCrary continued, "Let me give you some history of the savagery we were facing. General Canby was the only general killed in the Indian Wars. On April 11, 1873, Canby was shot twice in the head and had his throat slashed by the Modoc chief with the help of one of the chief's lieutenants at a peace parley in the Northwest. General Canby was unarmed.

In 1876 Custer had orders to force Sitting Bull and his band back onto the reservation or destroy the Lakota Sioux if they refused. The 7th Cavalry was more concerned about the Indians escaping and how they would capture them than about the great number of warriors they were about to face. This would be their downfall.

Custer and his men were literally massacred in the Battle of the Little Bighorn in western Montana on June 25, 1876. That's just 2-½ years ago. It was mostly the Lakotas and Northern Cheyenne with just a few Arapahos who fought against Custer and the 7th Cavalry. It was a two-day battle, which will never be forgotten. We lost 268 men. They were hugely outnumbered and to make things worse, many of the hostiles were armed with repeating Winchesters, Spencers, and Henry rifles while the 7th Cavalry carried single-shot Springfield Model 1873 carbines. Gentlemen, our men didn't have a chance.

While Custer and his troops were being slaughtered by Chief Gall, Crazy Horse, Sitting Bull and their warriors about 2,000 strong, ironically our first official World's Fair was being celebrated in Philadelphia, Pennsylvania between May 10th and November 10th (It was officially known as the International Exhibition of Arts, Manufactures and Products of the Soil and Mine). It commemorated the 100th anniversary of the signing of the Declaration of Independence. Twenty percent of the United States population attended the fair. They were totally oblivious to the horrid battles between the Sioux and the United States Army going on at the same time.

Custer also had several relatives killed in the same battle. They were two of his brothers (Boston and Thomas), a nephew (Henry Reed) and a brother-in-law (James Calhoun)."

At this point Sherman stopped McCrary and asked,

"What about now, are Crazy Horse, Sitting Bull and Gall potential problems to us and our operation?"

"No sir, after the Battle of the Little Bighorn, the Sioux and the Cheyenne packed up and fled fearing major retaliation from us. In May of 1877, Sitting Bull escaped to Canada. Later Crazy Horse surrendered. He was later killed on September 5th trying to escape.

We believe Chief Gall and Sitting Bull are both hiding out in Wood Mountain, Saskatchewan."

And so they were.

"Gentlemen, The Great Sioux Wars of 1876, which were a series of battles in the Montana, Dakota, and Wyoming Territories, actually occurred between 1876 and 1877. They were due to Indians leaving the reservations to go back to their original lands and/or seeking out food for survival. It was our migration west, us destroying their food source, and us moving them off their own land, which caused the problems we had and still continue to have with the Native Americans whom we now refer to as hostiles.

The Sioux Wars are over and the Apaches are too far to the southwest to worry about. However, there are still Indians on reservations who are starving and causing havoc as they become angry at the way they are treated and forced to live. Many are still breaking out of reservations.

There is one area we need to be concerned about as it relates to our operation. A storm is brewing with the White River Utes in White River, Colorado, which is located in northwestern Colorado."

McCrary was so concerned about the timing of the uprising, that he had prepared a map to show the group the exact location. He had it rolled up and placed on the table during the meeting. It was tied with a piece of thin leather. As he talked about the uprising, he unrolled the map and spread it out onto the table for everyone to see. They all stood up as he pointed to the location of the Indian reservation where the White River Utes were located.

"There is an Indian agent living right here whose name is Nathan C. Meeker. He has requested military assistance because he fears an uprising by the White River Utes.

We are dispatching Major Thomas T. Thornburgh and about 150 troops and a few militiamen to the scene."

"What is the cause for this alarm?" Sherman asked.

"Sir, Meeker is attempting to convert these Ute Indians to a European style culture introducing Christianity and agriculture. The Utes have no desire to change. In addition, the Utes are upset at the way the settlers are plowing up their grazing land and horse racetracks. Once again it's us pushing our lifestyles on the Native Americans. I fear that war may break out right about the time our gold shipment is passing through Colorado."

Just then, one of the railroad men asked to speak,

"What is even more precarious is the fact that our train will be stopping just one to two miles from the Ute's reservation for water and wood for the steam engine."

McCrary showed great concern on his face, as did everyone else in the room.

McCrary was indeed correct about war breaking out that year. It would become known as the White River War.

The White River War consisted of the Battle of Milk Creek and the Meeker Massacre and it commenced on September 29, 1879 when Major Thornburgh advanced his troops across Milk Creek into the reservation. The Utes were waiting on high ground to defend their land contemplating that peace talks would not materialize. A shot rang out and the battle began. Even though the Army outnumbered the Utes, the Indians were able to inflict significant troop losses. It was there that Major Thornburgh was killed. The fight became known as the Battle of Milk Creek.

While this encounter was taking place, a separate band of Utes raided the Indian Agency and killed Nathan Meeker and ten of his employees. This slaughter became known as the Meeker Massacre.

Meanwhile, the Battle of Milk Creek lasted six days until reinforcements arrived. The first to arrive were Captain Frances Dodge and his Buffalo Soldiers from Fort Lewis in southern Colorado. They arrived on the third day of the battle. Then Colonel Wesley Merritt with about 450 troops rode in and the Utes subsequently retreated.

Eventually, the Utes were moved to a new reservation in Utah, which opened up millions of acres of new settlements for Midwesterners and Easterners.

McCrary continued,

"There have recently been uprisings of the Shoshones, Bannocks and Paiutes but they are outside of our operation's proposed train route. I don't foresee problems with hostiles in Kansas, Missouri or east of the Mississippi River either.

I will conclude this part of my presentation here by asking if there are any questions."

Sherman immediately inquired, "If I understand you correctly Secretary McCrary, when our train arrives in northwestern Colorado, we should be extra vigilant."

"Yes sir, that is correct."

"Very well then, I will make note of that. Continue please."

"The second part of my assignment was to identify guards for the gold shipment and who would ultimately be in charge of the project on the train.

I am recommending that the U.S. Army guard the shipment. I believe about twelve men along with a commanding officer will suffice as long as we are able to keep this shipment top secret.

I am also suggesting that Colonel John J. Jeffrey command this operation from the very beginning and on the train while in route. He is a decorated Civil War hero and fought at Bull Run, Gettysburg, Shiloh, and Vicksburg. He was seriously wounded three times but always recovered and headed back to the battlefields. He is a man of determination and honor.

He is also an Indian fighter. He fought against the Sioux with Colonel Miles and the 5th Infantry in the fall of 1876 in what is now known as the Miles Campaign. In 1877 he fought the Sioux at the Battle of Wolf Mountain. This soldier is a proven fighter and never shows fear at the sight of the enemy no matter who it may be. I believe he is the perfect man for this job. He is currently stationed in California, which is perfect."

Sherman then asked this question, "Who should we select as the other twelve soldiers for the job?"

"Sir, I believe we should select men who are not acquainted with each other or with Jeffrey. There are several regiments stationed in California and we can acquire recommendations from commanding officers at those posts."

Sherman responded, "Sounds like a great idea. Proceed then with that plan. However, I must remind you that neither the twelve chosen men nor their commanding officers should be made aware of *Operation Last Spike*. For the time being they should only be aware that they will be involved in a top secret operation. They will be told the exact details at the right time which will be at my discretion.

Is there anything else you have for the group?" Sherman asked.

"No sir."

"Well then, let's take a 15 minute break."

Sherman opened the doors and asked the White House staff to bring in a tray of fruits and cheeses which had been prepared for the break. The staff also refilled the coffee urns with freshly made Columbian coffee. Hot water was also brought in for tea.

A couple of the gentlemen lit up Cuban cigars in the hallway even though it was still morning.

At 10:45 a.m., Secretary Sherman asked the group to return to the meeting room. Everyone filled up their coffee and teacups before sitting down while Sherman closed the double doors and again bolted them shut as the formal meeting commenced once again.

Sherman then spoke, "Gentlemen we are making very good progress but we still have a lot of work in front of us so let's get right to it. Vice President Wheeler, I believe you are up."

"Thank you, sir. My assignment was to identify the railroad lines to use and then meet with the appropriate people. Secondly, I am to discuss the routes, stopping points for refueling, related issues and exact departure and estimated arrival timetables.

In the room with us today are three railroad executives representing the three main lines we will use for this operation. We have met previous to this meeting and have outlined our route. Since we are beginning the route in San Francisco, we will use the Central Pacific line, then transfer to the newly installed Santa Fe tracks to Dodge City and then on to Kansas City, Missouri where we will pick up the Union Pacific line. From then on it's…"

Just then, Sherman stopped the Vice President in his tracks and asked in disbelief, "Why are we stopping in Dodge City? That's not along the straight route."

"Sir, it's part of the plan Secretary of State Evarts and I developed to serve as a diversionary tactic. I don't want to steal Evarts' thunder but we felt it necessary to make this train appear as if it were a normal passenger/cattle train for the purpose of averting suspicion or attracting undue attention."

Sherman looked straight into Wheeler's eyes for what seemed to be a long minute without saying a word as the room became very silent. Sherman thought about it for a few more seconds and then conceded that it was a creative idea.

Sherman then inquired of Wheeler, "Tell me more about the train."

"Sir, it will be a 15-car train consisting of the engine, the wood/fuel car, two passenger cars, one freight car, one mail/payroll car, eight cattle cars, and a caboose.

I would like to let Evarts explain the significance of each during his presentation.

The Santa Fe Railroad and The Central Pacific are building a connecting line to Dodge City because of the cattle boom there. This will allow a good flow of hauls and backhauls from east to west through Dodge City. The connection will be completed in mid-May. Gentlemen, this timing couldn't be any better."

Pointing to locations on a map of the United States which he had placed on an easel, Vice President Wheeler took another twenty minutes explaining the rest of the route all the way to Philadelphia. He estimated the trip to be about 3,000 miles and that it would take approximately 75 hours running time at 40 miles per hour. Then it would be necessary to add in all of the stops for refueling, passenger transfers, the cattle pickup and the dropping off point at the Chicago stockyard. With all of that added together, he estimated another 115 hours. So the total trip would take about 190 hours or about 8 to 9 days.

At this point the Vice President completed his presentation and the group then broke for lunch. Since it was still a little cool outside, the committee was escorted to another room in the White House, which was set up specifically for their lunch.

The chef had prepared a hearty meal for the committee members; roast beef, boiled new red potatoes with beef gravy, carrots, greens and corn bread. The beverage served was lemonade. There's a great story about lemonade in the Hayes' White House. In fact, it was Vice President Wheeler who told the story at lunch.

"President Hayes and his wife Lucy now have a 'no-alcohol' policy in the White House. It seemed that too much wine was served during the first White House party and many of the guests became inebriated. It was extremely embarrassing for the First Lady and the President. Lucy asked the President to never serve alcohol again at White House functions. President Hayes agreed with the request and from then on Lucy Hayes was known as Lemonade Lucy."

This story got quite a chuckle from the railroad men and even though most of the Cabinet members already heard the story, they were still quite amused.

There were many other topics brought up at lunch that afternoon including the most important source of food and clothing for the Native Americans, which dates back several thousand years, i.e. the bison. The president of the Santa Fe Railroad was well informed about the Native Americans and their usage of the bison for meat and other essentials for survival on the Plains. So he decided to offer up his knowledge about the subject.

"The great buffalo herd was split in half when the railroad divided the Great Plains. The railroad brought many hunters who hunted the buffalo for their hides or just for sport. Consequently, the great buffalo herd numbers are way down. It's well known that the Indians relied on the buffalos for their survival. Buffalos provided meat, clothing, leather, grease, dried dung for fire starters, and more. The Indians also made pemmican, similar to jerky, out of the tougher meats of the buffalos, which could be taken as food on hunting trips or search parties.

I was always impressed with the way the natives captured buffalos before they had horses. They would actually create stampedes by various means and drive them off of cliffs. If the cliffs weren't too high, the fall would just break the animals' legs making for an easy kill. Later, when the natives acquired horses, they could easily lance or shoot the buffalos. If you wonder why some Indians would rather live on reservations now, it's because of the depletion of the great buffalo herd."

"Not to change the subject," Sherman said, "but did any of you railroad men get to go to Philadelphia for the World's Fair?"

None of the railroad men replied in the affirmative.

"Well, I did and I was impressed with some of the new consumer products that were introduced there."

"Give us some examples," Schurz requested.

"Well, Alexander Graham Bell's telephone was displayed there. In fact, President Hayes is the first President to install a phone in the White House. His telephone number is "1". The problem is he can't use it much because hardly anybody else has a telephone in Washington, D.C."

They all laughed at that.

"What else did you see at the fair?" the Vice President asked.

"Some of the other things introduced there were Heinz Ketchup, a condiment made from tomatoes I suppose, Hires Root Beer, a soft drink, Remington's typographic machine, they called it a typewriter, and a plant from Japan and China called Kudzu used for erosion control amongst other things."

By now it was time to end the informal lunch and small talk and get back to serious work. So the committee members convened back into the Red Room for the afternoon session. It was now Secretary of State William M. Evarts' turn to speak. His assignment was to identify diversionary tactics and to identify workable timetables for each phase of the plan.

"Gentlemen, I have been giving a lot of thought to the plan I am about to present to you. I have met with several of you prior to this meeting in order that I might be able to effectively formulate a strategically workable plan which would aid in moving this gold shipment from the west coast to the east coast, safely and without a hitch.

Let's start once again with the types of cars we want on the train as was mentioned earlier. This is where we need the help from the president of the Central Pacific Railroad. Here is how we would need to set up the train: the engine, the fuel car, two passenger cars, the freight car, the mail/payroll car, eight cattle cars and the caboose. The more normal the setup of the train appears to the public, the better our chances are that we will have a safe and successful journey.

Each passenger car can accommodate about fifty people. However, we will need to save seven seats for soldiers. Six will sit in the last rows of the second passenger car next to the freight car and pretend to be traveling home to the East. One will sit in the first passenger car."

Then Secretary of State Evarts added a little levity.

"By the way, I believe that the passengers will thank us for putting the smelly old cattle cars at the rear of the train behind them. What do you think?"

The assertion and rhetorical question drew a measured laugh from the group but the tone of the meeting continued to be very serious and formal.

Evarts continued, "The mail/payroll car will carry just that; the mail, payroll, cash, bonds, etc. in the train's safe. There will be one soldier stationed there."

"Where will the gold bars be stored?" Sherman asked.

"In the freight car," Evarts replied. "Let me explain. My plan is to box the gold bars in wooden crates. There will be 6 bars per crate. Each bar weighs about 25 pounds. Therefore, each crate will net weigh about 150 pounds. Add another 5 pounds for the crate and you'll have a total weight of 155 pounds. Let's say the price of gold is about $18.00 per ounce. That equates to about $288 per pound. If my calculations are correct and I'm sure they are,

$1,000,000 in gold will weigh about 3,472 pounds. Figuring 6 bars per case at 150 pounds net weight, we will be shipping roughly 25 cases of gold on this train, give or take one or two crates.

Each crate will be labeled 'Ranch Supplies'. This is the only cargo which will be shipped on this train and in the freight car. Three soldiers will be locked in from the inside of the freight car with the gold. They will be the colonel in charge of the operation and two of his men. We will also station two soldiers in the caboose and one in the mail/payroll car. The final soldier will be stationed in the first row aisle seat of the first passenger car, which will be behind the fuel car. He will be the first one available to help the engineers in case of trouble."

Sherman then requested, "Secretary Evarts, please recap for me and the committee once again, for the sake of clarity, where the soldiers will be stationed on the train."

"Yes sir," Evarts responded. "Here is how I perceive it.

- 1 soldier will be positioned in the front row (aisle seat) of the first passenger car, which will come right after the fuel car.
- 6 soldiers will be seated in the back seats of the second passenger car, three on each side of the aisle. This car is right in front of the freight car.
- The colonel in charge plus 2 of his troops will be stationed in the freight car with the gold shipment. They will be locked in from the inside.
- There will be 1 soldier in the mail/payroll car.
- And lastly, there will be 2 soldiers in the caboose.

This will give us excellent coverage across the entire train."

The committee seemed to agree with the plan so far.

Sherman then asked, "Where will we load the gold into the crates and how will we get it to the train depot?"

Without hesitation, Evarts quickly responded. It was obvious that he was on his game with a well thought out plan.

"Sir, it is important that we follow a path of normalcy. Here's my plan:

- A soldier in civilian clothes will order the wood crates from a box manufacturer in San Francisco. The crates will be labeled 'Ranch Supplies'. It will take the manufacturer about one week to make the 25 crates.

- Another soldier in civilian clothes will then pick up the crates in a wagon, cover the boxes with a canvas and during the night, deliver the crates to the San Francisco Mint. The guard on duty will be aware of the project.
- The soldiers who will eventually be on the train will box the gold into the crates and haul it during the night in two wagons to Scranton's General Store and Ranch Supplies where it will secretly be unloaded in the back of the store. Obviously, Scranton will need to be part of the plan and he will be made aware of the contents of the shipment. We can trust him because he is a retired decorated soldier who fought for the North during the Civil War and fought against the Apaches in New Mexico with the U.S. Cavalry. He received high honors for his patriotism and heroic acts and dedication to his duty. Also, we have used him for other clandestine projects before.
- Soldiers in civilian clothes, in full view of everyone, will reload the crates onto the wagons, the next morning. The soldiers we select will have to be of good size and very strong to be able to lift those crates.
- They will then drive the wagons to the train depot and load the cargo onto the freight car.

After the men load the cargo, they will quietly and secretly move to the caboose, change into their uniforms and take their positions on the train. I don't remember if we discussed this before but the railroad will not have a person stationed in the mail/payroll car. There will just be one of our soldiers. He will pick up and drop off the mail at the various stops.

Everything I detailed at the loading point will happen two hours before the passengers board the train, which will be at 11:00 a.m.

Just for the record, the train we use will arrive the evening before like all trains do and stay in place until departure, which will be at 11:15 a.m.

We will begin loading the gold at about 9:15 a.m. and should be done by 9:45 a.m.

Incidentally, the engineers and the conductor should not be made aware of the contents of the crates."

Sherman then spoke, "This is indeed a well thought out plan and I believe, if executed properly, it should ensure the secrecy of the gold shipment which will mean we can expect to have a successful operation. I am impressed, please continue."

The next thing that Evarts did was to point out on a map the route and the stopping off points for passengers along with the fuel (wood) and water stops for the steam engine.

Four stops were of interest and created some anxiety amongst the committee members. The railroad men showed the greatest concern. Those stops were; the one near The White River Indian Agency in Colorado where the Ute Indians were close to going on the warpath, the fuel and water stop one mile prior to arriving in Dodge City, the stop in Dodge City for the cattle, and the stop near the Kansas/ Missouri border where the James Gang was said to be regrouping.

Sherman then commented and raised a question, "I am personally most concerned about the Kansas/Missouri border with the James Gang. They have a long history of holding up trains and I suspect they will continue their criminal ways. I believe this is where we need to be the most vigilant. The question I have though is, how far is our stop from the Utes and The White River Indian Agency?"

"We will be refueling about two miles from there, sir," Evarts replied.

"Will Thornburgh and his troops be in the area at that time?" Sherman asked.

"Yes sir, they will," Evarts responded.

"Well, that gives me some relief," Sherman said with a sigh. "What about the stop off for refueling before Dodge City and the stop in Dodge City itself? Can you assure us of getting through those areas without incident?"

"Obviously, I can't guarantee it but I think the steps are in place that will ensure us a high degree of safety," Evarts responded. "The thirteen soldiers on the train should adequately protect our cargo at all of the stops.

Dodge City itself should be safe because they have a few notoriously famous lawmen there, James Masterson, and James and Wyatt Earp. These three men have really tamed Dodge City and it is now a more civilized town from what it was just a few years ago."

What Evarts didn't know at that time was that the Earp brothers had plans to leave Dodge City that year because they had no interest in that town anymore and they both were searching out a new life and a new adventure.

Sherman then once again reiterated his concern about the James Gang but Evarts reassured him that the soldiers stationed at various locations on the train would be able to adequately defend the gold shipment against Jesse's new gang who would most likely be less of a threat than the original James-Younger Gang.

Then Evarts proceeded to discuss the balance of the trip; the additional fuel and water stops, the passenger stop in St. Louis, the cattle stop at the stockyards in Chicago, and the balance of the passenger stops and transfers between Chicago and Philadelphia. The Philadelphia Mint was the final destination.

He also explained that when they reached Philadelphia, there would be no need for the soldiers to be incognito as they were in San Francisco. More U.S. Army troops would meet the train at the depot and they would subsequently unload the gold onto the wagons and haul it to the mint.

Evarts concluded his presentation at this point and asked if there were any questions.

The Vice President asked the railroad men if they saw any problems with Evarts' plan.

The railroad men all looked at each other and virtually in unison, shook their heads, no.

The president of the Santa Fe Railroad then offered his opinion, "This is probably one of the most thought out and most thorough plans I have ever heard. The Santa Fe Railroad won't have any skin in the game but if we did, I'd feel very comfortable that this mission would proceed as planned without a hitch." The other two railroad men agreed.

"So be it," Sherman concluded. "Thank you for your excellent effort and sharing your well thought out strategy with complete clarity and unprecedented attention to details."

Sherman then added, "What I would like to do now is to spend the rest of our meeting time reading over my notes in a recap fashion just to be sure I fully understand your plans and recommendations. I want to be sure that I have all the facts straight so that I can adequately and correctly present this Master Plan for *Operation Last Spike* to President Hayes for his approval."

So after a short afternoon break, the committee spent 2-1/2 tedious hours going over all of the plans from start to finish rehashing specific issues related to the soldiers' responsibilities, the railroad's responsibilities, etc.

By the end of the meeting, everyone was completely exhausted as they all had a right to be.

One of the last comments Sherman made before ending the meeting was this tongue-in-cheek wish.

"With the buffalos on the plains and around the tracks, Indians on the warpath, and outlaws on the horizon, let's hope our transcontinental train trip is not a bumpy one."

After that comment, Sherman literally went around the conference room table shaking hands with each member and personally thanking them for their plans, strategies and participation.

"Gentlemen," he said, "I am very proud of our accomplishments today and I believe that because of you, we will successfully transport, for the first time ever in the history of our country, $1,000,000 in gold bullion from coast to coast by rail. How exciting!

You all have about a half an hour before we meet in the garden for dinner. The temperature is a perfect 72 degrees outside and that's fairly warm for the first week of April in Washington, D.C. And as a small treat for a job well done, I have convinced Lemonade Lucy with the permission of her husband, the President, to allow me to serve up a toast at dinner with one of the finest imported French champagnes on the market today. So, I will see you all at dinner, gentlemen."

Dinner was served in the garden at 5:15 p.m. To the relief of all, formal gave way to informal. The menu consisted of T-bone steaks, baked yams from Louisiana, fresh creamed peas and carrots, cooked greens, and corn bread.

Sherman started the dinner with a prayer of thanks and then stood up and proposed the toast as he promised, "To our President, Rutherford B. Hayes, and his bold plan for the first transcontinental gold shipment."

"Here, Here!" the others responded.

Several of the White House staff looked at each other and realized that they had heard something that was probably not meant for their ears. The committee members thought nothing of it.

During dinner, there was a lot of small talk. However, there were several conversations focusing on the continuing Indian Wars out west.

McCrary was asked by one of the railroad men if it was true what he had heard about Custer's horse at Little Bighorn. McCrary responded, "Yes and no; I believe the horse you are referring to is Comanche. Is that correct?"

"It is," responded the railroad president.

McCrary then explained, "Comanche was one of those wild stallions that was gathered up, gelded and sold to the U.S. Cavalry on April 3rd, this very day, in 1868, for $90. It was a bay horse that weighed about 950 pounds and stood about 15 hands. That's a pretty nice size horse. They think it was about 14 years old at the time of the battle. The misconception is that Comanche was Custer's horse. The horse actually belonged to Captain Myles Walter Keogh who was Captain of Company 1, 7th U.S. Cavalry Regiment commanded by George Armstrong Custer. Keogh was one of the poor souls killed at the Battle of the Little Bighorn with Custer.

I heard that Custer's brother, First Lieutenant Thomas W. Custer, picked up Comanche in St. Louis, along with other horses of course. Comanche and 40 other horses were loaded on the train and shipped to Fort Leavenworth, Kansas and later further west. Keogh loved the animal and bought it for himself for the same money the Army paid, 90 greenbacks.

Comanche was wounded in several battles but healed quickly. He was thought to be part Mustang and part Morgan and was a proven battle partner for Keogh.

Well, what we know is this. Two days after the 7th Cavalry was defeated at Little Bighorn, a burial detail found Keogh's horse severely wounded but still breathing. The Indians took the other horses that were not injured but left Comanche remain on the battlefield because of his wounds. He was the only living being found at the Battle of the Little Bighorn.

He was transported by the steamer named Far West to Fort Lincoln in the Dakota Territory, which happened to be about 950 miles away by water. Comanche spent the rest of the year recuperating and the orders were that no one would ever ride him again. I understand that he's still living and is free to meander around the fort."

Everyone at the dinner table that evening, in the White House Garden, listened attentively to that remarkable story.

However, what would have really amazed the group is if they knew the rest of the story.

Comanche died of colic on November 7, 1891. It is believed that he was 29 years old. When he died, he was sent to a well-known taxidermist in Kansas whose name was Lewis Dyche. Dyche mounted Comanche and this famous horse was exhibited at the World's Fair in Chicago in 1893.

Comanche is currently displayed in an enclosed, humidity controlled, glass case at the University Of Kansas Museum Of Natural History in Lawrence, Kansas and is forever claimed to be the only survivor of the Battle of the Little Bighorn.

That famous steamer, Far West, which originally hauled supplies from Fort Lincoln to the 7th Cavalry troops near the Sioux nations, and which eventually hauled 52 wounded soldiers (wounded in battles on June 25th and 26th in surrounding battles other than the Little Bighorn), and transported Comanche back to Fort Lincoln, hit a snag near St. Charles, MO. and sank in the Missouri River in October of 1883.

Eventually the conversation changed from Indians to railroads thanks to Evarts.

Always a curious soul, he got the attention of one of the railroad men and told him he was enamored with the sheer power of steam engines (locomotives). Railroad business was expanding rapidly around the country and was considered one of the biggest catalysts toward progress in the 19th century and certainly would play a major role in *Operation Last Spike*.

Evarts asked the president of the Union Pacific to explain how this mountain of steel, the locomotive, really worked.

The president of the Union Pacific, a railroad man for all of his life, was excited to be able to demonstrate his knowledge of the workings of a locomotive to President Hayes' distinguished Cabinet.

So he began with a sense of enthusiasm that was written all over his face.

"A steam engine, though seemingly a very complicated looking machine, is powered by a very simple concept. The power comes from steam. Boiling water makes steam to push a piston. Steam power is a simple operation but it is very complex to control. Let me explain where the power to move a locomotive engine and consequently an entire train comes from."

At this point everyone turned his head toward the president of the Union Pacific Railroad.

"A locomotive can be divided into three basic areas. They are: the backend that contains the firebox where heat is produced, the boiler which contains the water in the center of the engine, and the smoke box and/or smoke stack in front of the engine which emits smoke and spent steam."

Now the president of the Union Pacific Railroad really got into it. He put down his knife and fork and began to explain using a copious amount of hand gestures. It was like he was a professor on a mission to teach his students in the most coherent and logical way possible so even a backwoods frontiersman could understand.

"Here's how it works:

- First, fuel is shoveled into the firebox. The fuel can be either coal or wood. Incidentally, the train coming from California, which will be carrying our gold shipment, will be using wood.
- When the fuel burns, it emits what is known as flue gases.
- These 'hot' gases are drawn through the long metal tubes contained in the boiler in the center of the engine. The movement of the gases is made possible by the airflow created by the help of the smokestack in front of the engine.
- Those hot gases flowing through the metal tubes in the boiler are what heat the water that creates the steam.
- The steam then rises into what is known as the steam dome, which is situated on top of the engine directly in front of the engineer. The steam dome is where the throttle body is located to control the power to the pistons.
- Now, as the steam enters the cylinders which are located by the front wheels on either side, it shoves the pistons back driving the main rod backwards that forces and pushes against the crank pin which turns the wheel and off you go.

Are you with me so far?" he asked. The group nodded their heads "yes" because the explanation was very precise.

"Well then let me continue:

- Next, the valve changes and puts steam on the backside of the piston. By the way, these pistons are fairly large and positioned horizontal and parallel to the tracks. The steam then pushes the piston ahead and the cycle starts all over again.
- The spent steam is then blown out creating that chug, chug, chug sound associated with a locomotive."

That drew a smile from the people around the table. About halfway through his explanation, he began to get the attention of the White House staff too. Then he continued, "To run a steam engine, the engineer has to be concerned about the level of water in the boiler, how much fuel you have and the intensity of the fire. You have to balance the pressure with the amount of fire being generated. Not enough water in the boiler will cause an enormous explosion and will be fatal to the crew. I am sorry to say that the railroads have had a few serious explosions over the years killing entire crews because of human error in managing the water levels and the steam pressure.

We've also experienced many other accidents throughout the years due to various other problems. Secretary Schurz, you said you were from Missouri, right?"

"That's right, I am," Schurz responded.

"Then you are probably familiar with the tragedy that happened over the Gasconade River in Gasconade, Missouri on November 1, 1855."

"Yes, I am. It was a horrible event, and I know about the incident very well because it was the worst train wreck in Missouri's history. On that fateful day the first large trestle bridge was opened out west. It was west of St. Louis over the Gasconade River just south of the Missouri River. Gasconade is situated just short of being halfway between St. Louis and Kansas City. For the people boarding the train, it was party-time. The champagne was flowing and everyone was jubilant because they were going to be part of history, crossing the first large trestle in the West.

There were railroad owners, politicians, the mayor of St. Louis and over 100 passengers boarding the train in St. Louis.

Unfortunately, that bridge was not inspected nor was it given approval to be crossed. The passengers were not aware of those facts.

As the engine reached the first pier, the trestle bridge gave way and collapsed into the cold Gasconade River. Many of the cars were pulled into the river and thirty-one passengers along with the engineer were trapped and drowned. The mayor was amongst all the others who were injured."

A deafening silence came over the group and that macabre story seemed to put an end to the evening, exposed the reality of the railroad tragedies of the past, and made them wonder what the future would hold for them and their bold and risky project.

The dinner in the White House Garden officially ended at 7:00 p.m. and afterwards, everyone went directly home since it was quite an exhausting day.

For the next few weeks it was up to John Sherman to organize all of the notes from the meeting and put them in a report form to present to President Hayes on the afternoon of May 4th.

As always, when working with complicated projects and under a specific deadline, time seemed to fly by for Sherman. However, on the morning of May 4th, Secretary of Treasury John Sherman was professionally well prepared and ready to present the committee's plan and strategy for a successful *Operation Last Spike* to President Hayes.

Sherman arrived at the President's office at 1:50 p.m. Immediately upon arrival, President Hayes offered Sherman a glass of brandy. Like a child hiding his candy from his older brother, he had the brandy hidden in the bottom left-hand drawer of his desk so Lemonade Lucy would not be aware of its existence.

After a few minutes of pleasantries, Hayes began the inquiry, "Well Sherman, what do you have for me?"

"Mr. President, I believe the committee and I have put together a very elaborate plan which will ensure that your request of successfully transporting $1,000,000 in gold bullion from the west coast to the east coast is safely and totally fulfilled."

President Hayes smiled and said, "Excellent! Continue please."

Sherman then spelled out the plan from the very beginning to the end. It took him about two hours to go through all of the exhausting details. President Hayes asked a few trivial questions but seemed to be confused about one part of the plan and why they should even take that risk. Overall though, he was well pleased with the endeavors of the committee and complimented Sherman and the group for a job well done.

When the two were finished, President Hayes offered Sherman a Cuban cigar. After Hayes lit his cigar, he leaned back in his chair, took about three large puffs, blew the smoke slowly into the air and said,

"So you really feel we need to stop off in Dodge City, ehh?"

CHAPTER TWO:

Gaming Houses, Brothels and Saloons

There were many circumstances that led up to the creation of Dodge City and the role it played in the Old West. Before it was Dodge City, it was nothing but a flat dusty stopping off place along the Santa Fe Trail.

This infamous city became a new cow town because of the Missouri and east Kansas ranchers' hatred toward Texas longhorn steers due to the ticks they carried which transferred to local herds, infected them with a deadly disease, and ultimately killed local cattle by the thousands. In addition, local residents got fed up with the uncontrollable vice, which exploded in the new cow towns that became the cowboys' playgrounds. The cow towns brought saloons, gunslingers, gambling halls and brothels. Eventually the townspeople outlawed the cattle drives into their towns, the action moved west, and the Dodge City boom years began.

Before and just up to the Civil War (1861-1865) and as early as the 1840's, Texas cattle were driven north up the Shawnee Trail, which was also known as the Texas Trail, the Kansas Trail, and the Sedalia Trail. This trail was the first major and the most eastern route used by cattle drovers from Texas. The route started in south Texas near Brownsville, and traveled through Austin, Waco, and Dallas. It then traveled through the Indian Territories (now Oklahoma) of the Cherokees, Choctaws, and Chickasaw nations, passing through the Fort Gibson area. From there it went on to Baxter Springs, Kansas where it branched off to Kansas City, Sedalia, St. Louis, and a few other towns.

During the Civil War, the Shawnee Trail was used by both the North and the South to transport troops and supplies so at that time it was virtually unused for cattle drives.

There were two notable Civil War clashes along this trail. They were The Battle of Honey Springs, fought on July 17, 1863 in Oklahoma, a Union victory commanded by James G. Blunt (July 21, 1826 – July 27, 1881, lived to age 55) and The Battle of Fort Blair fought on October 6, 1863 in Cherokee County, Kansas, a Confederate victory commanded by William C. Quantrill (July 31, 1837- June 6, 1865, lived to age 27).

But even before the Civil War, deadly and bloody clashes began breaking out on the northern leg of the Shawnee Trail. It was in the month of June in the year of 1853 when a group of Texas drovers hit a snag. A herd of about 3,000 longhorns, while trailing through western Missouri, were forced to turn back by local

Missouri farmers and ranchers. The reason was that Texas longhorns transported a tick that transmitted a disease known as Texas fever. Texas fever at one time threatened the very welfare of the nation's cattle industry. The sickness was caused by parasitic protozoa and the results were high fever, emaciation, anemia, numerous other symptoms and eventually death for the infected animals. The ticks, transported by the Texas longhorns, hosted the protozoa.

Local herds would pick up the ticks when they bedded down in the same places as the longhorns. The Texas steers were immune to the disease but the local cattle died by the hundreds and eventually thousands. Whole herds were even wiped out.

In 1855 angry ranchers and farmers in central and western Missouri were fed up. They began forming vigilante committees and armed bands, stopping herds and even killing Texas cattle that entered their counties. Many herds were turned back but some also made it through.

A group of angry Missouri cattlemen called on their legislature for action and in December of 1855 a frivolous law in Missouri was passed. It was a failure from the beginning because the law banned "diseased" cattle from entering into the state. The problem was that those long legged, strange looking Texas longhorns were "immune" to the disease and never showed signs of sickness.

Because of the vigilante style resistance in southwest Missouri, some of the drovers circumvented this dangerous and often deadly territory and attempted to drive their herds through eastern Kansas searching out a safer route.

However, they began meeting resistance there as well for the very same reasons. Eventually farmers and ranchers in eastern Kansas convinced their territorial legislature to pass a law in 1859, which attempted to restrict Texas longhorns from entering their part of the state.

Then came the Civil War in 1861. Men between the ages of fifteen and thirty-five years, on both sides, left their homes, farms, and ranches and went off to war.

Cattle herds were not managed in Texas during the War and they multiplied ten-fold and ran free. The number of feral cattle literally exploded into the millions and would potentially become a gold mine for anyone who possessed an adventurous entrepreneurial spirit and the raw grit to match it.

Immediately after the War, there was no real market for cattle in the South. So, 200,000 to 260,000 longhorns were herded and driven north to the railhead towns in Missouri and Kansas. If you were lucky, you made it through. If you were not and met with vigilante groups or Northern sympathizers, you were pistol-whipped or even killed and your herd was dispersed or killed as well. That's just the way it was.

There was a young Texas man who was only sixteen years old at the time. His name was James M. Daugherty. He gathered a few willing cowpokes and they herded about 500 maverick longhorns and drove them northward along the Shawnee Trail.

When they entered southeast Kansas, they were brutally attacked by farmers and ranchers, some say Jayhawkers dressed as hunters. This vicious militant band scattered the herd, killed one of the drovers, and captured and roughed up Daugherty within an inch of his life. He was just trying to get his cattle to market but probably got caught up in the anti-slavery/pro-slavery clashes of that time. If the militants were truly farmers or ranchers, then it was the tick fever or crop damage that became the catalyst for the deadly conflict.

Jayhawker was a name that became well known just prior to the Civil War in east Kansas, which became known as "Bleeding Kansas" (the term "Bleeding Kansas" was coined by none other than Horace Greeley of the New York Tribune). These ruthless guerrilla fighters known as Jayhawkers were affiliated with the "free-state" cause. They were the anti-slavery settlers. The infamous John Brown supported their cause with violence in the name of righteousness. They often clashed and fought against pro-slavery groups out of western Missouri called "Border Ruffians".

The Jayhawkers were anti-slavery fighters at first but were later described in this seemingly accurate manner,

"Confederated at first for defense against pro-slavery outrages, but ultimately falling more or less completely into the vocation of robbers and assassins". Daugherty and his Texas drovers were unfortunately victims of the times.

Daugherty was able to gather up about 350 of his cattle and drive them at night to Fort Scott in southeast Kansas along the Missouri border where he was able to sell them at a profit.

In 1867, more states enacted laws against trailing and it became obvious to drovers and cattle buyers that it was time to find a new route from Texas to other railheads up north.

Enter Joseph G. McCoy (December 21, 1837 – October 19, 1915, lived to age 77), and the story about how his ingenious idea became the "model" for the new cow towns of the West. Along with his venture came the establishment of a new cattle route known as the famous "Chisholm Trail". If you understand the building of the first cow town in Kansas, then you will know what it took to build what was known as the last cow town in Kansas, Dodge City.

Some people claim that McCoy is known as the godfather of the cowboy. Others call him the "Poster Boy for Capitalism" in the West. He was born in Sangamon County, Illinois and grew up in the cattle business becoming an affluent cattle buyer and an aspiring entrepreneur with very big ideas.

McCoy saw a great moneymaking opportunity and was determined to take advantage of it. He recognized that there was an ever-growing population in the East; before the Civil War they consumed mostly pork for their meat. However, now they craved beef for variety, flavor and protein. He also knew that there were millions of cattle in Texas that the cowboys needed to get to market. If he could figure out a way to connect the two, it would make him one of the richest cattle brokers in the country.

During the Civil War, Texas longhorns were running wild and multiplied into the millions. They were so abundant that they weren't worth much in Texas; about $4.00 per head. Conversely, they were worth up to $40 per head in Chicago and many of the eastern cities.

However, the trip from Texas to east Kansas and Missouri became very precarious for the drovers. Not only was the journey along the trail dangerous, but also when they arrived in east Kansas and Missouri, they were faced with irate farmers and ranchers carrying guns. The reason for this was twofold; the damage the longhorn cattle did to the local crops, and most importantly because of the tick fever the Texas longhorns brought with them, which killed thousands of local cattle. At that time, the farmers and ranchers had no idea what caused the tick fever. They only knew that it was most likely related somehow to those strange looking, long legged Texas longhorns.

McCoy figured that for the cattle business to survive and prosper, he needed to shift the railheads (shipping points) farther west. In 1867 there was a major auspicious break through. The Union Pacific finished its railroad line through Kansas. In addition, unlike Missouri, Kansas was wide open and much of the state was not yet settled making it possible to build a financial empire from the ground up.

McCoy knew that the railroad was looking for new business and he had just the plan to accommodate their needs and make him rich at the same time. He saw gold in them there Texas longhorns.

On a rudimentary map that he acquired, McCoy discovered a small settlement along a creek in Kansas, later named Abilene, which had been a stagecoach stop since 1860. There was a small population of only 35 people living in small buildings, which McCoy described as log cabin huts. However, the most important thing was that this underdeveloped settlement sat on the edge of the new Union Pacific railroad tracks.

McCoy chose this spot as the town he would build for the purpose of receiving cattle from Texas to ship by rail to the East. He was determined to make Abilene (considered a cow town from 1867 to 1871) the "cattle trade capital" of the West.

There was a problem though. Abilene was a town that was situated in a quarantine area for Texas fever. Longhorns were not allowed in that part of the state. The quarantine was made up of the top half and about 30% of the eastern half of the state.

But McCoy was adamant and determined to make his initial plan work. So he got creative. He did some lobbying with settlers, townspeople, farmers, ranchers and the local legislature. He told them that he would reimburse the farmers and ranchers for any loss of cattle due to Texas fever. He also convinced the townspeople that bringing the cattle business to Abilene would certainly make the town prosper along with everyone in it. The townspeople saw dollar signs and were enamored with the idea and so building the cow town commenced. One person has said that this was "venture capitalism" (a daring use of money to gain profit) at its best.

Then things happened quickly. The first project to be built was the stockyards adjacent to the railroad tracks where cattle would be corralled and loaded onto the cattle cars. It took three months to build the stockyards. Then McCoy built an office, a bank, and a hotel of elaborate proportions. The hotel was named "Drovers Cottage". It was unique in that it accommodated 175 guests, stabled 50 carriages and 100 horses. On a side note, when the cow town era ended in Abilene, the building was dismantled, moved westward and reconstructed in Ellsworth, Kansas (a bona fide cow town from 1872-1875) which was considered the wickedest and one of the most deadliest of all the notorious Kansas cow towns.

McCoy needed a trail from Texas to Abilene. Fortunately, there was a trail about 120 miles south of Abilene in a town called Wichita, (a bona fide cow town between 1872 –1876) which already connected Wichita to Texas. This trail as of yet had no name but later, it would be known as the famous "Chisholm Trail".

At first this north to south path was nothing more than a buffalo trail, which followed the natural contour of the land. Indians also used it following the great buffalo herd.

The trail was named after an Indian trader named Jesse Chisholm (1805 or '06 – 1868, lived to age 62/63). Jesse would use the trail to haul Indian goods and supplies to the Indian camps from his trading post in Wichita.

Jesse's father was Scottish and his mother was a Cherokee woman. Jesse was the eldest of three sons. He was an Indian trader, a guide, and an interpreter. He was a trusted man and translated at treaty councils in Texas, the Indian Nations, and Kansas.

It is said that Jesse died of food poisoning in 1868 after eating rancid bear meat at Left Hand Spring, near the site of the present Geary, Oklahoma.

The Chisholm Trail was considered the most famous trail of the cattle drive era.

It is estimated that an unprecedented 5,000,000 head of Texas longhorns reached Kansas by way of the Chisholm Trail. It is also interesting to note that Jesse Chisholm never drove cattle himself on the famous trail named after him.

In 1867 Kansas was a wide-open frontier, virtually all prairie, excellent grazing ground and flat as far as the eye could see.

The disappearance of the buffalo on these plains helped make the cowboy era possible. This is not often talked about but it is a fact; at one time Kansas was literally swarming with buffalo.

Records show that a staggering 60,000,000 buffalo roamed the Great Plains before the Civil War. Buffalo was the main source of food, clothing and such for the Indians. However by 1870, the great herds had all but vanished from the Kansas Plains as hunters slaughtered them for their hides and left the meat rotting on the ground. This was considered, by some, as one of the great tragedies during this time period. These buffalo killings destroyed the Indians' way of life and were no doubt one of the catalysts that caused the Indian Wars of the Great Plains.

Now it was necessary for McCoy to identify a trail from Wichita to Abilene. So he hired men to make landmarks of dirt mounds with signposts that would guide the drovers from Wichita to the stockyard and railhead in Abilene.

He then sent thousands of circulars to Texas to tell the drovers to bring their cattle to Abilene. And so they did. They came by the thousands between the months of June through October. They came as far away as 1,500 miles from the southern tip of Texas.

By 1868 about 75,000 cattle arrived in Abilene worth over $2,000,000. By 1869, that number doubled.

Some people say Joseph McCoy earned the name "The Real McCoy" because he promised, and he delivered.

But it was a mixed blessing for the town. Eventually, the town that McCoy built turned against him.

With the cattle business came saloons, which were tents at first but then they became bigger and better and many. Then there were gambling houses and brothels. The town exploded with pimps, prostitutes and gamblers. Vice was everywhere.

Ever present were the foul odor of cattle and the seemingly never-ending sound of bellowing. Of course you also had the constant railroad traffic and the deafening shrieks of the locomotive whistles. The towns were dusty in the summer and muddy in the late fall and early spring.

Saloons were open all day but extremely busy at night and were rivaled by dance halls and brothels.

The cowboys from Texas were mostly young men, some even in their teens. The cattle drives were hard and grueling dirty work. The days were long and tedious and the cowboys were in their saddles from 12 to 15 hours each day. The pay wasn't great and generally came at the end of the drive.

Cattle can only travel 12 to 15 miles per day, which added to the length of the journey that could take up to 3 months to complete.

The only thing that kept those worn out cowboys going was the excitement they knew would be awaiting them at the end of the trail.

Once the cattle were counted and sold, the cowboys' job was not finished until all the cattle were loaded into the train cars and ready for shipping; and that was no easy task either for it is not a normal thing for cattle to walk up a ramp and into a dark and enclosed railroad car. However, if a drover could use his experience and skill to get just one steer to commit, then the rest would follow because of their herd instinct.

After the cattle were loaded into the railcars, the cowboys received their pay, around $150. Then they had a lot of time on their hands before they rode back to Texas or headed elsewhere.

The first thing many of the cowboys did was to spend their money on new clothes, hats and boots. Some then took a much-needed bath, got a shave for two bits, and headed to the saloons, many looking for female companionship.

That was the time of the year when the town really prospered due to the cowboys spending a good portion of their earnings, but there was bad with the good. The cowboys were rowdy, drunken and fights broke out in the saloons and gunsmoke filled the air.

From June through late September, the population of the town grew from 2,000 to 10,000. It was like living a double life if you were a citizen of Abilene; from October to May, it was fairly peaceful, from June to late September, pandemonium ruled.

The Abilene settlers eventually grew to become weary of the noise and vice, and fed up with the whole arrangement, threatening McCoy's gold mine.

The town was growing and more farmers were settling in the area, which made it more difficult for the drovers to get their cattle through the fields without damaging the farmers' crops. Moreover, Texas fever loomed large once again and threatened local herds more now than ever before. Four out of every five heads were dying from Texas fever.

In order to take control of the situation, McCoy got himself elected mayor of the town. He then moved the brothels to the other side of the tracks (some people called it "The Devil's

Addition") but saloons, gambling and dance halls were still part of the main part of town.

McCoy then went out and hired the most notorious person he could find who could control the wild life in Abilene. Enter the infamous Wild Bill Hickok (May 27, 1837 – August 2, 1876, lived to age 39). On April 15, 1871, Hickok became Marshal of Abilene. He was hired for $150 per month plus he received 25% of the fines from the people he arrested.

There was only one problem. Ole Wild Bill joined the party and spent most of his time gambling in the Alamo Saloon and hung out with prostitutes, so the story goes.

He was fast, fast on the draw, and an excellent marksman. He carried two pistols (a pair of cap-and-ball Colt 1851 .36 Navy Model pistols). They had ivory handles, silver plating, and were engraved with "J. B. Hickok – 1869" on the back strap of the pistols. (J.B. Hickok stood for James Butler Hickok, which was Wild Bill's real name). His guns were as flashy as the clothes he wore. He rarely wore a holster. Instead, he carried the guns backwards in his belt. When he drew his pistols, he used what was known as a "reverse twist" or "cavalry draw".

On October 5, 1871, Hickok had a shootout on the street with a saloon owner and rival named Phil Coe (1839 – circa October 5, 1871, lived to age 31/32). There was a street brawl and Hickok was trying to break it up when Coe, who abhorred Hickok with a passion, unwisely drew his gun on Wild Bill. He shot and missed but Hickok put a slug right through Coe's belly.

Hickok then heard the sound of someone running at him from behind. Wild Bill instinctively turned around quickly, aimed high and shot. What a tragedy, he mistakenly shot his deputy, Mike Williams in the head and killed him instantly. Hickok was devastated. Some say he cried. This incident haunted him the rest of his life and he never shot another person after that.

The townspeople were fed up with Hickok and his vices, which were as bad as the cowboys'. Two months later, Hickok was voted out of office and he left Abilene.

For the record, Hickok eventually found his way to Deadwood, in the Black Hills of the Dakota Territory. It was August 2, 1876. Wild Bill showed up at the Nuttal & Mann's Saloon No. 10. He sat down at a table to gamble. Now Hickok always sat in a chair next to a wall so that his back was always protected. However, the only chair left at this table on that fateful day was situated in front of a door. Wild Bill reluctantly sat on that chair and began to play poker.

A coward named John (Jack) McCall (1853/1853 – March 1, 1877, lived to age 23/24) walked through the door behind Hickok unnoticed, pulled a pistol and blasted Hickok in the back of the head. Hickok's head slammed to the table and he died instantly. The hand he was holding has forever been known as the *Dead Man's Hand*. It was a pair of aces and eights, all black.

There were two trials. It was in the second trial that Jack McCall was found guilty of killing Wild Bill. On March 1, 1877, he was hung and then buried with the noose still around his neck.

Moving on…

Now the town was really turning against McCoy. They had enough. Conflict with the farmers came to a head. The homesteaders formed the Farmers' Protective Association, which was a grass roots campaign against the cattle trade. The biggest complaint was the Texas fever, which still was a mystery to the northerners. But farmers were also upset at the drovers driving their cattle through their local crops. And of course the town was fed up with all of the vices and bad behavior that existed within their cow town.

The tide finally turned and the townspeople and farmers barred cattle from entering Abilene and told McCoy and the cowboys to find another town.

In 1872 the Kansas Legislature ruled that any county in Kansas could legally bar the cattle trade from its borders. Abilene did and the cattle trade was over. Civilization came to Abilene and the city continued to grow and prosper.

With that, the cattle trade moved farther west to Ellsworth and then ultimately to Dodge City. McCoy moved west too but never again experienced the success he had in Abilene.

McCoy will always be famous for creating the model that was used to build future cow towns like Ellsworth and the Queen of the Cow Towns, Dodge City.

The story of Abilene presents a vivid and realistic picture of how a cow town came into existence.

First you find a location close to the railroad tracks where the land is flat and suitable for building a town.

Then you get the railroad to build a spur to load cattle cars.

Now you build a stockyard to corral the cattle arriving in town.

Then you need to build an office, a bank and a hotel to accommodate the drovers and the cattle buyers.

Next came the supply stores and general merchandise stores built in close proximity to the hotel and railroad depot.

To lure the cowboys, you build the saloons, brothels, gambling houses and dance halls.

Now you need a good marshal and a jail.

As the cattle business booms, the town and the townspeople prosper. Then more people show up and begin building more houses near town, along with houses and farms just outside of town.

However, over time, townspeople will rebel and refuse to be held captive in their own homes as the rowdy cowboys ride up and down the streets shooting off their pistols and breaking out windows in barroom brawls.

Eventually, the townspeople will ban the arrival of cattle drives.

This was the evolution of the cow towns in Kansas and how it all began and ended in the Queen of the Cow Towns, Dodge City.

Dodge City became one of the most notorious cow towns of the Old West. It didn't begin its existence for the purpose of becoming a cow town as Abilene did. However, its growth to become the most famous cow town of all followed the Abilene model.

The history of Dodge City actually begins with the Santa Fe Trail. This was a transportation route blazed by a pioneer named William Becknell (1787/1788 – April 30, 1865, lived to age 77/78). This famous trail connected Franklin, Missouri to Santa Fe, New Mexico.

Franklin, Missouri was located in central Missouri and on the north shores of the Missouri River. Becknell lived on a farm just northwest of Franklin. In 1821 he took a group of adventurers and blazed the new trail. Another notable person grew up in Franklin. His name was Kit Carson (December 24, 1809 – May 23, 1868, lived to age 58).

The Santa Fe Trail was used as a commercial and a military route. The travelers needed protection from the hostile Indians so civilian settlers, in the area that later became Dodge City, built Fort

Mann in 1847. However, one year later, an Indian attack destroyed the fort.

Two years later the U.S. Army arrived and built Fort Atkinson on the exact same site as Fort Mann. Their main charge was to provide protection for civilians against the Native Americans in this untamed territory. This fort was closed in 1853 and it wasn't until after the Civil War that the area that would become known as Dodge City had a new fort named after Brigadier General Grenville M. Dodge (April 12, 1831 – January 3, 1916, lived to age 84). Fort Dodge opened in 1865 just east of where Dodge City would spring up. This was a welcome advantage to the people traveling the Santa Fe Trail and also to the people who were about to inhabit the area.

Some say Dodge City can be traced back to a man named Henry J. Sitler who had a cattle operation in the area. In 1871 he built a sod house. These living quarters were fairly popular in that area and on the Great Plains since there was very little wood material available to construct log huts. Sod houses were made of rectangular patches of sod with the following dimensions: 2' x 1' x 6". These pieces would be piled up to make fairly strong and sturdy walls. Sod structures did have normal type doors and walls with roofs made in a number of different ways; but these houses were musty, damp, and full of insects and were easily damaged by the rain. However, they did their job for the time being. Sod houses were even used in Fort Dodge.

Henry Sitler's sod house was near the Santa Fe Trail and became a stopping off place for travelers who traversed the trail going southwest or northeast.

Within a year, many people saw the potential of the area with the railroad approaching full speed ahead from the east. So in 1872, a group of settlers plotted out an area just about five miles or so west of Fort Dodge and founded the town of Dodge City.

This town was initially settled by mostly men and served as a civilian community for Fort Dodge. Traditional buildings began springing up. George M. Hoover founded the first tent saloon, which serviced the soldiers. Early settlers traded buffalo hides and bones. Then local stores began to be built where you could find whiskey, clothing, hats, boots, guns and ammunition. Then came a billiard hall, more saloons and more shops.

With the Texas fever plaguing cow towns farther east and the Kansas Legislature outlawing Texas cattle in many parts of Kansas, the opportunity stage was set for Dodge City to become the next cow town.

And so it began. A railhead was established with a railroad spur built to load cattle onto railroad cars. Then a stockyard and a corral were built next to the railroad spur. A hotel was constructed for the cattle drovers as well as more saloons, gaming houses, dance halls and brothels. Dodge City had it all and they boasted the best and most elaborate businesses of any cow town.

The Texans and the new cow town needed a cattle trail, and they found one. The trail started in Texas, sprung off the Chisholm Trail, and became known as the Great Western Cattle Trail. It started just west of San Antonio in a town named Bandera, went through the Nations and ended in Dodge City, Kansas.

Now Dodge City was ready to receive cattle and boy did it. From 1875 to 1885, over 75,000 head were shipped out of Dodge City by rail each year. And this town knew how to cater to the cowboys from Texas with some of the most upscale saloons, dance halls, brothels, and gaming houses of their time. Card games were the most popular in the gaming houses. The favorite card games were poker, faro, and monte. Dice games and keno were popular as well.

As did the other cow towns, Dodge also had great clothing stores. One of the most desirable pieces of clothing to a drover fresh off the drive was new boots. A man by the name of John Mueller moved his boot shop from Ellsworth to Dodge City when the cattle business ended in Ellsworth. This was the place to pick up custom-made boots and that's just what those Texans preferred.

Many of the cowboys also purchased new hats which were a critical part of a cowboy's gear during the drives. It was every bit as important as their bandannas which kept them from eating dust on the trail, their chaps which protected their legs and pants from briers and branches, their boots which protected against snake bites, and their spurs which reinforced leg cues they gave to their horses.

As many Easterners moved west for adventure, improving their lives, and following their dreams, they brought with them many different styles of hats: derbies, top hats, Civil War headgear, sailor hats and every other hat imaginable. Originally, the most popular hat of the West was the "bowler hat", not the traditional cowboy hat. The bowler hat was known as the coke hat, billycock or bombin, and was originally created in 1849 for the British soldiers.

In the United States the bowler hat became known as the derby.

It's hard to imagine that at one time, the bowler hat was more popular than the cowboy hat or the sombrero. The benefit of the bowler hat was that it would not blow off easily in the wind while riding a horse or sticking your head out the window of a speeding train to view a herd of buffalo.

The bowler hat was popular with both outlaws and lawmen. Some of the more famous people who wore the bowler hats were Bat Masterson, Black Bart, Butch Cassidy, and Billy the Kid.

There was also another famous outlaw who sported the bowler. His name was Marion Hedgepeth (April 14, 1856 - December 31, 1909, lived to 53). He became known as the Derby Kid. He was born in Prairie Home, Missouri and was an outlaw by the time he was 20, having robbed trains and murdered people in both Colorado and Wyoming. He was known as one of the fastest guns in the Wild West.

The invention of the original cowboy hat is credited to John Batterson Stetson (May 5, 1830 - February 18, 1906, lived to age 75) a hat maker who worked for his father.

John was diagnosed with tuberculosis and the opinion from his doctor was that his time on this earth was very limited. This turned out to be inaccurate. However, because of the prognosis, Stetson left his roots and headed west fearing that if he didn't do it now, he would never have the chance and his curiosity about the New Frontier would never be satisfied. As they say, "the rest is history".

Out West he was able to witness the needs of the drovers and cowboys out on the trail.

In 1865 Stetson traveled back to Philadelphia to begin a hat manufacturing business that suited the needs of the American cowboys. The hat that he made was called the "Boss of the Plains". It was a practical hat for the cowboys of the West. Its high crown provided insulation on the top of the head and the stiff wide brim provided shelter for the face, neck and shoulders from both the sun and rain. The original fur-felt hat shed the rain because it was waterproof.

But this new fangled cowboy hat had other uses besides just sitting on top of the head. For instance, they were also used as buckets by cowboys to water and grain their horses, and used to fan fires as well.

As time went on, cowboys preferred to crease the crowns of their hats and reshape the brims. This caused manufacturers to begin to add variety to their hat styles and as a result, the cowboy hat industry grew to great proportions.

But out of this industry came a colloquial phrase which is used to describe a crazy person. That phrase is "Mad as a Hatter" or "Mad Hatter".

In the eighteenth and nineteenth centuries, mercury was used in the production of felt which was used to make hats.

People who made hats were exposed to this dangerous metal every day. Over time, the mercury had an accumulative effect in their bodies causing dementia by mercury poisoning. The mercury also caused violent or uncontrollable muscle twitching appearing that the individuals were mad or crazy. No one realized that the mercury was causing the muscular reaction. People of that time equated the hatters' reaction to madness. Thus the term "Mad as a Hatter".

Inside most cowboy hats is what is known as a "memorial bow" to past hatters who developed brain damage due to mercury poisoning. The bow resembles a skull and crossbones.

Back to Dodge City...

Dodge City became a profitable city because it levied a sin tax on liquor, prostitution and gambling and the tax income was used to finance the addition of even more businesses which attracted new people to this growing boom town.

Another reason Dodge City became so popular was because of the notable lawmen (to keep the peace) and gunslingers that passed through Dodge City at one time or another. There were notables like Wyatt Earp, James Earp, Bat Masterson, Ed Masterson, James Masterson, Doc Holliday, Bill Tilghman (lawman and gunslinger), Clay Allison (notorious gunslinger), Luke Short (gunfighter by hearsay) and Dave Mather (lawman and gunfighter). The terms gunslingers and gunfighters were used interchangeably meaning they were men who had a reputation for being dangerous with a gun. "Gunman" was more commonly used in the 19th century.

Between 1877 and 1879 the Earps and the Mastersons were lawmen in Dodge City and Ford County; Dodge City was located in Ford County. These two families had the most recognizable names of the Old West and were in Dodge City around the time that President Hayes' Cabinet was putting together their plans to transport gold bullion across the country.

James Earp (June 28, 1841 - January 25, 1926, lived to age 84) Soldier, saloonkeeper, deputy marshal.

James Earp, Wyatt's older brother, enlisted in the U.S. Army in 1861 at the start up of the Civil War. He was a young lad, only 19 at the time. James was wounded in a battle near Fredericktown, Missouri losing the use of his left arm. After some years of traveling, he ended up in Dodge City and became deputy marshal to Marshal Charlie Bassett. He left Dodge City with Wyatt in the early fall of 1879. Even though James was in Tombstone, he was not at the OK Corral during that famous shootout. However, he did ride side by side with Wyatt chasing after Morgan Earp's killers.

Wyatt Earp (March 19 1848 – January 13, 1929, lived to age 80) Gambler, lawman, saloonkeeper.

Wyatt became a deputy lawman for a while in Wichita, Kansas. His career ended there on April 2, 1876 when Wyatt got into a fight with former Marshal Bill Smith and was fired. He then moved to Dodge City where he was eventually appointed assistant marshal under Marshal Larry Deger in 1876. Contrary to popular belief, Wyatt was never the marshal of Dodge City. Wyatt left Dodge for a while to gamble throughout Texas. Speculation has it that he met Doc Holliday while in Texas.

Earp returned to Dodge City in 1878 to become the deputy marshal to Charlie Bassett. He resigned from the police force on September 9, 1879 and left Dodge to move on to New Mexico and eventually Tombstone, Arizona.

This date is extremely important since the gold shipment coming on the train from San Francisco would be arriving in Dodge City around the first of October to pick up a load of cattle to transport to Chicago.

By the way, it was in Dodge City where Bat Masterson and Wyatt Earp became friends and were both lawmen.

William Barclay "Bat" Masterson (November 26, 1853 – October 25 1921, lived to age 67) Gambler, lawman, journalist, buffalo hunter, Army scout.

Bat was born in Canada. He and two of his brothers, Ed and James, left their family farm to become buffalo hunters, as did many adventurous frontiersmen.

All three ended up in Dodge City in 1877, Jim and Ed arriving before Bat. Bat and Wyatt served together as sheriff's deputies and within a few months Bat was elected as County Sheriff of Ford County, Kansas. He did well as sheriff but was voted out of office in 1879.

Again it is important to note here that Bat Masterson and Wyatt and James Earp were no longer lawmen in Dodge around the time the gold train would arrive in Dodge City.

Hayes' Cabinet members were obviously not aware of these future circumstances when formulating their plans in the spring of 1879. Their impression was that Dodge City would be a safe place for a cattle stop because of the presence of the excellent and well-known lawmen in town.

Ed Masterson (September 22, 1822 – April 9, 1878, lived to age 56) Lawman, buffalo hunter.

Ed did not possess the characteristics of his brothers Bat and Jim, which were needed to survive the ruthless times of the Wild West. He was more easygoing and would rather try to solve dangerous situations with talk rather than the use of a gun. This strategy proved to be a fatal one for him.

Ed became town marshal of Dodge City in June of 1877. Bat warned Ed that he needed to change his ways and become more forceful with the troublemakers but stubborn ole Ed had his own ways of dealing with the problems.

In late March of 1878, Ed introduced a new gun policy. No one was allowed to carry guns in the city limits with the idea that it would eliminate street violence. On April 9, 1878, Ed attempted to disarm a drunken cowboy named Jack Wagner. Wagner pulled his pistol and shot Ed at close range in the side. Ed turned away and staring straight ahead, walked down the street, collapsed and died.

Bat, who was across the street at the time, ran into the street with his pistol drawn and shot Wagner who died the very next day.

After Ed's death, Charlie Bassett became the new marshal. His famous deputies were Wyatt Earp, James Earp, and Ed's brother, James Masterson.

James Masterson (September 18, 1855 – March 31, 1895, lived to age 40) Buffalo hunter, deputy marshal.

James never did receive the notoriety through history that his brother Bat did. However, between the three brothers, James was the best with the gun and probably the better lawman. In June of 1878 James became a deputy marshal in Dodge City, some say assistant marshal. Both of the Earp brothers, Wyatt and James, were also deputy marshals at the same time. They were deputies to Marshal Charlie Bassett (1847 – 1896, lived to age 48/49).

Between 1878 and 1879 James Masterson made several hundred arrests. When Charlie Bassett resigned in November of 1879, James became the new marshal of Dodge City.

A word about the arrival of the gold train…

The train, which would carry the gold bullion, would arrive in Dodge City on October 5, 1879 while Charlie Bassett was still marshal. Wyatt Earp, James Earp, Doc Holliday (Wyatt's friend), and Bat Masterson had left Dodge City by this time. James Masterson was out of town on the trail of bandits who held up a local saloon.

Since it was getting late in the year, most of the cattle drives were over for the season and that suited most of the local townspeople just fine. There was only one more drive due around October 4th, but the trail boss of that drive and his cowboys were well known in town and respected because they were men who were older and more mature than other drovers.

So the town was about to settle down and the community would have a quieter life until June of next year when cattle would begin arriving from Texas once again.

At least, that's what they thought.

CHAPTER THREE:

Eastward Bound

President Hayes felt fairly confident about the plan his committee had formulated to transport the $1,000,000 in gold bullion across the continental U.S. His only concern was still the stop off in Dodge City, Kansas to pick up cattle to be hauled to Chicago. He considered it an unnecessary risk to stop in Dodge City but as it was, he bought into the idea to make the train appear as normal as possible.

Directly after his meeting with President Hayes, which occurred on May 4, 1879, Secretary of Treasury John Sherman, working with a new member of his staff named Billy Daniels, a young man from Atlanta, Georgia, put the wheels of the committee's plans in motion.

Sherman, who decided that it was appropriate for a one-on-one conversation with some of the key players, made the long train trip to California. He arrived in San Francisco in mid-May and met with Colonel Jeffrey's commanding officer, General Schumacher, to inform him of their selection of Colonel Jeffrey to lead *Operation Last Spike*.

Before Sherman arrived in California, General Schumacher had received a telegram from Sherman with orders to identify twelve good men for a secret operation. These men would basically be sequestered from June 1st until the end of the operation and located in an abandoned fort north of San Francisco. If those soldiers had families, they would be allowed two visitations between July and September before the departure of the gold train. The schedule of the visitations would be at the discretion of the officer in charge, Colonel Jeffrey.

In addition, Sherman recommended that since the soldiers would be isolated for several months, that they be assigned additional duties which would be beneficial to the U.S. Army. He suggested that some of the soldiers train horses for the cavalry while others work on reconstructing the old fort and making it suitable for future use.

In his first meeting with Schumacher, he explained the reason for the selection of Colonel Jeffrey.

"We chose Colonel Jeffrey for this mission because he is a respected officer, a man we can trust, a great leader and a brave soldier. I even like the way they say he presents himself. I hear he has that West Point look about him, you know: clean-shaven, boots always shined and his uniform always pressed. I like that in a commanding officer. I'm sure I will be very impressed when I meet him for the first time. He will be in charge of the mission and the twelve soldiers who will escort the gold to Philadelphia. He and two other soldiers of his choosing will be positioned with the gold in the freight car."

Sherman laid out all of the details of the plan with the General and stressed that secrecy was of the utmost importance to the success of this mission.

During their second meeting, on May 20, 1879, at 8:00 a.m., Sherman and General Schumacher met one last time before summoning Colonel Jeffrey to the meeting. Not only did they discuss details about the operation but they also finalized the list of the other twelve soldiers who were to join Jeffrey on the mission.

Because of General Schumacher's prior notice by Sherman, he had already worked out a list with the other commanding officers around California. He had what he thought was the final group of soldiers who were exceptional marksmen and brave men who were extremely capable of handling any type of danger they would encounter in route. These men were the crème of the crop.

After Sherman and Schumacher discussed the mission for about an hour, the General's aide summoned Colonel Jeffrey to the meeting. Jeffrey had no idea that he was being considered for such an important mission. The General's aide rapped on the General's office door and walked in with Jeffrey.

"You can be excused now," the General said to his aide.

"Yes sir," he responded as he saluted the General and waited for the General's return salute as per Army regulations. Then the General looked at Jeffrey and said,

"Colonel Jeffrey, I want you to meet the Secretary of Treasury of the United States, John Sherman."

Jeffrey had a puzzled look on his face as he extended his arm for a handshake with the Secretary.

"Sir, it is an honor to meet you."

"Thank you Colonel Jeffrey," Sherman said. "Now let's talk business, shall we?"

With that, they all sat down to carry on a formal conversation; the General behind his desk and the other two men in chairs in front of the General's desk.

Sherman then looked Jeffrey directly into his eyes and said,

"Colonel Jeffrey, I'm going to get right to the point. You have been selected and are being ordered to lead an extremely important mission given to us by the President of the United States himself, President Hayes. The mission has been named, *Operation Last Spike*. The goal of this operation is to successfully transport $1,000,000 in gold bullion from the San Francisco Mint to the Philadelphia Mint by rail. You and twelve of the best Army soldiers we have will escort the shipment from the time the gold is removed from the San Francisco Mint until it arrives at the Philadelphia Mint."

"I'm assuming you have a grand plan to make this a successful venture, Mr. Secretary," Jeffrey replied in a very serious tone.

"Yes we do and I intend to go over the entire plan with you right now," Sherman responded.

"Sir, before you do that, could you please tell me why you chose me for this job?"

"Yes I can colonel."

Sherman leaned forward in his chair and said,

"You come highly recommended. You're a Civil War veteran and an Indian fighter. That experience will be extremely useful for this dangerous mission. You could face many precarious challenges along the way like hostiles and outlaw gangs whose intent is to rob the passengers and steal the payroll. They might even stumble upon our gold shipment."

"What if I don't accept the mission, sir?"

"Let me be blunt, Jeffrey. You have no choice. You are being ordered to lead this mission," General Schumacher said with a commanding attitude in his voice as he jumped into the conversation.

Then Jeffrey looked at Sherman with a smile on his face and said, "Well Mr. Secretary, since my commanding officer says I have no choice in the matter, then let's go over the plans, shall we?"

Just then, General Schumacher stood up and while walking over to the door said, "I'll have my aide put on a fresh pot of coffee for us since it appears that we will be here for quite awhile."

The meeting between the three lasted almost two hours. Sherman outlined the plan in great detail and meticulously went over many parts of it several times until it was fully understood by Jeffrey. Jeffrey and the General were not permitted to take any notes on the plan because Sherman feared that the notes could get into the wrong hands and compromise the security of the mission.

Unbeknownst to anyone, the General's aide was sitting right outside the General's office and overheard every single word of the entire plan.

Sherman gave General Schumacher and Colonel Jeffrey the official orders to coordinate the notification and hiring of the twelve soldiers who would guard the gold train. He insisted that the men be pulled in as soon as possible to begin their training. He also asked that they begin execution of the plans according to the deadlines that he gave to the two officers. Sherman insisted that there could not be any changes to the original plans.

He then stood up, followed by the other two, and said with a commanding tone in his voice and a stern look on his face,

"One last thing gentlemen, I must warn you; these plans have been approved and cleared by President Hayes and any changes by anyone would result in strict military discipline. Is that absolutely clear?" Sherman asked while looking at General Schumacher and then Colonel Jeffrey.

"Yes sir," they both responded simultaneously.

With that, Sherman shook hands with each and was escorted to his horse and carriage by the general's aide, and was off to more meetings with key players. He had placed his full trust of the implementation of the plans in Schumacher and Jeffrey's hands.

Over the next thirty days, the twelve selected soldiers were ordered to the old abandoned fort for the purpose of meeting with Colonel Jeffrey. They were strong soldiers, excellent marksmen and of the highest caliber the U.S. Army had to offer.

These thirteen men, who included Colonel Jeffrey, were to spend several months preparing for *Operation Last Spike*. The old abandoned fort was chosen because of its privacy and seclusion. There they would be able to practice their marksmanship skills with their Springfield '73 rifles and their Smith & Wesson Schofields. They would also be given their group and individual assignments.

The selected soldiers were a diverse group of men and ranks. Some of the soldiers were married and had children while a few were bachelors. All had planned a lifetime career with the U.S. Army.

The twelve soldiers were:

Captain Jon Shultz, 10 years of service, married, two children
Captain Billy Blaylock, 12 years of service, married, three children

Captain Joey Fuller, 12 years of service, married, no children
Major Lance Trent, 10 years of service, bachelor
Major Ray Kranes, 9 years of service, married, one child
Major Bob Thomas, 9 years of service, bachelor
Sergeant Daniel Snider, 7 years of service, bachelor
Sergeant John Maloney, 12 years of service, married, no children
Sergeant Ray Patrick, 14 years of service, married, two children
Corporal Todd Jackson, 6 years of service, married, two children
Corporal John Wilcox, 5 years of service, bachelor
Corporal Jesse Taylor, 6 years of service, married, four children

By June 25th, the last three soldiers of the twelve had arrived at the abandoned fort. Jeffrey set up his first formal meeting on June 26th. However, on the evening of the 25th, Jeffrey arranged an outdoor cookout for the troops and officially welcomed them to the "party". None of the soldiers knew exactly why they were there. However, they all had figured that whatever the purpose or the reason, they speculated amongst each other that it was a top-secret mission that they had been ordered to participate in.

Before the evening came to an end, Colonel Jeffrey ordered the soldiers to be in full uniform and arrive at the assembly hall at 7:45 sharp the next morning. He had adjusted the old assembly hall to make it appear like a small classroom, with chairs in the middle and a chalkboard in front of the room.

As ordered, all of the soldiers arrived on time for the meeting. They were greeted with coffee, eggs, biscuits and gravy, bacon, sausage and grits for breakfast. None of them expected an elaborate breakfast like this. The breakfast tables were set up at the opposite end of the assembly hall from the chalkboard.

After breakfast, the doors were closed and locked. Everyone in the room took his seat. The mood became very solemn as they all waited with anticipation to be told the reason for their presence. You could hear a pin drop in the room. It was that quiet.

Then Colonel Jeffrey walked to the front of the room and began to speak in a formal and direct manner like a West Point graduate.

"Good morning gentlemen, by now you all know who I am and during the last couple of days, especially last night, you were able to become acquainted with each other.

Because of your abilities, you have been selected and ordered to participate in a secret mission ordered by President Hayes himself. He has named this clandestine mission *Operation Last Spike*.

You are being asked, or should I say ordered, to safely escort $1,000,000 in gold bullion across the country by rail from the San Francisco Mint to the Philadelphia Mint. This may or may not be a dangerous operation. It all depends on several things. First and foremost, the mission must and will remain classified. You are not to speak of this mission to anyone outside of this room. In fact, you are not to speak of this mission to each other outside of this room. If anyone disobeys these two "official orders", you will be treated as a common criminal and will spend the next two years behind bars. Do I make myself clear?"

All the soldiers responded, "Yes sir!"

Colonel Jeffrey continued,

"The other factor which could negatively influence the success of this mission are the hostiles and outlaw gangs we may encounter along the way. We need men with great marksmanship skills who have the courage to stand up and fight in the face of any and all danger, and that is why you have been selected. The President is relying on you men to get the job done.

I will spend the rest of the day outlining the mission. Every detail has a critical significance so you will need to pay close attention. If at any time something seems ambiguous to you as I proceed through these plans, I expect for you to stop me and ask questions."

Jeffrey proceeded to cover all of the plans in great detail: everything from the setup of the train cars, how the gold would be crated and hidden at a local general store the night before it was to be loaded onto the train, the actual loading of the gold bullion onto the freight car, stops along the way, etc.

Finally, he spent about forty-five minutes discussing where each soldier would be positioned on the train and what his responsibilities would be.

"Gentlemen," Jeffrey began while pointing to the drawing on his chalkboard, "The makeup of the train will be this: the engine, the fuel car, two passenger cars, the freight car, the mail/payroll car, eight cattle cars, and the caboose.

Now I'll give you your actual positions on the train. They will not change unless I say so. In other words, your car and seat assignments will remain the same throughout the entire trip.

Corporal Jesse Taylor, you will be stationed in the aisle seat in the first row, on the left-hand side of the first passenger car. You will guard the first passenger car and the engineers as well. I want someone young there who can move quickly between the passenger car, the fuel car and the engine. You fit the bill perfectly.

Captains Shultz, Blaylock and Fuller, you will be seated in the last row on the left-hand side in the second passenger car.

Majors Trent, Kranes and Thomas, you three will take your places in the last row on the right-hand side of the second passenger car.

Because of your ranks and ages, you six will be assigned to sit in with the passengers during the whole trip. However, the key is that all six of you will be directly in front of the freight car that will house the gold bullion. You will be my extra protection.

Corporal John Wilcox and Corporal Todd Jackson, both of you will be stationed with me in the freight car with the gold. We will be locked in from the inside so nobody will be able to open the railroad car doors except for us. The doors will not be opened unless ordered by me.

Sergeant Snider, you will be stationed in the mail/payroll car. You will be the only one in that car, so you will have additional duties consistent with the duties of the post office man who is normally stationed in this car. We'll make sure you get the additional training you need to perform those duties. I also wanted you there because this is where we will keep the remote telegraph equipment. From what I understand, you are experienced in sending telegrams, is that correct Sergeant?"

"Yes sir, it is," Sergeant Snider confirmed.

Jeffrey continued, "Nobody will be guarding the cattle cars. If someone wants to rustle the cattle, more power to them, we are protecting the gold, not Texas longhorns.

Sergeants Maloney and Patrick will be positioned in the caboose and be on the lookout for hostiles or outlaw gangs approaching from behind.

Are there any questions at this point?" Jeffrey asked.

"Sir, I have one," Corporal Jesse Taylor shouted out as he raised his hand at the same time.

"What is it?" Jeffrey asked.

"Sir, will there actually be passengers on this train?" Taylor inquired.

"Yes there will be. I expect that the train will carry a full load of passengers from California to Pennsylvania. One thing for sure is that we want to keep it absolutely safe for those passengers too. If luck is on our side and this mission is kept confidential, I do not foresee any real trouble along the way. Are there any other questions?"

"I have one sir," Major Ray Kranes requested.

"What is it?"

"Sir, it seems to me that there are so many people involved in the planning and execution of this mission that it will be impossible for this to remain a covert operation. I mean many in Washington, D.C. know about it, don't they? The members of the mint know about it, railroad men know about it, and even Scranton the general store owner knows about it. If any one of these people mouths off to their friends or relatives about this mission, it could put not only this mission in jeopardy but also our lives and the lives of the passengers as well. Don't you agree Colonel?"

"Yes I do," Jeffrey admitted. "I told you from the start that this would likely be a dangerous mission. As I said before, that's why we selected you men for this job. You are the best that the U.S. Army has to offer. Let me make this clear, the President of the United States is counting on us to see this operation through to the end. We will not disappoint him. Are there any other questions?"

"I have a couple," Sergeant Patrick said.

"When do we start loading the train and what do we do between now and then?"

Jeffrey responded, "The train will leave the San Francisco station on September 29th and should arrive at the halfway mark by October 5th. The halfway mark is Dodge City, Kansas. There we will pick up cattle; Texas longhorns I suppose. I'm not sure how long it will take for the cattle to be loaded so we will have to be very vigilant during that stop.

Those cattle will be dropped off in Chicago. We could have a passenger exchange there also. In case you are wondering why this gold train is picking up cattle, I will tell you. The bigwigs in Washington decided to make this train appear as normal as possible. By the way, if you were to be asked by any passengers why you are on this train, the answer is that you are on your way home to the East coast, understood?

As to your other question, we will keep going over the plans and practicing your marksmanship skills. We have planned two dates for your families to come and visit while you are here. However, they are not to be made aware of the objective of this mission. Do I make myself perfectly clear?" Jeffrey asked.

"By the way, in case you are wondering why you are being sequestered so long, it is because some of you have unknowingly volunteered to train wild mustangs for the U.S. Cavalry and others have unknowingly volunteered to help reconstruct this abandoned fort to get it back into shape to be used in the future.

In fact, we would like people outside of the operation to assume that our primary purpose for being here is to perform those specific duties for the Army.

Your families will be the only ones who will know that you are training for a secret mission.

Since there were no more questions, Jeffrey dismissed the soldiers for the day.

In the meantime, Secretary Sherman continued to visit the key players around San Francisco.

His first stop after meeting with General Schumacher and Colonel Jeffrey was the San Francisco Mint. There he met with the Director of the Mint and the Chief of Security. He let them in on the entire plan, i.e., how soldiers in civilian clothes would come during the dark of the night with two wagons and about 25 empty wood crates marked "Ranch Supplies". They would load the gold bullion into the crates and then transport the gold to Scranton's General Store where the crates would be unloaded and stored in the backroom until the next morning when they would be once again loaded into the wagons and then transferred onto the train.

Sherman made it clear to the Director of the Mint and the Chief of Security that no one else should be on duty that night with the exception of the Director, the Chief of Security and just two additional guards who could be trusted and would be sworn to secrecy about the mission under the penalty of severe discipline if they breached their orders.

Since the President of the United States initiated this mission, the Director of the Mint wanted more information and asked several questions of Sherman.

"Mr. Secretary, I am assuming I will be able to meet Colonel Jeffrey before the mission. I want to be sure I open the doors to the mint for the right person," the Director said with a chuckle.

"Good point," Sherman said as he gave a smile back to the Director. "I will make sure he is scheduled to come by and meet with you some time in July. What other questions do you have for me?"

"Sir, is it possible to give me an exact time and date when the gold will be removed from this mint?" the Director asked.

"Here's my plan. If there are any changes, I will let you know in advance. The gold will be picked up on September 28th at 10:00 p.m. I want this pickup to occur very rapidly so I expect you to be ready to go a minimum of one hour before this scheduled pickup, clear?"

"Yes sir, we'll be ready," the Director confidently responded. "You can count on us."

"Good, do you have any other questions before I leave?"

"No sir, I don't."

"Alright then, I'll keep in touch with you through Colonel Jeffrey if there are any changes to the plan. If there are not, then be ready to open your doors to Colonel Jeffrey and his soldiers at 10:00 p.m. on September 28th."

Sherman then left the San Francisco Mint and headed to Scranton's General Store and Ranch Supplies Co. to discuss the plans with him. At this point, Scranton was not aware of his participation in *Operation Last Spike*. However, Scranton had participated in other covert operations for the U.S. Army before and Sherman felt that Scranton could be trusted.

In addition, his warehouse would work perfectly for the mission. Scranton never had to leave his store since his home occupied the second story of his place of business. It was a cozy two-bedroom living quarters with a kitchen and dining area along with a small parlor. He was available to open his store for freight deliveries anytime during the night hours, which would be very convenient for Sherman's plan.

Scranton lived with his young and lovely wife Lisa. His brother-in-law, Ray Albers, moved to California from the East in 1878 and lived and worked with the Scrantons through 1878 and 1879. He stayed in the second bedroom above the store.

Sherman had not previously been aware of Ray Albers'
presence in the house and felt a little uncomfortable with this
because he was not familiar with Albers' background. Sherman
now had second thoughts about having the gold shipped to
Scranton's store but because the operation's plans were so far
along, he made the decision to proceed with his original plans
anyway.

Sherman asked to meet with Scranton privately. So after
introductions and greetings, Scranton took Sherman upstairs to his
kitchen while Lisa and Albers took care of the store's business.

When they sat down at the table, Sherman began the
conversation.

"Scranton you have been a very loyal patriot over the years
and you are someone our country can trust. Well, the U.S.
Government wants to solicit your service once again."

"I'll do whatever I can to help, sir. You know that. What is it
you want me to do?"

"Scranton, I want you to participate in an operation ordered
by the President himself, President Hayes. The mission has been
coined *Operation Last Spike*. It's a clandestine mission and you will
be sworn to the utmost secrecy. Not even your wife, and certainly
not your brother-in-law, should be made aware of this mission."

"OK, you have my word. Keep talking."

"We need to use your store as a decoy," Sherman said.

"A decoy, how's that going to work?" Scranton asked with an
askance look on his face.

"Here's the deal." Sherman then proceeded to fill in Scranton
on the entire mission, its goals and objectives and all of the details
that were designed to make this mission a success. "The success of
this operation will depend upon how well we can maintain its
secrecy. To do that, we need to disguise every part of this shipment
and operation. That's where you come into play.

You see, the gold will be picked up at the San Francisco Mint
during the night by soldiers dressed in civilian clothes and loaded
into wooden crates labeled 'Ranch Supplies'."

"I'm beginning to get the picture," Scranton said confidently
as he started piecing the plan together in his own mind.

"That's good. The shipment will then be delivered to the back
of your store during the middle of the night and stored there and
guarded by our soldiers until they reload it onto the wagons the

next morning. I want the crates to come through your back door and go out the front door. I want this to appear like a normal sale as if you are shipping ranch supplies by rail to an out-of-town customer.

There is one problem that I foresee though and that is how we are going to keep this operation from your wife and brother-in-law," Sherman said as he thought about a quick solution to the dilemma.

"On the evening of the arrival, if they ask you about the shipment, just inform them that the crates will be shipped the next day. Tell them that the Army is involved and that the crates are filled with new special ammunition being secretly tested by the U.S. Government. Then say that you were sworn to secrecy about the project and that's all you can tell them."

Scranton was comfortable with Sherman's suggested explanation and felt certain that he could handle that job.

"I'm with you so far, Secretary Sherman. I guess what I need to know now is, when do you deliver the goods?"

"It will be on the night of September 28th or the very early morning of September 29th. And by the way, while I'm thinking about it, a soldier in civilian clothes has been assigned to order the wood crates. He may have to tell the box manufacturer that he is ordering them for you. Just keep that in mind in case there are any questions that come to you from the manufacturer. If there are, just say you are preparing for an out-of-town shipment. Do you have any other questions at this point?"

"No sir I don't."

"OK then, there's one last thing. If you require any additional communications between us in regards to this operation, the exchanges need to be between you and Colonel Jeffrey who is in charge of this mission. I will make sure he contacts you personally before the operation commences whether he needs to or not. I want you to personally know who you will be dealing with after today."

With that, the two shook hands and Sherman was off to his next meeting, which would be with the president of the Central Pacific Railroad; that meeting was scheduled to be held in San Francisco, as well.

The president of the Central Pacific Railroad was Leland Stanford (March 9, 1824 – June 21, 1893, lived to age 69). Stanford was the 8th Governor of California and served a two-year term from January 10, 1862 to December 10, 1863. He also later served as a United States Senator from California from March 4, 1885 to March 4, 1893.

One of eight children and born in Watervliet, New York which is now the Town of Colonie, he was a tycoon, politician, railroad builder and founder of Stanford University.

In 1861 Leland Stanford, Collis P. Huntington, Mark Hopkins and Charles Crocker organized the Central Pacific Railroad, which was built eastward to meet the westward bound Union Pacific Railroad. The two railroads met in Promontory Summit, Utah on May 10, 1869. Stanford was one of two men who drove in the "Last Spike", a golden spike made in California, to connect the East to the West by rail.

Stanford became president of the Central Pacific Railroad, Collis P. Huntington took care of eastern financial and political arrangements, Mark Hopkins was in charge of the company's finances and Charles Crocker supervised construction.

Stanford and Sherman met incognito in a hotel room in San Francisco because they wanted complete privacy and secrecy since the railroad was playing such an important role in this operation. One of Stanford's associates signed for the room with no knowledge of the reason except to be told that the purpose was for an important business meeting.

The hotel they met in was the famous Palace Hotel (1875 – 1906). The Palace was opened on October 2, 1875. It was the largest hotel in the western United States at that time and had 755 guest rooms. Ill fortune destroyed the hotel when it was consumed by fire late in the afternoon on April 18, 1906 following the great San Francisco earthquake that struck early that morning.

Sherman chose the Palace because of the hustle and bustle there; he was certain he would go unnoticed. Since they had met each other at the meeting in Washington, D.C., they both knew who to look for in the lobby that afternoon. After they met and shook hands, they went up to the 6th floor, room 625, and immediately ordered room service for a bottle of brandy and a light meal.

While waiting for room service, they did a lot of small talk discussing the weather, their families and some political issues.

When the room service arrived, Sherman broke open the brandy and they toasted to the success of *Operation Last Spike.*

After a couple of snifters of brandy, Sherman just had to get something off of his mind.

"Say Leland, you didn't bring it up in Washington but weren't you one of the key participants in Promontory Summit, Utah when the last spike was driven to connect the Central Pacific Railroad to the Union Pacific Railroad?"

"Yes John, I was," Stanford admitted.

"Well then, why didn't you mention it when I talked about the reason why President Hayes chose the name of this operation?"

Stanford laughed and said, "First let me pour myself another drink and I'll tell you."

So while pouring himself more brandy, Stanford began, "You see, John, it was quite an embarrassing moment for me even though it was quite a momentous occasion," Stanford said.

"One locomotive came from the West and one from the East. They drove right up within a couple of feet from each other waiting to touch after the last spike was driven.

People came from all around the country for the celebration; they came from the East coast, the West coast, and the Midwest. There were photographers, newspapermen, journalists, authors and politicians, and a special telegraph unit was set up so they could give a blow by blow account of the activities to the entire country as they happened.

The locals even had a twelve piece brass band playing. And because of the magnitude of this event, champagne was flowing like the rapids of the Colorado River. Well I went swimming in that Colorado River that day and imbibed in several tributaries as did most everyone else."

That analogy made both men laugh out loud.

"What happened after that?" Sherman asked.

"This is when it became embarrassing but quite hilarious. Two guys were selected to drive in the last spike. I was one and T. C. Durant, the Vice President of the Union Pacific Railroad, was the other one. Keep in mind that by now we had consumed more than our share of champagne. Well Durant let me go first. I placed the golden spike in its final location to where it was standing upright. Then I picked up the sledgehammer, reared back, swung forward and 'missed' the spike, hitting the rail.

Well, a howl went up, louder than a clash of thunder, which was heard from the East coast to the West coast. Everyone laughed, hooted and hollered and yelled, 'He missed!'. The engineers blew their whistles and rang their bells. It would have been a really embarrassing moment for me if I were sober enough to know how silly I must have looked. Then I decided to regroup. Luckily I was able to hit the spike just by tapping.

Then I gave the sledgehammer to Durant and dang nation if he didn't miss the spike too on his first swing. It was even funnier than my miss. Everyone yelled, 'He missed too!' I almost fell over in laughter, as did everyone in the crowd when the engineers began blowing their whistles again and ringing their bells. We finally got the spike driven and the two locomotives drove up to each other until they touched. The engineers got out of their locomotives and shook hands while the photographers snapped pictures of everyone. There were speeches given before and after the event. It was quite a celebration.

It was an honor for me to drive the last spike but I only wish I would have drank a little less champagne so I could have nailed that spike the first time. And that, Mr. Sherman, is why I didn't bring it up at the White House in April."

They both got a big chuckle out of that story. Then Sherman said, "I'm glad you took the time to share that story with me. I needed a little humor after spending many hours of serious time on this project. But let's talk about the project now and put these two brandy snifters down.

Leland, you were at the meeting in D.C. and are familiar with the details of the plan. I have already met with many key players here in San Francisco: Scranton, Colonel Jeffrey and the Director of the San Francisco Mint. We have also selected the twelve soldiers who will guard the shipment from the pickup of the gold at the mint here in San Francisco to the delivery of the gold in Philadelphia.

What I want to do today is to go over the makeup of the train, when it needs to be in place to load the gold and the passengers, the various stops along the way, and a few other details. In addition, I'm leaving it up to you to choose the engineer of the train. As much as I hate to do this, I think the engineer needs to be made aware of the gold shipment. That means we need somebody who can be trusted to keep his mouth shut about the cargo."

"I'll need to have my vice president help me with that one since he's closer to my engineers than I am," Stanford said.

"That's fine. But I guess my question is, can your vice president be trusted to keep this project a secret?" Sherman asked.

"I guess we'll have to assume he can. We have no other choice. I'll be sure to tell him the importance of maintaining a covert-type operation."

"Good, now here's the makeup of the train and there cannot be any variations to this because we have already made specific plans on where the soldiers will be stationed. I want the train set up in this exact order."

Stanford then stopped Sherman, "If you're going to be that specific, then let me make a few notes."

Stanford removed a notepad and pencil from his carrying case, and said, "OK, I'm ready."

Then Sherman continued, "Here is the planned layout of the train: the steam engine, the fuel car, two passenger cars, the freight car, this will house the gold, the mail/payroll car, eight cattle cars, remember, we are stopping in Dodge City for a cattle pickup, and the caboose.

Here are a couple other points. We do not need anyone managing the mail car. We will have a soldier do that. I also need an adjustment made on the inside of the freight car. I need a guard to be able to lock or latch all four doors from the inside: the two doors on the ends, and the two side doors. Do you see any problems with that?"

"Not at all," Stanford said. "What else?"

"I need this train in place to be ready to load passengers and the gold on September 29th. In fact, it would be best if the train arrived the evening of September 28th. Do you see any issues with that?" Sherman again asked.

"We can handle that too, with ease. I'll plan to have it there on the 28th," Stanford said as he made a note of it.

"Great," Sherman responded. "If we have any more questions for each other, let's keep the communications between ourselves and we can forward information to the respective parties if the situation dictates. Do you agree?"

"Sounds good to me John."

With that, they toasted to the success of the operation and went their individual ways.

Sherman traveled back to visit with Colonel Jeffrey while Stanford immediately called for a meeting with his vice president to fill him in on the operation and to delegate various responsibilities to him regarding the mission.

Stanford gave his vice president the task of requisitioning the correct number of railroad cars to be available at the proper time, selecting a good crew to engineer the train, and scheduling the route activities along with various other things agreed upon by Stanford and Sherman.

The engineer selected for this special train was a man named Bret Jackson. Bret came from Tennessee and engineered trains for the South during the Civil War. After the War, he engineered trains along the East coast and eventually through Indian territories out West. He had the privilege of driving the first train from Kansas to California and afterwards was acknowledged by the Union Pacific Railroad for his safety record and "on-time" performances.

Jackson was informed of the entire plan, sworn to secrecy, and was told to tell no one of the mission. He was also allowed to choose his own assistant crewmember. His choice was a long time friend with a slightly shady past. His name was Timothy Day and he was from Kentucky, a border state during the Civil War. Timothy was a Southern sympathizer.

Even though Jackson was told not to tell anyone of the clandestine plan, Jackson could not keep his mouth shut. One evening after he brought a train up from Fresno to San Francisco, which was directly after he was informed that he would be the engineer for the gold train, Jackson took Timothy to a local bar named the Southern Comfort Saloon. They sat in the corner of the poorly lit saloon and consumed several shot glasses of California whiskey. It was there that Jackson spilled the beans about the gold shipment and the plan designed to get it safely to Philadelphia. Jackson made Timothy swear that he would not tell a soul about the shipment. Timothy agreed to keep it quiet, but did he?

Everyone who needed to know about the plan had now been informed. Some who were not supposed to know about it, unfortunately found out as well.

When Sherman met with Colonel Jeffrey one last time, he informed Jeffrey of his meetings with all of the participants. He explained to Jeffrey everyone's role in the mission and ordered

Jeffery to be the go-between and to follow up with all the participants, as the time got closer to the actual shipping date.

Sherman then left for Washington, D.C. to discuss his progress with President Hayes. He reassured the President that all of the committee's plans were in place and he felt confident that *Operation Last Spike* would be a success. At least, that's what he told the President.

Sherman then caught a train to Philadelphia to meet with the Director of the Philadelphia Mint.

The plans were finalized and it was now a waiting game; waiting for September 28th to put all the wheels in motion.

On September 28th, the train pulled up at the San Francisco Train Depot. Jeffrey received a very short telegram on September 27th informing him that the train would arrive on the 28th so Jeffrey had his men ready to go to the mint the night of the 28th.

In Sherman's telegram to Jeffrey, Sherman asked Jeffrey to ride over to the depot and check to see if the number of cars was correct and if they were positioned according to the plan.

Jeffrey did and found a slight variation. There were ten cattle cars instead of only eight. However, Jeffrey did not see the addition of two extra cattle cars as a problem, even though it was a variation from the original arrangement.

Sherman however, was visibly displeased with the change to the plan and telegraphed Stanford questioning the motive for the unauthorized modification. Stanford sensed an angry tone in the telegram and he likewise shared Sherman's disapproval. When Stanford inquired about the change he discovered that his vice president took the initiative to increase the number of cattle cars because of the large herds of cattle coming up from Texas that summer. His decision was a smart business one. However, since it went against Stanford's specific instructions, Stanford reprimanded his vice president for the alteration and blindsiding him with the change.

Now things were moving fast. It was important that timetables be kept and that the soldiers and all the players involved act with a sense of urgency to stay on time.

The two wagons arrived at the San Francisco Mint at 11:00 p.m. sharp on the 28th escorted by all 13 soldiers. This was one hour later than originally planned. Two soldiers were seated on each wagon and nine rode on horseback.

All of the gold was loaded into the 25 wooden crates. Thirteen cases were put in one wagon and 12 cases were loaded into the second wagon.

Then the rush was on to get the gold to Scranton's General Store unnoticed. They rode fast and hard down the dirt road in the dark of the night with just enough light to see due to a rustler's moon.

They arrived at the back of the store at 1:00 a.m. on the 29th. Scranton was waiting for them at the back door. Jeffrey ordered his men to be swift and quiet and unload the crates and carry them into the backroom of the store. They did so and they had the wagons unloaded in less than 30 minutes. It took two men to lift each case. In order to go unnoticed, there were no lanterns lit that night; rather they worked by the light of the quarter moon.

Then all of the soldiers bunked out for the night in the storage room. Scranton had blankets available for the men so that they would at least be able to enjoy a small degree of comfort during the night sleeping on a hard wood floor.

When morning arrived, the soldiers took turns going to the café for breakfast, six at one time then seven the next, but splitting up into smaller groups. They were still in civilian clothes.

The soldiers were not aware of it but Scranton had told his wife and brother-in-law about the gold shipment directly after Sherman informed him of the plan. This was not supposed to happen, but it did. Jeffrey sensed that Scranton's wife and brother-in-law already knew about the plans because they were not asking any questions. Jeffrey had no time to worry about who knew what at this point. His only concern was that he had a job to do, orders to follow, and a timetable to keep.

After breakfast, all the soldiers returned to the backroom of the store and waited for orders from Jeffrey. Jeffrey saddled up his horse and rode over to the train to check the freight car to make sure he could latch all four doors from the inside as the plan called for. Everything checked out perfectly.

Then at 8:45 a.m. two soldiers drove the two wagons around to the front of the store where they loaded the gold, which was in wood freight boxes marked "Ranch Supplies".

Everything appeared to be normal. Scranton pretended that it was nothing more than a normal sale for an out-of-town shipment. Four soldiers in civilian clothes loaded the gold into the two wagons while the other nine men just hung around hiding in plain sight keeping an eye out for potential trouble. All of them were packing a Smith & Wesson variation of the Model 3 .45 caliber revolver.

After the gold was loaded, the four soldiers drove the two wagons down to the train depot while the other eight soldiers plus Colonel Jeffrey mounted up and rode their horses down to the depot as well keeping a close eye on the situation but trying to make it appear that they had no involvement with the shipment.

The wagons were guided to the side of the train that was opposite the depot so that no one could watch the cargo being loaded into the freight car. When the loading was complete, all of the soldiers meandered back to the caboose where they changed into their Army uniforms. Corporal Taylor had placed the uniforms along with their Springfield '73 rifles in the caboose the night before. Meanwhile, Scranton and Albers gathered the soldiers' horses and wagons to be picked up later by the U.S. Army.

It was there, in the caboose, that Jeffrey gave the men their last pep talk.

"Gentlemen, you are performing admirably. Everything has gone very well so far and as planned. From here on out, we all need to remain very vigilant. It's going to be a long trip but we cannot let our guard down at any time. Good luck to all of you and Godspeed. Now, let's take our positions men," Jeffrey ordered.

Making sure that the coast was indeed clear, all the soldiers departed from the caboose, one at a time, with their rifle in hand and their .45 strapped to their side as they proceeded to take their respective positions on the train. Jeffrey and the two corporals, who would be stationed with him in the freight car, were the last to go.

When all three were in the freight car, Jeffrey latched all four doors. After locking the fourth door, a feeling of relief came over him because the first leg of the journey went off without a hitch.

By now, passengers were arriving at the depot. It appeared that everything was proceeding as planned. The engineer and his assistant knew that the soldiers were already on the train but ignored their presence knowing that the soldiers would take care of their own responsibilities.

The conductor of the train was informed that the soldiers were on board because they were guarding the Army's payroll in the mail car. The conductor bought into that story.

The passengers were made up of men, women, and families with children. Some were dressed in their Sunday suits and dresses while others were dressed in casual attire. All were headed to various cities along the route like St. Louis, Chicago, and cities further east.

It was a beautiful September morning in the Bay City. The temperature was 56 degrees and there wasn't a cloud in the sky. If you would listen closely, you could hear the screeching calls of the seagulls coming from the seashore. But those sounds would soon be drowned out by the start-up sounds of the big black iron horse.

Smoke began belching from the steam engine's smokestack as the engineer and his assistant threw more wood into the firebox. Every once in awhile the engineer would release some steam while the passengers watched as it shot out the sides near the wheels making its signature hissing sounds.

Many passengers had family and friends seeing them off that morning at the train depot wishing them a hearty farewell. There were smiles and there were tears. However, there were no brass bands to see them off, only the familiar yell of the conductor while the steam engine blew its deafening high pitched whistle,

"All aboard!"

Then at 11:15 a.m. on September 29, 1879, the most important train trip since the completion of the Transcontinental Railroad, carrying an unprecedented cargo of $1,000,000 in gold bullion, departed from the San Francisco Train Depot on an adventurous cross-country journey traversing some of the most dangerous lands and times in these great United States.

As the steam from the engine's boiler filled the piston chambers pushing the rods, which turned the magnificent steel wheels, you could hear the traditional chug, chug, chug, chug from the locomotive while President Hayes' train with its special envoy, guarding its precious cargo, departed from the San Francisco depot.

Nobody on that beautiful September morning, not the passengers nor the soldiers, knew what fate was awaiting them somewhere west of the Mississippi River between the golden state of California and the border state of Missouri.

There were many stops along the way for passenger transfers and for fuel and water pickups. Secretary Sherman ordered the telegraph-experienced soldier, Sergeant Snider, to send him an update of the journey by wire at each stop. This was made possible by the piece of equipment that most trains carried. It was a long wooden rod with a metal hook on the end that was placed on the telegraph wire. A wire ran from the hook through the rod and connected to a portable telegraph box where a Morse code message was transmitted to a specific party.

It was during the second stop in Nevada that Sergeant Snider received a telegram from Sherman informing him about the massacre at Milk Creek in Colorado.

This was the message:

Colonel Jeffrey
Regarding Operation Last Spike
NOTE: Ute Indians are on the warpath!

Secretary of War McCrary has informed me that Major Thornburgh has been killed at Milk Creek, Colorado while leading his troops against the Ute Indians.

Utes also raided The Indian Agency and massacred Nathan Meeker and ten of his employees.

Don't know how long battle will continue. Be very vigilant when crossing Colorado. Do not take any unnecessary risks. We will not be able to deploy troops your way if you encounter belligerent hostiles. Continue to keep me informed of your progress.

Secretary of Treasury John Sherman

Sergeant Snider decoded the Morse code message and ran it to the freight car as fast as he could.

Urgently rapping on the door, he called out to Colonel Jeffrey, "Colonel Jeffrey, it's Sergeant Snider with an urgent message from Secretary Sherman."

Jeffrey quickly unlatched and opened the door of the freight car and read the message out loud in disbelief.

"Major Thornburgh killed? That's horrible. Before we leave this watering hole Snider, very calmly collect all the soldiers and the engineer and ask them to meet me in the mail car immediately, but do not panic the passengers."

"Yes sir," Snider said as he ran off to round up the soldiers and the engineer.

Within minutes, the soldiers and the engineer were in the mail car. Jeffrey had told the two corporals to stay with the gold since they already knew what was in the message.

Jeffrey quickly read the telegram to the group and then told the engineer to keep a look out for hostiles and not to slow up or stop the train for anything unless it's a scheduled stop.

He also told the soldiers to keep their eyes open for hostiles.

"Stay in your seats unless you see hostiles approaching the train and keep your rifles close by. Now go back to your posts and keep this information to yourselves," Jeffrey ordered. "We don't want to have a bunch of panicking passengers on our hands."

Everyone returned to their positions and the engineers stoked up the fire and began moving the train down the tracks, eastward bound toward Colorado. The next fuel and water stop would be in a small town just a few miles north of the Meeker Massacre location.

Anxiety levels amongst the soldiers were running sky high as the train approached the Colorado stop. As far as the soldiers knew, the battle at Milk Creek was still going on. They were accurate with their assumption. The battle went on through October 5th.

When the engineer brought the train to a complete stop and the locomotive steam engine became silent, everyone could hear the gunshots from the battle, which was occurring just south of their location. The soldiers, except for the ones watching over the gold, all left their posts and guarded the outside of the train until logs for the firebox were loaded and the boiler was filled with water. By now the passengers were on edge because they too could hear the gunfire coming from the south. Even though they were not made aware of the Battle at Milk Creek, they put two and two together and figured that this was a battle with hostiles in the area.

When the engineer was ready to depart, he gave one pull of the whistle's rope and that familiar shrill told the soldiers to get back on board; and so they did. The train then continued its journey eastward, making one more stop in Colorado before moving on to western Kansas.

The next scheduled stop would be a fuel and water stop one mile west of Dodge City. Now that they were about ten miles east of the gunfire, the soldiers felt relieved that the threat of danger was behind them and they became a bit complacent and let their guards down.

CHAPTER FOUR:

The Insider

The date was June 14, 1879. The place was the Big Horn Mountains of Johnson County in northern Wyoming. Specifically, the location was known as "Hole-in-the-Wall". It was a perfect outlaw hideout because the only entrance in was through a tight passage, which was heavily guarded. This made it impossible for lawmen to enter without being detected and ripped to shreds by a barrage of gunfire.

It was the remote hideout for numerous outlaw gangs. There were cattle rustlers, bank robbers, train robbers and murderers. Many were of historical notoriety and desired to become famous while others were outlaws who would rather remain anonymous.

Mick Stonehill was one of those ruthless outlaws who preferred to remain in the shadows, at least for now. He was born in Sedalia, Missouri, and at the age of six years old was adopted by a foster family. Mick killed his first man when he was only thirteen years old.

Sedalia, Missouri was founded by General George Rappeen Smith (1804 – 1879, lived to age 75). The origin of the city is traced back to November 30, 1857. After the Civil War, as the railroads expanded their lines through Sedalia, it exhibited that boomtown like atmosphere and environment. From 1866-1874, it was one of those railheads for cattle drives from Texas and had all the traditional cow town vices attached to it like saloons, brothels, gambling houses and dance halls. The cowboys would arrive in late spring through early fall with their cattle and load them into railroad cars to be shipped to the slaughterhouses in Chicago.

Sedalia was not a great place for a kid to grow up. In 1877 the St. Louis Post-Dispatch named Sedalia the "Sodom and Gomorrah of the 19th Century" because of all the illegal prostitution in and around the city. Even though prostitution was illegal on the books, no one seemed to enforce the law. Mick was exposed to all of this vice during his childhood and early teen years.

Mick's mother died of consumption when he was only six years old. She worked part-time in a brothel to earn money for her family. Her name was Cynthia. She was a prostitute with a heart of gold who did her best to support her child and put food on the table for her family. During the same year when Cynthia passed on, Mick's father, who was a no-good drunken, child-beating criminal, left town that spring and never returned, leaving Mick homeless. Luckily, a respectable family allowed Mick to live with them.

Mick did odd jobs around town while he was growing up and became quite a handyman. One year he worked at the livery stable cleaning stalls, brushing down horses and cleaning tack. Another year he did various jobs for the town's blacksmith and learned to trim hooves and shoe horses at an early age. He even swept floors in the brothel where his mother previously worked. There, as one would expect, he grew up quite quickly.

Then he even got a small job at the town's general store. This store sold everything from food and clothing to some ranch and farming supplies.

While Mick was working at the general store one day sweeping the front steps, the owner, Patrick Murphy, a quick tempered redheaded Irishman, came out of the store, yelled at him for doing a poor job and whacked Mick across the back of his head with his open hand. Mick fell to the ground due to the force of the blow while the owner simply laughed, turned around and walked back into his store. Several onlookers witnessed the event.

Mick had experienced more than enough abuse growing up and wasn't about to take any more. He ran as fast as he could back to his foster parents' house. No one was home at the time. He knew the exact location in the study where his foster father stored a pistol. He went right to that spot, grabbed the loaded revolver, and ran back to the store.

When he quietly walked in, the owner was stocking shelves along the wall and had his back to the door. Mick looked around to make sure there were no customers in the store. He then aimed, pulled back the hammer of the single-action Colt .44 and shot Murphy in the middle of his back. The bullet went straight through his heart. Murphy fell to the floor and died instantly. Mick then walked up to the body, calm and collect, and shot Murphy in the back of the head, execution style.

For a minute he felt elation. Then panic set in as he watched the blood from the lifeless body slowly flow across the floor from Murphy's wounds. He threw the gun down and ran out the back door and headed home as fast as his legs could carry him. Mick knew he would be in trouble but he would have no remorse for his evil deed.

Several of the townspeople heard the two gunshots and ran to the store. They were in shock and disbelief when they found the store owner lying in a pool of blood. Next to him was the pistol with two spent shells in the cylinder. One of the onlookers ran to get the town's marshal. When the marshal arrived, he picked up the pistol and immediately tried to identify and locate the owner.

After a few hours of inquiries, the gun was traced back to Mick's foster parents and Mick was arrested. Within a week, even though he was only 13 years old, he was tried. However, Mick was acquitted for two reasons: First, witnesses saw the store's owner strike Mick in front of the store; and second, there were no witnesses inside the store to deny Mick's story at the trial.

Mick had lied and told the jury that Mr. Murphy had threatened him the day before. So he decided to carry a gun with him the next day. He also told the jury that Mr. Murphy was beating him just before the shooting, and when he turned around to get a shovel handle to make the beating even more severe, "That's when I shot the slob," Mick said. He claimed it was self-defense and that's how the jury saw it.

Mick had another skirmish two years later and killed a U.S Army soldier. This time he knew he would be in serious trouble so he left town hell bent for leather with a posse and several soldiers chasing after him. He avoided capture by riding hard and hiding out in the thick white oak woods of southeast Missouri.

He spent the next several years traveling through Missouri, Kansas, Arkansas, and Colorado and ended up in Deadwood in the Dakota Territory.

During those eight traveling years, he gambled, robbed stores, small banks, and stagecoaches and murdered several more people. He toted two pistols and worked on becoming quick on the draw and a sharpshooter with both hands. He even briefly joined a gang in Missouri who robbed two passenger trains and got away with a total of $25,000 in gold and silver.

There was no doubt that he desired to live the life of crime. Yet, he was extremely determined to be discreet in every which way possible. He knew that if he was not well known, there would be little chance of seeing his picture on wanted posters, *Dead or Alive.*

A 6'1" dark haired, always unshaven bandit, with bushy eyebrows, dark brown almost black beady eyes and a pockmarked face, Mick was a man who always wore black from the top of his Boss of the Plains Stetson to his custom made leather cowboy boots. He even rode a tall black stallion with an attitude to match his own.

At the age of 24 he had more experience in criminal activities than most outlaws around the country. As he grew older, he took more risks but his risks were measured with well thought out plans and meticulous details.

When he was 25, he assembled a gang of thugs in Deadwood, outlaws of the worse breed. They were all evil criminals in their own right and very good at their trade. Each and everyone was as cautious as Mick and would not take risks unless they knew there was a high percentage of success attached to them.

In November of 1878, the gang left Deadwood and headed to a safe haven for criminals in Wyoming. Along the way they robbed banks, held up stagecoaches, town stores and committed several more murders.

There were eight thugs in Mick Stonehill's gang including himself. They were Frank Rickets, Jay Johnson, Tex Mex, Bobby "Whiskers" McFarland, Lance Carter, Johnny Reb Sanders and Danny O'Brien. Each one came with their own story of growing up in broken homes or mixed breed families and had parents who mistreated them. They were bullies, troublemakers and desirous of lawless endeavors for a quick buck.

All were excellent sharpshooters with their pistols. They all carried the latest single-action .44 revolvers with ten inch barrels for accuracy, and cylinders that housed six bullets. This was a requirement by Mick. He wanted to make sure that everyone in his gang toted the best and most powerful pistol on the market. He jokingly called his gang the "Forty-Fours". However, that name came to stick with the gang.

About the gang members…

Frank Rickets

Frank Rickets came from 75 miles northeast of Liberty, Missouri in Clay County and was a Southern sympathizer. Clay County was part of the area known as Little Dixie.

Frank's father was Charlie Rickets and his mother was named Sarah Slone Rickets. His parents grew up on plantations in Logan County, Kentucky where their families raised tobacco and hemp. In the early 1800's the Rickets family and a group of young Kentucky families packed up their belongings and many of their slaves and headed west by wagon train to Missouri in search of land and soil that was similar to their homeland. In this group of pioneers were Robert S. James and Zerelda Cole James, the father and mother of the infamous brothers, Frank and Jesse James.

This wagon train of over 150 couples and families homesteaded in Missouri counties on land mostly adjacent to the Missouri River where the soil was rich and fertile and the land was flat. These counties became known as *Little Dixie*. This name was given to a 13 to 17 county area, which was homesteaded by people who came from the tobacco and hemp growing areas of Tennessee, Kentucky, and Virginia. They brought with them their southern cultures along with their slaves to work their newly discovered lands.

Hemp became the main commercially grown commodity in the area. The use of hemp is said to date back over 10,000 years. For centuries, hemp fiber has been used to make pendants, pennants, rope, sails, canvas, clothing, flags, and the paper used for maps, logs, and even Bibles.

In the early years, George Washington, Thomas Jefferson, and Benjamin Franklin all raised hemp on their plantations.

In the mid 19th century, the census showed that there were over 8,400 hemp plantations that had at least 2,000 acres or more.

Since hemp is part of the marijuana family (but not narcotic nor has the same euphoric effect) growing it has been outlawed in the U.S. because it looks identical to the marijuana plant.

The Rickets family settled northeast of Liberty, Missouri, while the James family settled just southwest of Kearny, Missouri. The two families remained friends and even held family picnics together when the James boys and Frank Rickets were young.

After the Civil War and before the James-Younger Gang began their notorious lawless rampage, Jesse James and Frank Rickets did a few small jobs together robbing stagecoaches along the Kansas/Missouri border.

Frank Rickets was always enamored with practicing his fast draw and target shot as often as he could to perfect his shooting accuracy. He was very adventurous and like many in those days, traveled from town to town looking for excitement, the lawless kind. He never earned money the legitimate way so he became a thief to help just get by. In 1877, he settled in the Black Hills of the Dakota Territory and eventually ended up in Deadwood where he became friends with a dance hall girl named Shelly. He admired Shelly because she was the type of person who could take care of herself. She was known to be as mean as a South Texas rattler, always carried a derringer pistol hidden in her garter, and was not afraid to use it. Shelly and Frank remained close friends until Frank joined up with Mick and the Forty-Fours.

Jay Johnson

Jay Johnson grew up in the Smoky Mountains of Tennessee. He did not participate in the Civil War and was neutral to the policies on both sides. He didn't care about anything unless it was directly related to his own survival. He was a cheat and a liar and loved to play poker every chance he could. He visited many of the cow towns in Kansas because of the gaming available. You could find him gambling everyday in Abilene, cheating at cards and making a bundle for himself. However, when Hickok came to town to become the town marshal, things changed for him in Abilene because Hickok was a gambler as well. Hickok came with a reputation and Jay Johnson knew it. In order to live another day and not get caught cheating at cards around Hickok, Jay moved on to Wichita. However, the lack of gaming there made him saddle up and head to Ellsworth, Kansas.

In Ellsworth he got more than he bargained for. Ellsworth was known as the wickedest of all cow towns. There were numerous shootings and killings between drunken cowboys and townspeople. It was similar to all of the rest of the cow towns, which had numerous saloons, brothels, gambling houses and dance halls. However, gun smoke in this cow town was more commonplace than the others. In 1876 while gambling in one of the gaming houses, Jay got caught cheating at cards and was shot twice right at the table by a cowboy who abhorred cheaters. He was shot once in the abdomen and once in the shoulder and immediately thrown out of the building onto the street and left for dead.

One of the girls working in the gaming house named Mandy, who was somewhat friendly with Jay, had two men put Jay in a buggy and drive him down to her house. She then sent one of them for the doctor.

When the doctor arrived, Jay was unconscious and bleeding profusely. The doctor examined the abdomen shot and discovered that the bullet had gone through the body without damaging any major organs. However, the other bullet was still lodged in his shoulder. So the doctor removed the bullet and bandaged both wounds. He told Mandy that Jay had a 50/50 chance of living.

Jay was in unbearable pain for three days. The doctor left a bottle of laudanum, an opium based painkiller and Jay used every bit of it quickly since his pain was so intense from the two gunshot wounds.

Mandy spent the next five weeks nursing Jay back to health. It was a miracle that he survived that incident. If it weren't for Mandy's quick action, he would have been another body in an unmarked grave on Boot Hill.

After three months, Jay was ready to leave Ellsworth. He thanked Mandy for saving his life and promised that he would return and call on her again. Mandy had grown quite fond of Jay and was very sad to see him leave. She took him seriously when she told her he would return some day.

Jay saddled up and headed west to Denver for some gambling action and then north to Dakota. He arrived in the gold mining town of Custer, in the Dakota Territory in the fall of 1876 and did a little gambling there before moving up to Deadwood when the snow melted in the spring of '77. He headed to Deadwood because he heard that an assassin had shot and killed Wild Bill Hickok on August 2, 1876. He felt that this opened the door for him to head up there for some gambling and once again cheat his way to a profit.

It was in Deadwood where he became a good friend of Mick Stonehill and they traded stories about their criminal adventures traveling through the Wild West. Mick was impressed with Jay's stories of survival and toughness and felt that Jay might be a perfect associate in his future gang. And so it came to pass. Jay joined the Forty-Fours and became a secondary leader of the group just under Mick.

Tex Mex

Tex Mex was born in Mexico and was called a "half-breed". His father was a Mexican who had served under Santa Anna in his early years, and his mother was an Apache. This was a strange combination since Apache and Mexicans had been bitter enemies for decades. He lived with the Apaches for a short while and learned how to live off the land. He had no problem stealing from or murdering gringos but later enjoyed being a member of a gringo gang named the Forty-Fours. Tex was a great horseman and was taught the vaquero way of horsemanship from his father's side of his family. He was also proficient at knife throwing ever since he was a kid. Later in life he carried a pistol and learned to be quite a marksman. Mick was the one who introduced him to the .44 pistols up in Deadwood.

Bobby "Whiskers" McFarland

Bobby "Whiskers" McFarland got his nickname because of the thick black beard he wore. He had a black patch over one eye but that did not take away nor diminish his shooting skills. McFarland came from Canada and spent many years in the mountains of Montana trapping and living off the land. He lost the use of his left eye in a knife fight with a Crow Indian who was trying to steal his horse. "Whiskers" killed the Crow and dismembered him in a rage of revenge for a serious eye injury. He then went on a virtual warpath against the Crow after going blind in that eye. Whiskers felt that it would be safer to be the aggressor and earn respect rather than staying on the defense and not being able to sleep at night.

After five hard years in the mountains, he made his way east from Montana to the Dakota Territory. His plan was to head to the Black Hills to mine gold but as he passed through Deadwood, he got into a fisticuffs with a drunken cowboy who made fun of his blind eye. McFarland beat the guy to death with his bare hands. He was arrested but was released after the jury found him not guilty because Mick paid off everyone on the jury. Mick witnessed the fight and was impressed with McFarland's hand-to-hand combat skills. They met after the trial and Mick offered him a job in the gang. Whiskers accepted and the gang began to grow in numbers.

The orders from Mick to his new gang members were to hang around Deadwood until he could find a few more men. Then they would ride out together.

Lance Carter

Lance Carter was from New Mexico and was also part Apache. His father was an Apache warrior and his mother was a young woman from Missouri who had traveled along the Santa Fe Trail with her family. One evening, her family's wagon train was ambushed by a war party of Apaches. All the men were butchered and scalped and the women were captured and were forced to become squaws. Flying Lance was the name of his father and his mother's maiden name was Carter, thus Lance Carter. Lance grew up speaking Apache most of the time but he also learned to speak English from his mother. He became a great horseman like his father and learned to shoot a bow quite effectively. He was also skilled at knife fighting. Later in life when he left the tribe, he became an outlaw and very proficient with a rifle and a pistol. Lance found his way to Deadwood in 1877 and became friends with Tex Mex since they had similar backgrounds. Both spoke Apache fluently and had similar weapon skills. After knowing each other for about three weeks, Tex asked Lance if he could buy him a drink at the saloon one afternoon. It was the same saloon where Hickok was killed, the Nuttal & Mann's Saloon No. 10.

Lance said "sure" and they headed across the street.

They walked up to the bar and ordered a bottle of whiskey and two glasses from the barkeep. Then they walked over to a table at the far side of the saloon where they could talk in private. Tex started the conversation.

"Amigo, you lookin' for some action the next few months?" Tex asked in a quiet voice.

"What type of action are you talkin' about?" Lance inquired.

"I'm talking about making a quick buck and not necessarily in the legal sense."

"I want in," Lance said. "What do I have to do to get in?"

"Leave it up to me amigo. I'll talk to our leader Mick Stonehill. He's lookin' for men like us who are good with guns and have the courage of a mountain lion. Now what do you say we roar through this bottle of whiskey." And so they did. The next day Tex talked to Mick and Mick accepted Tex's recommendation. Lance was now a member of the gang.

Johnny "Reb" Sanders

Johnny Reb Sanders was from Vicksburg, Mississippi and fought in what became known as the "Siege of Vicksburg". The Confederates were beaten badly by the Union soldiers there. At 15 years of age he had joined the Confederate forces in Vicksburg and served under Lt. Gen. John C. Pemberton (August 10, 1814 – July, 13, 1881, lived to age 66). It was one of the bloodiest battles of the War. Johnny Reb was captured in June of 1863 and was a prisoner of war for two years until the War ended in '65. After his release, he headed north to the Kansas/Missouri border and was involved in various bloody clashes along the border. He became an outlaw eventually making his way up to Deadwood with the objective of paying back Northerners for the death and destruction they brought upon his hometown. He sought revenge his whole life for Grant's destruction of Vicksburg and his suffering in a damp and cold U.S. Army prison for two years. Johnny was more than willing to join up with Mick Stonehill's gang when Mick offered him a job. Ole Johnny Reb was the oldest of the Forty-Fours.

Danny O'Brien

Danny O'Brien was the son of Irish emigrants. He lived on a cattle farm in rural Pennsylvania with his parents until the age of sixteen. He was one of two sons. While in school, he was known as a bully. He was an Irish redhead and had a short fuse, which caused him to get into fights quite often. At the age of sixteen, he nearly beat a kid to death. To keep from getting arrested, he packed up some clothes and headed west to Missouri and then eventually ended up in Abilene where he worked at the stockyards when the cowpokes from Texas rode into town. One year he went back to Texas with the cowboys and helped them bring a herd of Texas longhorns to Ellsworth, Kansas. Ellsworth was the most dangerous of all cow towns. It was there where Danny killed a local citizen with his fist in a drunken rage. However, he was sober enough to jump on his horse and high-tailed it out of town, quicker that a snake could slither into his hole, before he was caught and hung. As he headed farther north, he too became very proficient with a six-shooter. Eventually, he ended up in Deadwood around the same time as the others and became good friends with Lance Carter as they both liked to gamble and play poker. Lance introduced him to Mick and Danny O'Brien became the very last person to join the Forty-Fours.

The Forty-Fours ended up in the Hole-in-the-Wall in the spring of 1879 honing their shooting skills through April and May and on occasion would head out to do a job. They were vicious outlaws and considered terrorists of their day. They would rob banks, stagecoaches and had grand aspirations to do a train heist when the time was right and the payoff was worth the risk.

After each job, they headed back to their safe haven, Hole-in-the-Wall, and hung low while they continued to sharpen up their shooting skills.

In July of 1879, Mick hitched up a team of horses to go to the nearest town to pick up supplies. As a youngster, Mick grew up with a cousin who he had kept in contact with over the years. His cousin's family moved away when Mick was young but Mick always kept track of him through telegrams and an occasional letter.

When Mick drove to town on this particular day, he discovered that he had a letter from his cousin waiting for him at the post office. It was in a large envelope and the letter was five pages long. Mick went over to the saloon, ordered a beer and sat at a table by himself on the far side of the room. He read the letter in disbelief. When he finished, he put all of the pages back into the envelope, drank the rest of his beer, smiled and walked over to the telegraph office.

Mick's cousin had asked him to send a telegram after reading the letter and to use the two enclosed code words if he was "in".

So Mick sent a telegram which read "Gray Dragon". Then Mick went over to the general store, bought his supplies and rushed back to Hole-in-the-Wall.

Upon his arrival back at the camp, he asked his gang to unload the supplies and told them that he had received a letter, which might be the break they've been looking for. It was the opportunity that could make them all rich for the rest of their lives. However, he needed time to analyze the information, and to put together a plan that would ensure success.

So Mick told his gang to leave him be and to spend their time the next couple of days target shooting with their .44's because down the road, their skills with their guns would be a matter of life or death. Mick had purchased several large boxes of ammunition in town for that very reason.

After two days of re-reading, analyzing and planning, Mick gathered his gang together in the old log cabin around the wooden rectangular table in the center of the room and said in a foul-mouthed discourse, "You smelly drunken lawless curs, when was the last time you saw $1,000,000 in gold bullion?"

"What? What are you talkin' about?" Jay asked as the rest looked on.

"Are you ready for this one? I'm talkin' about stealin' $1,000,000 in gold bullion right from underneath those fancy talkin' politicians' noses. We'll be the most famous outlaws of our time. They'll probably write some of those fancy Eastern dime novels about us."

"Are you crazy?" O'Brien asked.

"Crazy like a fox," Mick answered.

"You're joking with us, right?" asked Lance.

"No, I'm not. I'm dead serious," Mick replied. "I have inside information and a plan that will make us the richest outlaws in the entire country."

"Keep talkin'," Tex Mex demanded.

"OK, here's the deal. President Hayes had some of his Cabinet staff put together a plan to secretly ship $1,000,000 in gold bullion by rail across the country from the San Francisco Mint to the Philadelphia Mint. I know every last detail of the plan which makes this thing as easy as blasting a hole in the side of a barn with a double barrel shotgun from just three yards away. I don't have exact dates yet, but my cousin said that our opportunity will come in early October."

They all laughed and started pouring drinks from half-filled whiskey bottles. Mick wouldn't have any of that and told them to put the corks back in the bottles. He told them that their minds needed to be absolutely clear while he explained to them Washington, D.C.'s plan and his strategy to steal the gold.

"We'll have our drinks when I'm finished," Mick said.

"Before you explain the plans, who's the insider you know?" inquired Whiskers.

"He's a relative of mine."

"Well where does he work?" Tex asked.

Mick sort of smiled and said, "I'll tell you later after we go over all of the details."

Then Lance showed a little anxiety and asked, "Before you start, how you gonna split the gold up?"

Mick looked at him in anger, "Look Lance, everybody gets the same share in this gang. There's only one thing I want you to remember. I call the shots. Is that clear?"

Lance agreed and so did everyone else.

Then Mick said, "We'll split up the loot up in nine ways."

"Why nine? There are only eight of us," O'Brien said.

"I thought you were brighter than that O'Brien. Did you forget about my cousin who's making all of this possible? I'm certainly not leaving him out of the equation."

"OK you Forty-Fours, hobble your lips and stop your jawing and let's get down to the business at hand."

"Let's do it," Whiskers replied.

"OK, I'll cover Washington, D.C.'s plan first and then I'll go over my plan. At that time I'll give you each specific assignments. There'll be no Plan B. If you guys go along with my plan and we succeed, I'll guarantee you that we'll walk away with an even million."

Mick then laid out on the table a roughly drawn map of the route which the train was scheduled to take. He also had a few other rough drawings of relative points of interest in California plus a sketch of the layout of Dodge City. Mick's cousin, whom he wanted to remain anonymous for now, mailed him all of these maps and various drawings.

Mick pointed to the first map of California. "The gold will be shipping from the San Francisco Mint which is right here. It's gonna be hauled to a general store in town by two or three wagons."

Why a general store?" Tex asked.

"If you can keep your trap shut for two minutes and let me go on, you'll probably get all the answers you're looking for. Got it?" Mick shouted.

"Go ahead," Tex said unabashed.

"OK, they're trying to make this train look as normal as possible carrying passengers, cattle, freight, mail and payroll. The freight that they'll be hauling will be our bonanza. It's the gold bullion.

The Army has already ordered wood crates marked 'Ranch Supplies'. When they're ready, a couple of soldiers will pick up the crates and deliver them to the mint. During the night, several soldiers dressed in civilian clothes will load the gold into the crates and then load the crates onto the wagons and deliver them to a general store in San Francisco.

The cargo will be unloaded during the night and placed in a storage room at the general store. The way I understand it is that soldiers in civilian clothes will be guarding the gold until the time of shipment.

When the right train arrives in town, the soldiers will load the gold into two wagons in plain sight."

"In plain sight, what are they crazy? Do they want the whole countryside to know that they're shipping gold?" inquired Jay.

"Dangit, you're not listening Jay. I told you that these crates would be marked 'Ranch Supplies'," Mick said in an angry voice. "Now, pay attention, would you!"

Mick went on,

"Like I told you before, the gold will be loaded onto a couple of wagons and the wagons will be driven over to the railroad to be loaded into a railroad car."

"In the mail/payroll car?" Whiskers asked.

"Thank goodness I'm in charge. You guys can't figure anything out," Mick said with a frustrated tone in his voice.

"Remember, those idiots in Washington want everyone to believe that this gold shipment is nothing more than 'Ranch Supplies'. So the gold will be loaded and shipped in the freight car, not the mail/payroll car.

Here's what I also understand. The soldiers in civilian clothes will then change back into their uniforms in one of the cars and take their positions on the train."

"Wait a minute," Johnny Reb said, "you mean to tell me that you expect us to hold up a U.S. Government gold train guarded by U.S. Army soldiers? How the hell are we gonna to do that without getting ourselves killed?"

"I'll tell you how, if you just give me a few more minutes. I can appreciate your anxiety Johnny but look at it this way. This is your opportunity to get back at those dang Yankee dogs for tearing up your hometown of Vicksburg and throwing you in jail to rot for two years," Mick said.

"Now listen up guys. The train will be pulling a couple of passenger cars and several cattle cars too. I absolutely do not want any passengers to get hurt during this raid so when we take over the train, it has to be quick and clean. I'll tell you how I intend to do that in just a few minutes."

"Alright, Mick, you told us a lot of stuff so far except for one thing. Just where do we intend to hold up this train?" Frank Rickets inquired.

"Dodge City, Kansas, the most famous cow town in the West."

"Are you out of your mind?" Frank yelled. "Dodge City is full of notorious lawmen like Wyatt and James Earp and the Masterson brothers. You mean to tell me you're talkin' about holding up a government train under the noses of the U.S. Army and the likes of the Earps and the Mastersons? Look Mick, I respect you as a leader but not even my ole buddy Jesse James would attempt to pull somethin' like that off."

The rest of the gang chimed in with Frank and were all skeptical about how they could make this robbery a successful one. Then Mick eased their anxiety with this piece of information.

"Look guys, I have it on good authority that Bat Masterson has left Dodge and there's only one Masterson left there and he's always leaving town for one thing or another. I also know that Wyatt and James Earp are heading to Tombstone with Doc Holliday in September, leaving Dodge for good. That leaves us with one marshal to deal with. His name is Charlie Bassett. He's so dang fat that it would take him two days to get down to the railroad tracks after finding out what we're doin'. By that time, we'd be long gone."

Mick continued, "OK guys, the rest of the stuff about this shipment, the events and people involved, will come out in my plans. So listen up because I'm only gonna cover it one time today, but it's gonna be in great detail.

Tomorrow, and the next day, and several days after that, we'll continue to go over it and over it until you know it in your sleep. Then we'll go outside and practice it, over and over again until it's time to head south to Dodge City.

Each and every one of you will have a specific job to do, including me; and we all will need to perform our jobs with precision and be successful with our responsibilities. If anyone of us fails our job assignment, it would jeopardize our whole attempt to get away with the gold and probably get us all killed. We have all lived a dangerous life up to now and all of us are survivors because we're all good at what we do; but to make this job successful, we need to be better, sharper and more skillful than ever before."

"Gee Mick, that there is the fanciest I ever heard you talk," Whiskers said.

Mick smiled at Whiskers' comment and just went on.

"Is everyone still in?" Mick asked.

Everybody looked at each other and said nothing.

"Well are you? I wanna know right now before I go over all my plans. If you aren't in, pack up and get out now!"

Frank said, "I'm in boss." Then they all followed suit.

"Good, then let's get to it."

Mick then threw two more sketches on the table. One was a drawing of the train and the other one was a drawing of the route with three points of interest. The drawings were from Mick's cousin. These were the details. The first point of interest was where the train needed to stop for water and fuel. This was generally a 30 to 45 minute stop and just about a mile before arriving in Dodge City. The second point on the map was Dodge City itself, which showed the railroad tracks in relationship to the town and the marshal's office. It also showed where the railroad spur and the stockyards were located to load the longhorns into the cattle cars. The third point of interest on the map was a point just one mile east of town. He would explain the significance of that later.

Mick now began to explain the layout of the train. He had an excellent drawing of the entire train that he would use, and point to, as he proceeded.

"My cousin found out how this train will be laid out and where the soldiers will be positioned. Here's what I know. This gold train will have 15 cars and laid out in this manner: the steam engine, the fuel car, two small passenger cars which hold about 50 passengers each, the freight car where the gold will be stored, the mail/payroll car, eight cattle cars which will pick up the cattle in Dodge City to be shipped to Chicago, and a caboose.

Now here is the most important information that I received from my cousin. It's where the soldiers are gonna be positioned on the train. There will be thirteen bluecoats. One will be the commanding officer and then there are twelve very skillful cavalry soldiers who will be armed to the max with pistols and Springfield '73 rifles. The good thing about it is that those Springfields have to be reloaded after each shot. I understand that the new Winchester repeating rifles are being supplied to the soldiers in the Indian territories first, so we really lucked out there.

I'll tell you where the soldiers are positioned by following the order of how the cars are laid out."

Mick then pointed to the train drawing on the table.

"There'll be one soldier positioned in the first passenger car. He'll be in the first row on the left-hand side sitting in an aisle seat right here. Remember, this is the car directly behind the fuel car.

Then there'll be six soldiers positioned in the second passenger car. They'll be back here in the last row, three on each side of the aisle.

The commanding officer and two of his soldiers will be stationed right here in the freight car with the gold. My source told me that the railroad car doors would be locked from the inside. But not to worry because I have that figured out too.

The mail/payroll car will be positioned right here after the freight car. As far as I know, there'll only be one soldier stationed there. The car will be hauling mail, payroll and such and I don't believe this car will be locked. If it is, that could pose us a slight problem.

The cattle cars will be positioned after the payroll car and then the caboose will be last. I'm told that there'll be two soldiers in the caboose.

Now, is everybody with me so far?" Mick asked.

Danny O'Brien commented, "Your insider must come from high places if he has detailed information like this."

Mick just smiled and said, "yep" and went on.

"Now, let me give you our overall plan and then I'll give each of you your assignment. When we pick up the right stuff from town, you guys are gonna cut down fifteen trees and lay them end to end just like rail cars in a train. Then the practicing begins."

The gang thought Mick's idea was a good one but they weren't real crazy about the manual labor involved. Nevertheless, they agreed that it was a good way to prepare for the job. With all of those armed soldiers aboard the train, they knew it was imperative to have their act together or they would never come out of this alive. Plus the rewards for success amounted to a whopping one hundred grand per person in gold. That was more money than they could individually steal in a lifetime.

"Are you guys ready to hear my plan?" Mick asked.

"Let's hear it," Frank said.

"OK then, pay close attention. The train will stop at the fuel and watering station a mile west of town. That's where most of us will be waiting. We will get there the day before the train is scheduled to arrive and gun down anybody who gets in our way.

When the train shows up the next day, we'll send those soldiers to their maker except for the three in the freight car with the gold. We'll take them out in Dodge City."

It was here that Lance Carter stopped Mick dead in his tracks.

"I don't get it Mick, why aren't we taking the gold at the fueling station?" Lance asked.

Everyone looked at Mick awaiting a reasonable answer.

"I'll tell you why," Mick shouted, "because I said so, that's why!" Mick was always quick-tempered when someone questioned his decisions.

"We need a better answer than that," Whiskers insisted. "We're putting our lives on the line here. We could all get killed."

"OK, here's the deal. I want the Forty-Fours to go down in history as the most notorious train robbery gang ever. That's why we're gonna do the gold heist in Dodge City."

Mick calmed down and said, "Look guys, stealing this gold in Dodge City will be as easy as blasting an empty whiskey bottle at five paces with a double barrel shotgun. There'll be plenty of cover for us where the train stops. I'll explain that to you in a few minutes. Plus, none of the townspeople have a dog in this hunt so they ain't gonna care what happens on that train."

Mick paused for a few seconds and then continued, "I don't want any passengers to get hurt at the fuel and water station nor in Dodge City. That's why we'll have all of the passengers get off the train at the fuel and water stop west of town. We don't want the whole U.S. Army down on our backs.

After the soldiers are eliminated and the passengers removed, we'll take the train to Dodge City. I'll ride with the engineer and have him pull the train into the railroad spur next to the stockyard. That's where the cover comes from. The train will park so that the freight car will be just past the stockyard. There, we'll break into the freight car and unload the gold into two wagons which will be waiting for us. We are unloading the gold on the stockyard side of the train and not the town side. The train itself along with the stockyard nearby will give us excellent cover from anyone trying to be a hero. If anybody and I mean anybody gets in our way, we'll gun 'em down outright. Got it?"

They all agreed and Mick continued, "After the gold is loaded into our two wagons, we'll drive them east along the tracks for about a mile. Then we'll cross over the tracks at a prepared crossing. I'll go into more detail on that in a few minutes.

Once we cross the tracks, we'll be on our way back to this hideout where we'll split the loot.

We'll take the same route both ways. When we leave from here, we'll travel to Ogallala, Nebraska and follow the new Western Trail to Dodge City. To play it safe, we'll travel in two groups. The wagons will be in one group and everyone else will be in the other. We'll stay about a mile apart from each other.

When we arrive about two miles north of Dodge, our two wagons will head southeast and stop about one mile east of town at the railroad tracks. The other group will head southwest of Dodge City to the fuel and water stop. Like I said before, we'll show up at those destinations a day before the train is scheduled to arrive.

OK then, here are the assignments.

Whiskers and Tex will each drive a wagon to Dodge City and drive the wagons back to Hole-in-the-Wall after we load up the gold."

Mick wasn't taking any chances with Whiskers having only one eye, that's why he made him the driver of one of the wagons.

"Before we head down to Dodge City, we'll load up one of the wagons with dirt. Make sure both of you pack shovels. When you reach your destination one mile east of Dodge, you'll use the dirt to make a ramp, up and over the tracks, making us a smooth path to cross. With all that gold weighing down the wagons, we don't wanna break a wheel goin' over those tracks.

After that job is done, find a secluded area outside of town to camp for the night. About 8:00 o'clock the next morning, drive the wagons to town and park them on the same side of the tracks as the stockyard. Be sure you are parked east of the stockyards because that's where we'll unload the gold from the freight car onto the wagons. Are there any questions at this point?"

Tex and Whiskers looked at each other and then looked at Mick and both said, "No."

"Good, now here are the rest of the assignments.

Remember, we need to take out all of the soldiers at the fuel and water station except for the three in the freight car. So Frank and Jay, since you are the best marksmen in the group, I'm giving you the toughest job; both of you will be entering the second passenger car from the back and gunning down the six soldiers sitting in the last row. Jay, you take out the three on the right and Frank, you take out the three on the left."

"Our pleasure," Frank said.

"I knew you would like that," Mick replied. "Jay, then you go up and get that blue belly sittin' in the first row of the first passenger car."

"Not a problem," Jay said.

Then Mick continued, "Lance, you and Johnny will take out the two soldiers in the caboose. Each of you should enter from different ends of the caboose but be careful not to shoot each other. Lance, you come in from the back and drill the soldier on the right side of the car and Johnny, you come in from the front and gun down the soldier on the left side of the car. We'll blow those blue bellies away in a cross-fire.

Danny, you waste the soldier in the mail/payroll car. Enter it from the backside near the cattle car; that door should be unlocked.

Once you guys take out your men, I want all of you to help get the passengers off the train. Take them off as quickly as possible. Remember, I don't want any passengers harmed unless it's you or them, understood?"

"What about the three soldiers in the freight car with the gold?" Johnny asked.

"If my thinking is right, those three won't open the door. They'll probably have orders to keep their doors locked until someone gives them a signal, so we'll deal with them in Dodge City.

While you guys are taking care of your business, I'll take control of the train up front with the engineers. As soon as all the passengers are off the train, give me a signal and we'll crank up that ole iron horse and head east to Dodge City.

Are there any more questions at this point?" Mick asked.

Everyone said, "No" because they were anxious to hear the rest of the plan.

"OK, good, when we get to town we'll be faced with several challenges. There'll probably be cattle in the stockyard waiting to be loaded onto the train. That means that there could be up to ten cowboys hanging around. If we get lucky though, most of those cowpokes will be on a bender, you know, in the saloon getting drunker than a bunch of liquored-up polecats.

Keep in mind though, nobody in town will have any idea what we're up too. Let's not do any shooting unless we have to. In fact, the only time we should have to skin our .44's is when we break into the freight car and take out the three soldiers guarding the gold."

"You still haven't told us how you intend to break into that locked freight car," Frank commented.

"It's simple ole buddy, you and I are gonna shoot our way in from the top," Mick said. "Freight cars have a trap door on top of their car. That door won't be locked so we'll climb on top of the car when the train comes to a complete stop, lift up the trap door and blast our way in."

"Sounds crazy but I like it," Frank said.

Mick continued, "All the unloading of the gold will take place on the stockyard side of the train. So the townspeople won't have a clue what's going on. They'll think the gunshots are the cowboys whooping it up again.

Once we get the side door open, I want everyone to get moving and unload the gold. We'll load up Whiskers' wagon first. When yours is loaded Whiskers, I want you to drive off east to the ramp you built outside of town and wait for us there. If you get any stupid ideas of leaving without us, we'll track you down, skin your hide and make buzzard bait out of you. Got it?

As soon as we fill up the second wagon, we'll head out and meet you guys at the crossing. Then we'll all ride back to Wyoming and celebrate the fact that the Forty-Fours pulled off the greatest gold heist in history.

Well all you sidewinders, how do you like the plan?"

"I think it's gutsy and just crazy enough to work," Lance said.

"And if it doesn't work, we'll all get killed," Mick added. "I'm not into dying before I get rich so after dinner, let's talk about how we're gonna practice for this Historic Grand Train Robbery.

Hey Frank, we're gonna make your friend Jesse James look like a novice outlaw."

They all laughed and got ready to eat. At this point, Mick told them to break open the bottles and have a few drinks before dinner; and so they did.

After dinner and when darkness set in, they lit up a couple of kerosene lanterns in the cabin and sat around the large table to listen to Mick's plan on how to practice for the train robbery. The plan was ingenious. They would build a makeshift train out of long pine logs about the length of real train cars. Then they would take the thick branches from the pine trees they cut down and pile them up where the stockyard would be. This would enable them to figure out the fastest and most efficient way to move the wagons in and out when loading up the gold.

Mick told Tex and Whiskers to go to town the next day and buy two buckboard wagons and four draft horses from the livery stable and then go over to the general store and pick up two shovels, three four-foot saws, three axes, two large canvases for the wagons and more .44 ammunition for target shooting. They were also to pick up more food; beans, bacon, coffee, flour and such. Mick made it clear that time was not on their side so they had to get "right to cutting down the pines and get to practicing."

The next morning, Tex and Whiskers rode out early and by noon they were back at camp with everything on Mick's list. They all took about an hour for lunch and then afterwards took the saws and axes to the woods and began cutting down pine trees. They cut them to the lengths of railroad cars just as Mick ordered and then pulled them one-by-one on horseback over to a cleared flat area designated to be the practice place.

By noon the next day they had the simulated train and stockyard area completely built and in place. Mick spent the rest of that afternoon outside with his gang, once more reviewing the plans and everyone's responsibilities.

Then the next day they began to practice their roles one at a time. It was like practicing for a Wild West Show. Every move was rehearsed with precision. They went over it and over it until they each knew every movement in their sleep. When they had their moves down, they began using live ammunition pretending they were blasting the soldiers.

Mick even set up a simulated passenger car for Frank and Jay. He put three stumps on either side of a makeshift aisle to mimic the six soldiers the two had to gun down.

Mick also had Tex and Whiskers hitch up the horses to the wagons and they practiced the most efficient way of moving the wagons close to the train, one at a time, and then moving them out quickly.

After Mick felt that they had the wagon situation down, he thought it was necessary to talk about how heavy the crates filled with gold would be. So one morning he stopped the practice and gathered the gang together and began a serious discussion about how best to prepare themselves to unload a very heavy cargo.

"Guys, one of the toughest parts of this job will be the actual lifting of the crates loaded with gold bricks. My cousin told me that there'll be about 25 crates of gold on the train and we're taking 'em all. Each box will weigh about 150 pounds. That's almost too heavy for one person to lift. Whiskers could probably do it but the rest of you skinny runts would give yourselves a hernia. The best way to prepare for this is to take one of the wagons out and gather some heavy rocks to practice lifting. We need rocks that are too heavy for one person to lift but light enough for two people to lift."

So that's what they did. Whiskers hitched up the horses, the men jumped into the back of the buckboard and they drove the wagon out to the side of the mountain nearby. There they found 13 boulders that weighed about 150 pounds each. They gauged the weight by how many men it took to lift the rocks. If one man could lift it, then it wasn't heavy enough. If two men could just barely lift it, then it passed the test.

They then loaded up the thirteen boulders and headed back to the practice site. Mick figured he needed a way to simulate unloading the gold from the train to the wagons so he came up with a brilliant idea.

He had Whiskers and Tex back up the wagons to each other. One of the wagons would represent the train car. Since it would take two men to lift a box of gold, he assigned two men on each wagon. His plan in Dodge City was to have Frank and himself be the lookouts while Jay, Lance, Johnny, and Danny would be the ones to unload the gold. Whiskers and Tex would be ready to drive off with the shipment when given the cue by Mick. Their plan was to put 13 cases on one wagon and 12 cases on the other.

The first thing Mick wanted to do was to have the four loaders get used to lifting the heavy weight without hurting themselves. So Mick put Jay and Lance on the wagon with the rocks, which simulated the railroad car, and Johnny and Danny on the empty wagon.

Mick then had them begin the practice. Jay and Lance picked up the first rock together and passed it to Johnny and Danny. Johnny and Danny carried it to the front of the wagon and gently set it down. They proceeded to lift and move the rest of the rocks, one right after the other. The lifting was arduous and painful on their backs.

Once the wagon was loaded with the thirteen rocks, they switched rolls and Johnny and Danny passed the rocks to Jay and Lance. To have a perfect practice, they needed to lift and pass twenty-five rocks, which represented the number of gold boxes that would be on the train.

After the first practice round, they took about a thirty-minute break. Oh there were complaints alright but the lifting was literally worth its weight in gold. Then they went at it again and again and again, taking breaks between each practice round. At the end of the day, the four lifters were plum tuckered out.

Over the next few days Mick and the gang felt that they were making great progress and becoming very proficient with their responsibilities. As the days continued on, they all became more assured that they could pull off this unprecedented heist with success; with each day of practice came a higher degree of confidence.

On the evening of August 1, 1879, Mick had one final meeting with his gang. After going over the plans one last time, Mick asked if there were any final questions.

Frank responded, "We're all excited about this gold heist but I just have one important question boss, just how are we gonna turn gold bullion into cash?"

"Not to worry. My cousin has already worked that out. He has a buyer out of Canada coming to Wyoming in November who has agreed to buy the gold from us, cash on the barrelhead. The buyer plans to haul it back to Canada and sell it up there for a profit.

As for me and my cousin, we prefer gold instead of paper money so I'm staying with the bullion."

"For what reason?" Danny asked.

"That's my business," Mick answered.

"Frankly," Lance said, "I don't care what you or that Canadian does with the gold. I just wanna be sure I get my share in American greenbacks."

"You will," Mick assured him.

After that brief discussion, Mick laid out the plans for the trip to Dodge City. He wanted to take plenty of food along to take care of most of the round-trip journey.

"Tomorrow, I want Whiskers and Tex to go to town and buy the supplies we need for the trip. While you guys are doing that, we'll load up dirt in the other wagon like we talked about before.

We'll rest our bodies for a couple of days and then on Thursday morning, we'll hit the trail to Dodge City by way of Ogallala and the Western Trail. We should arrive in the area of Dodge around October 4th. As I said before, we'll travel in two groups but meet up every night and camp together so we can all have a hearty meal at dinner and breakfast.

Guys keep this in mind; we are more prepared than any gang that ever held up a bank, stagecoach or a train. We have inside information of the government's plan even down to the last detail and most importantly, we will have the element of surprise on our side. Our speed and all the practicing we did will make the difference.

Now you ugly polecats, break open the bottles and let's have some whiskey and drink to us being the richest outlaws in the West!"

They all whooped and hollered and proceeded to get drunker than a bunch of cowpokes after a three month long cattle drive.

On Thursday, August 4, 1879, Mick's gang, known as the Forty-Fours, packed up their equipment and supplies and headed southeast to Dodge City, Kansas.

CHAPTER FIVE:

Caldwell's Last Cattle Drive

The year was 1830. The date was June 14th. It was a scorching hot sunny afternoon in the area we now call Austin, Texas. Texas has had a dry spell for months now so the breeze that day was blowing up clouds of dust, which layered and blanketed every nook and cranny around this old homestead.

Many Native Americans like the Tonkawa tribe, the Comanches and the Lipan Apaches were known to travel through the area following the great buffalo herds, which were their natural source for food, clothing and such. So the threat of hostile Indian raids was always a real possibility for the pioneers and settlers of that time and place.

This 3,500-acre spread, which was located near the site of the southern leg of the Chisholm Trail, sat between the Colorado and the Brazos Rivers. A tributary from the Colorado River flowed through this beautiful grassy plains ranch and the abundance of grass for grazing, along with the crystal clear water from the river, made this ranch premier land for raising cattle.

It was the home of Thomas H. Caldwell and his lovely wife Sarah Tranton Caldwell and today this ranch would be witness to the birth of the Caldwell's first of three children. For on this date in the sweltering heat of a lazy Texas afternoon, a baby boy by the name of Jesse Caldwell was born.

Thomas was the son of early immigrants from Scotland who migrated to Texas because the land was flat and had an abundance of good grazing areas and an excellent source of water for raising cattle. The Caldwells came from a long line of cattle ranchers in Scotland and searched out a new life for themselves in the land with open ranges, new challenges, and high rewards for people willing to put in a good honest day's work.

The Caldwells were Christians and were very religious people who attended church at an old Spanish mission named San Xavier. The Spanish Padre was Father Jose Vasquez who was a good friend of the family.

In addition to working his ranch, Thomas Caldwell would help the Padre at the mission with Sunday services. The Padre was blessed to have the Caldwells living nearby because the Caldwell family brought wealth with them from the Old Country and were willing to donate food for the Padre to distribute to the needy families in the area.

Thomas felt that he was blessed to be able to help the less fortunate families and swore that he would raise his children the same way his parents raised him; that is, to respect his neighbors and offer a helping hand to the poor folks who needed it.

During the next four years, Thomas and Sarah had two more children; they were both girls and their names were Mary and Ruth.

At a very early age, Jesse showed a lot of interest in horses and cattle and enjoyed riding double in the saddle with his father, rounding up stray cows and calves. He also enjoyed helping his pa do chores around the homestead like cleaning the tack, graining the horses and even milking the cows. It was easy to see that Jesse was a natural born rancher.

Due to the constant threat of Indian raids, Jesse's father taught him how to shoot a rifle at an early age. When Jesse went target shooting, taking long shots at Texas prickly pear cactus leaves, his pa always told him to "aim small". This advice made Jesse focus in on his target with a keen eye.

Over the years, Jesse learned to love target shooting and enjoyed working to improve his marksmanship skills with both a rifle and a pistol. He soon became a crack shot.

On his 10th birthday, his father surprised him with what Jesse called "the best birthday presents ever". They were a new long barrel musket and a pistol.

Now Jesse, like his parents, grew up to be a devout Christian. He would attend services at the old Mission on Sundays with his parents and even assisted the Padre before Mass by lighting the candles and preparing the water and wine. He seemed to be a chip off the old block. In fact, the Padre jokingly nicknamed him Chipper.

During the early 1830's, Texas was still a territory belonging to Mexico. In December of 1832 Sam Houston (March 2, 1793 – July 26, 1863, lived to age 70) relocated to Texas. Although there is no supporting written evidence of the following, it was highly speculated that Houston was commissioned by President Jackson to facilitate a U.S. annexation of the territory.

From 1833 to 1836 Houston, along with many others, promoted and planned independence from Mexico. Santa Anna, who cherished his dictatorship over what he reasoned to be his land, got wind of this and began sending troops north to squelch the idea.

In November of 1835, the Texas Army commissioned Sam Houston as Major General. In addition, the Texans held a convention in March of 1836 and it was there on March 2nd that Houston signed the Texas Declaration of Independence. It was also at that same convention that Houston was declared Commander-in-Chief of Texas.

Now, while all of this was taking place and while Santa Anna was marching north and increasing his army, volunteers were gathering in an old mission, known as the Alamo, in San Antonio de Bexar, later to become San Antonio, Texas.

These volunteers were converting the old mission into a fortress to withstand the oncoming attack of the Mexican Army. However, as future events would soon unfold, it would become fatally obvious that the former Spanish mission was designed to withstand only Indian attacks and not the full force of artillery bombardments by Santa Anna's Mexican Army.

Originally, Houston knew that he was critically short of troops to stage a successful defense at the Alamo so he sent Jim Bowie (circa 1796 – March 6, 1836, lived to age circa 40) and 30 men to remove the abandoned Mexican cannons and bring them north. In addition, he instructed Bowie to destroy the Alamo, fearing that Santa Anna would use the Alamo as a supply depot.

Unfortunately, when Bowie arrived at the Alamo, he too discovered that there were no draft horses available to move the heavy artillery.

Then James C. Neil, the acting Alamo commander at that time, convinced Bowie that the Alamo held strategic importance and needed to be defended. Bowie agreed with Neil's assessment and sent a request to Houston for more troops. On February 3, 1836, William B. Travis (August 1, 1809 – March 6, 1836, lived to age 26) arrived with 30 men. Then, only five days later, Davy Crockett (August 17, 1786 – March 6, 1836, lived to age 49) and a small group of volunteers from Tennessee arrived as well.

Neil left the makeshift fort on February 11th supposedly in search of more men. In Neil's absence, Travis and Bowie alternated being commanders of the Alamo a couple of times due to several circumstances and at one time, shared command. However, Travis ultimately assumed sole command because of Bowie's untimely illness.

Around the first of March approximately 3,000 Mexican troops were now present and ready to take on the brave Texans. On March 5th and under tremendous distress knowing that they were outnumbered at least six to one, Travis gathered his men together and informed them that there would be no more troops arriving and said that if any men wanted to leave, they should do so now. A few did, but most stayed.

On March 6th before the early morning sunrise on a cool pre-spring morning, Santa Anna's Army advanced forward toward the walls of the Alamo. The brave volunteers, with their muskets blazing away, and the cannons echoing across the countryside were able to stand off the first two grueling attacks of Santa Anna's ruthless army. But as history has recorded it, the third attack was just too much.

On that day at the Alamo, 182 to 260 brave and courageous men, who stood for the independent Texas, sacrificed their precious lives and defended their independence from Mexico. But even being tremendously outnumbered, they managed to inflict enormous casualties on the Mexican Army in the form of 400 to 600 killed or wounded.

News of the fate of the Alamo spread throughout Texas like a wildfire blazing across the Great Plains and came to the attention of Sam Houston on March 11th. Santa Anna felt that the slaughter at the Alamo would spoil the attempt of the Texans to push further for independence. He mistakenly thought that Texans would just turn and run from his fierce army like frightened jackrabbits. Some did, but most did not. In fact, it had quite the opposite effect. Men who were not soldiers but instead, ranchers, farmers and homesteaders left their domiciles and joined up with Sam Houston's Army to battle for their independence from Mexico.

One of the volunteer soldiers was Thomas H. Caldwell who lived about 85 miles northeast of San Antonio. He heard about the siege at the Alamo and knew that if his children were going to have independence from Mexico and Santa Anna's dictatorship, the time to fight for it, was now. So he made immediate plans to join Sam Houston's Army.

Jesse Caldwell, Thomas' son, was now 6 years old and still just a child. However, he was tall for his age and already knew quite a bit about ranching. Jesse's mother was a strong and independent type woman who also did a lot of work around the ranch but she also had two young daughters to care for. Luckily, the Caldwells had a neighbor with two teenage boys who Thomas hired to assist his wife and son with ranch chores. It was because of them that Thomas was able to leave his family and join Sam Houston. At this point he had no idea how long he would be gone.

So Thomas packed up his gear, his rifle and extra ammunition and headed east along the Brazos River where he met up with Houston's forces. He found the army on the evening of April 2nd and was able to personally meet Sam Houston himself.

On April 11th Houston accumulated 1,500 troops. Right around then, Santa Anna made a critical mistake. He split his army into three groups thinking they could surround Houston's men and wipe them out.

But it was not to be because on April 21, 1836, at San Jacinto, Houston and his army surprised Santa Anna and his troops during their afternoon siesta. Houston learned where Santa Anna was camping and snuck up to check things out. He noticed that there were only a few soldiers on guard and everyone else was taking their siesta. Houston passed the word around and said, "This is it, this is what we have been waiting for. It's time to get even and let our battle cry be, Remember the Alamo!"

So Houston's Army, 1,500 strong, bravely and slowly advanced forward toward the Mexicans, some on horseback and others on foot, and then charged, crying out loudly and often, "Remember the Alamo! Remember the Alamo!"

Their rifles and pistols were blazing. The smell and sight of black powder smoke filled the air. The Mexicans were in complete disarray and disoriented. Some of them began to run away while the Texans pushed forward in a historical gallant charge.

In just eighteen minutes, the Texans won a "decisive victory" over Santa Anna's Army. Not only was his army destroyed, but Santa Anna himself was captured as well. With his army badly beaten, Santa Anna was forced to sign the Treaty of Velasco, which granted Texas its final and everlasting independence. This was Texas' finest hour.

The Texans did not suffer many casualties during the Battle of San Jacinto. Although amongst the injured were Sam Houston and Thomas Caldwell. Both suffered from gunshots to the legs but Caldwell's wound was much more serious. His right leg was shattered from a 50-caliber musket ball, and had to be amputated at the knee. He was taken to a hospital in the area, which is now known as the city of Houston where he recuperated for eight months. During those long days and long nights he was able to keep in contact with his family by writing them a letter each week. He was happy to learn that his family and his ranch were doing just fine. His wife told him that Jesse was really a big help with chores and that the two neighbor boys were worth their weight in gold.

While recuperating, Thomas had plenty of time to think about his ranch, going forward. He loved their homestead and he was determined to figure out how he and his family could continue to ranch even with the handicap he was dealt with at San Jacinto. He was determined that having only one leg would in no way detour his dreams and his future.

In January of 1837, Thomas arrived home riding in a horse drawn wagon, which he purchased in town. He discovered that with only one leg, it was much easier to ride in a wagon versus riding on a saddled horse.

His family was extremely happy to see him. They insisted that he continue to rest and recuperate for a couple of months, and so he did. Thomas had nothing to worry about. His family had plenty of food stored away for the winter and the neighbors had cut an abundant amount of mesquite wood for the fireplace to keep the old cabin warm and the stove fires hot for cooking. It was a joyous time once again at the Caldwell homestead.

Thomas spent many lantern lit evenings telling his family about his exploits and the time he spent with Sam Houston. In fact, he sang high praises of Houston everyday during the first couple of months he was home and for years to follow. Jesse learned to respect and look up to Houston because of the strategic role Houston played in earning their independence from Mexico.

As the years passed, Jesse grew in maturity and strength. He was a handsome young man who was much taller than his father standing at 6' 2" tall. Jesse was a cowboy's cowboy with a deeply tanned square face, sporting a full long moustache, broad at the shoulders, and slim at the waist. His arms were the size of cannons and his hands were so big he could pick up and palm a San Antonio military cannonball with one hand. His father taught him everything he knew about ranching and raising Texas longhorn cattle. As their herd grew, it was necessary to build a bunkhouse on the ranch and hire several ranch hands to assist him with those grueling spring and fall cattle roundups, which consisted of roping, branding new calves, and castrating bull calves to make into steers.

In 1855, sorrow filled the hearts of the Caldwell clan. Jesse's father took ill and passed on leaving the ranch to his wife, his son and his two daughters. Jesse's mother passed away two years later as well. His two sisters, Mary and Ruth married local boys in 1857 and 1858 and they built houses on the Caldwell ranch while Jesse continued to live in the original homestead cabin. As time went by Jesse became a prosperous local cattle baron. As his herd grew, so did the number of ranch hands that were required to run his operation.

He had heard about the demand for beef on the east coast and discovered that he could obtain five to eight times more money for his cattle up north than selling them in Texas because Texas was overrun with cattle on the hoof. It was a matter of supply and demand.

So in January of 1861 he planned his first cattle drive to Missouri. Unfortunately, the Civil War began and his cattle drive dreams were shattered.

On February 1, 1861, the state of Texas declared its secession from the Unites States and on March 2nd of the same year, Texas joined the Confederate States of America.

Sam Houston was the Governor of Texas at that time. He agreed to secede from the Union but had no desire to join the Confederate States of America. He instead tried to convince the politicians and the folks to revert to their former status and become an independent republic and remain neutral during the war. Well the Texans would not have anything to do with that idea.

On March 4th a convention assembled for the purpose of declaring Texas out of the Union and to approve the Constitution of the Confederate States of America.

On March 16th, all state officials were to take an oath of allegiance to the Confederacy. Houston, who was in attendance, adamantly refused to take the oath. Consequently, he was deposed from his office.

Even though over 70,000 Texans served in the Confederate Army, there were still quite a few who were not Southern sympathizers. They were called Unionists. However, if you were found out, it was better than two to one odds that it would cost you your life.

Among the people who considered themselves Unionists were the Caldwells. Jesse and his two sisters grew up listening to their pa's tales of Sam Houston and his unprecedented courage and they grew to respect him enormously for what he stood for. Hearing that Sam Houston refused to take an oath to the Confederacy fortified their own position on the same. However, they kept their beliefs clandestine, fearing reprisal.

The state of Texas itself did not see any large battles during the Civil War. It was generally considered a supply state to the Confederacy, supplying mainly cattle and horses. There was also an abundance of cotton grown in the state but that made its way to Europe via Mexico.

Jesse Caldwell was 31 years old now and considered to be too old to fight in the War by many so he stayed on his ranch with his ranch hands who were of similar age. While the Civil War was being fought, Jesse spent the next four years increasing the size of his herd.

The Caldwells being the Christians that they were, would not deprive anyone cattle for food so they donated cattle to the Confederacy when asked to do so. However, Jesse also had to protect his herd from rustlers and guerrilla fighters who fought, killed and stole in the name of the Confederacy looking for ways to make an easy buck.

Jesse knew that he and his ranch hands had to be better than average marksmen to protect his herd so he constantly made his men practice their shooting skills on the range. He had no problem spending money for extra ammunition because he knew it would eventually pay off in the long run.

Because of his passion for guns and the desire to improve his shooting skills, he became well known around town as a skilled marksman. But what was also known was the fact that he would only use those skills when it was necessary to protect his property, his ranch hands or himself. Jesse was a good man in these regards.

It was now the spring of 1863.

One day while Jesse was picking up supplies in the town of Austin, he came across an old friend named Doc Flanagan. Doc just came back from a buffalo hunting trip in the west and acquired a couple of new rifles, which just came onto the market.

Doc knew about Jesse's passion for guns as did everyone in town. When Jesse jumped off of his buckboard, hitched the horses to the rail and began walking up the two steps to the general store, Doc called out from across the street while standing next to his own buckboard, "Hey, Jesse, do you have a minute?"

Jesse turned around, saw Doc and said, "Sure." So he headed across the street.

He shook hands with Doc, asked him how he was doing and then Doc said, "I just came back from a hunting trip in New Mexico with a friend of mine who lives out East. He's a gunsmith and sold me a few rifles, which have just been manufactured. Would you like to see them?"

"You bet," Jesse responded.

."Well, then come on back here with me and I'll show you what I have."

They both walked to the back of the buckboard, which was filled with supplies and covered with a white tarp.

Doc untied the tarp twines from the hooks on the sides of the wagon and threw back the canvas to expose the contents.

The first two words out of Jesse's mouth were, "My word."

Jesse then said, "What are those, and where did you get 'em?"

"Go ahead, pick one up."

So Jesse did with great care and in a manner as if it were a piece of his mother's fine china.

"You are holding one of the first newly manufactured repeating rifles," Doc said.

"What's it called?"

"It's a Henry rifle which was designed by Benjamin Tyler Henry in the late 1850's. About 900 of these beauties were made between the summer and fall of last year and they just hit the streets."

"Well don't just stand there," Jesse said, "tell me all about it."

"OK, it's a .44 caliber, lever action, breech loading repeating rifle that holds 16 bullets and it shoots them faster than any firearm in existence.

Some of the Union troops are buying them on their own but neither army has made them an official part of their arsenal because the ammunition is not that easy to find. However, look in here, Jesse."

Doc opened up a wood crate that was full of boxes of .44 caliber ammunition.

"Where the heck did you get that mother lode from?" Jesse asked.

"From the gunsmith who I bought these rifles from."

Then Doc made a surprising offer, "Look Jesse, I have always respected you and your family and know how you've been enamored with firearms for all the right reasons. I have three of these beauts which is one too many for me. So, if you're interested, I'll be more than happy to sell you one of them for $150, which is only $10 over what I paid for them. Plus I'll sell you a few boxes of ammunition as well. Is it a deal, my friend?"

"Are you kidding me? Give me ten minutes to run over to the bank and I'll meet you right back here."

"Wait a minute Jesse. I have one more thing I want you to look at, before you run off. It's a new pistol that's been on the market for just a couple of years. It's a Model 1860 Colt Army .44 caliber experimental model with a fluted cylinder. I actually have two of them along with dual holsters. I'll sell you the whole getup, two pistols and holsters for $50 if you're interested. I haven't tried it but I think you should be able to use the same ammunition that you use for the Henry rifle. Are you interested?"

"You bet I am," Jesse said with a big grin on his face. "You just wait right here friend and I'll be back from the bank faster than a badger can chew off the back leg of a fat and sassy crippled feral hog."

So ole Jesse ran over to the bank as fast as he could, which was directly across the street and next to the supply store he initially intended to visit. Within minutes he withdrew $250 and bought the two pistols and the Henry rifle along with several boxes of ammunition.

He then walked over to the gunsmith shop and bought a leather rifle scabbard for his new Henry repeating rifle to attach to his saddle. In fact, he was so excited, he climbed onto his buckboard, whipped the reins on his horse's hindquarters and took off down the road as fast as his horse could carry him. About a half a mile outside of town he realized he forgot to buy what he went to town for in the first place. So pulling the reins back to stop the horse while laughing at himself, he turned his buckboard around and drove back to the general store to buy his supplies: coffee, beans, flour, slab bacon and various other food staples that would take care of him and his ranch hands for another month.

When he arrived home he unloaded the supplies, gathered the ranch hands around to show them his new Henry rifle and the Colt pistols and then he immediately began to load them up and target shoot. He was acting like a kid with a new toy at Christmas. These firearms were his pride and joy and they would be by his side for the next twenty years.

Two years have gone by now...

The year was 1865 and the Civil War had just ended. Many of the 70,000 Texans who fought for the Confederacy were killed in the War while many others were wounded, losing arms and legs and were crippled both physically and sometimes mentally for life. Others who survived without a scratch had aspirations to begin a renewed life of ranching and farming once again on the vast southern Plains.

Throughout the state of Texas there were many ranches, which were unattended during the years of the Civil War. So cattle herds ran wild and multiplied into the millions. Since most of the cattle were not branded, they were there for the taking.

Word spread around Texas about the huge demand for beef in the East and if one could gather up a nice herd and successfully head it north to Missouri, he could get rich quick.

Jesse had a leg up on most of the Texas ranchers since he already had a number of ranch hands on the payroll. Plus he spent the last three years roping and branding every stray longhorn he could round up. His brand was a simple one. It was JC, which stood for Jesse Caldwell.

Jesse always had dreams of driving cattle up to Missouri and now the time was right to do just that. His plan was to leave in March of the following year, 1866, and head up the Shawnee Trail to the railhead in Sedalia, Missouri where cattle would be loaded on railroad cars and shipped to the slaughterhouses in Chicago.

Over the years, Jesse had put his brand on well over 10,000 head of maverick longhorns. Since he could only drive about 2,000 head up north at one time, he was forced to hire a few more ranch hands to take care of his ranch and the remaining herd while he would be gone.

In January of 1866, he did his research on the path of the Shawnee Trail. From his ranch near Austin, the trail would lead him through Waco, Dallas, cross the Red River near Denison, and head north through the Indian Territory (now Oklahoma) to Fort

Gibson. From Fort Gibson he would drive the herd to Baxter Springs, Kansas and then head northeast to Sedalia. He figured the trip would take about two to three months to complete depending on the weather.

On February 2nd, he met with his 15 ranch hands in their bunkhouse. It was a Saturday evening and quite chilly outside. There was a hot fire burning in the wood-burning stove and they had just finished their dinner. It was a tradition on the Caldwell ranch to fry up some thick medium rare beefsteaks on Saturday evening after a long hard workweek out on the open range. Then they would sit around the warm stove, soak up their favorite rye and tell stories about their exploits of the past week.

However, this evening was a little different. After eating a hearty cowboy dinner, Jesse asked them to hold up on the rye until he was finished talking about his plans.

Jesse gathered the guys around the large ranch dinner table, lifted up one boot onto a chair and began, "Guys, I've been dreaming about this for a lifetime and the time has finally arrived. I'm planning to take 2,000 head of longhorn steers, all with the JC brand, up to Sedalia, Missouri next month. I need ten men plus the cook to make the trip with me and the rest will stay here and take care of the ranch and the cattle while we're gone.

I'm looking for volunteers. The pay will be $150 per man and you'll get paid for the drive when the job is done. To be clear, that's in addition to your normal monthly pay. The job will be completed when the cattle are loaded on the railroad cars. I'll supply the food, ammunition, rain gear and the extra horses for the trip. We'll take a total of 45 horses with us: three for each man and twelve for the two supply wagons.

You'll take orders from me, and Jack will be second in command.

I'll tell you right now: this will not be an easy trip. You'll be in the saddle for 15 miles and a total of 12 hours per day. The total trip is about 900 miles and it will take close to three months to complete depending on the elements. I have no idea how long the distance is between water holes. We'll get up every morning at 4:30, eat breakfast and then hit the trail again. We'll run into rain and snow and will probably see some dust storms too.

When we cross the Red River, we'll be in Indian Territory. We could have a few run-ins with some small bands of Apaches or

Comanches who left their reservations. Chances are they'll just be looking for food so we'll let them have a few head. However, we will not let them steal our horses. If they do, we'll hunt 'em down and get 'em back.

When we get up near the Kansas/Missouri border we'll most likely have run-ins with Jayhawkers and Red Legs. These guys take no prisoners. They're mean, and steal and kill just for fun.

I think you're starting to get the idea why I have insisted over the years that you become extremely skilled marksmen with your pistols and rifles. There's no doubt in my mind that we'll be forced to put our marksmanship skills to work especially north of the Red River and near the Kansas/Missouri border, as well.

Are there any questions?" Jesse asked.

Jack spoke up, "I have one. What's the plan after we load the cattle onto the train and finish the job?"

"What do you mean?" Jesse asked.

"I mean do we saddle up and head back right away or do we rest for a few days in town before coming home?"

Jesse responded, "I hear Sedalia is a booming cattle town and that they have saloons, dance halls, gambling houses and clothing stores. They also tell me that there are three women for every one man in town. We'll stay in town for three days after we load up the train. I'll want you to rest up, stay sober and not get into too much trouble. We definitely don't want to break the law while we're there. I need you back at the ranch in August to get the herd ready for the next drive. OK, who's in?" Jesse asked, "I need ten volunteers from you fifteen."

There was no problem signing up ten men plus the cook. Actually, eleven men volunteered so two ranch hands arm wrestled for the drive. The loser would have to stay home.

Then Jesse added, "When we head north, I'm placing my cousin Tom in charge of the ranch. Everyone will answer to him. Tom, I'll leave it up to you to select your second in command.

Lastly, I have found out that we won't be the only ones traveling the Shawnee Trail. I heard in town that Texas ranchers and drovers would be driving about 250,000 cattle up to Missouri this spring. We're leaving in March to be one of the first ones on the trail. We might get a better price that way."

Little did the Texas drovers know that the Missourians would be waiting for them with vigilante groups near the border because they feared crop loss from the cattle herds tramping through their plowed fields plus they had no idea why, but Texas cattle seemed to fatally infect their local herds. They would discover later that it was the infamous Texas fever carried by ticks traveling on the Texas longhorns causing the problem.

Then Jesse concluded, "Now if there aren't any more questions, let's uncork some of those jugs and toast to our first of many cattle drives."

They all gave a "hoot and a howler" and the homemade rye flowed faster than a flash flood on the Rio Grande.

The next day was a much needed "sobering-up" day. However the following Texas sunrise witnessed the commencement of the preparations for the cattle drive with the breaking of 30 wild mustangs.

Not everyone on the ranch knew how to train horses to ride. However, there were three wranglers who were in their late twenties and were of Mexican descent from the California area. They were vaqueros (Spanish pronunciation: ba'kero) (a horse-mounted livestock herder of a tradition that originated in the Iberian Peninsula and brought to the Americas from Spain. The vaqueros were the first real cowboys).

They brought with them new techniques from the Old World for taming wild horses. Today it's called "Natural Horsemanship": back then it was known as the "Vaquero Tradition". These techniques of the Spanish origin employed a more humane way of breaking horses.

These three wranglers were equestrians and cattle herders of the highest caliber and could train a horse to ride within dos dias (two days). Their names were Juan, Carlos, and Jose. Jesse along with many from the Austin area were bilingual and spoke fluent Spanish which was a tremendous asset because Jesse was able to hire and communicate with three of the best horsemen of that era.

So Juan, Carlos, and Jose began to gather the wild mustangs in the area and break them to ride. After two weeks of arduous and exhausting work, the 30 horses were green broke to ride and subsequently corralled nearby. After their job was completed, the three amigos proudly shouted together, "Viva los Vaqueros!" Then with Jesse's blessing, they popped open a bottle of the finest Mexican tequila, brought in from central Mexico, and proceeded to wallow in the fine art of inebriation. Most cowboys preferred straight whiskey. However, the vaqueros preferred their traditional tequila, which they would drink straight up, right out of the bottle, squeezing in a little lime juice for additional flavor.

Tequila was a popular Mexican fermented beverage from the agave plant. It actually was North America's first indigenous (native) distilled spirits distilled by the Spanish conquistadors when they ran out of their treasured brandy back in the 16th century.

Conquistador is a Spanish/Portuguese word meaning "conqueror". They were soldiers, explorers, and adventurers for Portugal and Spain who brought much of the Americas under the control of Spain in the 16th century.

While the horses were being trained to ride, a couple of the cowboys worked on the two wagons ensuring that the wheels were in good working order and that the axles were properly greased.

Others were cleaning their tack and their guns and preparing the clothing they would need for the trip.

The cook's name was Juan Sanchez. His nickname was Cooky. He was a Mexican American who spoke both Spanish and English fluently and worked for Jesse for about five years preparing meals on the Caldwell's ranch.

Jesse gave ole Cooky a bankroll to take to town and load up one of the supply wagons with grub. He bought 50 pounds of coffee, 200 pounds of dried pinto beans, 200 pounds of flour, 50 pounds of salt, 200 pounds of ground corn, plus salt pork, lard, cured slab bacon, cured salted ham and a variety of other food supplies.

He also purchased medical supplies (the cooks on cattle drives were responsible to learn what they could about helping with injuries and such on the trail).

The list also included three thirty gallon barrels for water, along with ammunition, eating utensils, slickers (rain gear), matches, and three canopy tents for the cooking and serving area, and for sleeping under during unwelcome rainstorms.

In the meantime, the other ranch hands were rounding up the cattle for the drive and corralling them nearby so that they would be ready to move out on time.

On February 28th, Jesse gathered his cowboys and vaqueros together and went over the cattle drive plans one more time. He, Jack and the cook made out a checklist of supplies and things that needed to be accomplished before and during the drive and covered it with all of the drovers. He even developed a list of chores to do for the ranch hands who would stay back and take care of things in his absence. Now they were set: the plans were made and it was time for the final preparations. Jesse told his drovers that they would be leaving at sunup on Monday morning, March 2nd, at 5:30 sharp and be heading to Waco, which was right at 100 miles and about six days away.

So on March 1st, everyone took care of his respective responsibilities. You could feel the excitement in the air. The husbands of Jesse's two sisters were also joining him on the drive so they too were making final plans with their wives Mary and Ruth as well.

The cook loaded up one of the wagons with all of the supplies and filled the water barrels that were attached to either side of the wagon with good clean well water. In addition, he also gathered up all of the cowboys' canteens and filled them with fresh artesian well water.

He then attached the hickory wood straps in place over the wagons, which became the frame for the canvas covers that converted the open buckboards to covered wagons. The second covered wagon was loaded with mesquite firewood, which was an obvious prerequisite for cooking and also for welcome campfires during the long cool nights.

The vaqueros had all the horses corralled and ready to go, as did the cowboys with the longhorn steers. At about 9:00 that evening, the kerosene lanterns were turned off and everyone lay in their beds in the bunkhouse trying to get some shut-eye, many to no avail. The anticipation of the commencement of tomorrow's drive was just too great for some. But it was a cool, clear, moonlit night and as they began to drift off one-by-one, they could faintly hear the coyotes singing their high-pitched prairie songs, howling across the grassy plains.

As was typical out on the lonesome prairie and cattle ranches throughout south Texas, the first one out of the sack was the cook. He awoke at 3:30 the next morning and began preparing a hearty breakfast for the drovers before they began their 900-mile grueling journey.

His first job was to grind the coffee beans he roasted on an open fire the day before. Then he took his oversized coffee pot and filled it with cool clear artesian well water and threw in a handful of coffee grounds. He then hung the pot on a hook on a tripod, which he had placed directly over the flaming mesquite campfire. Making cowboy coffee would be his first task every morning the next two to three months. For it was well known that a cowboy could never begin his day without his first cup of thick black coffee.

Then using flour, baking powder, chopped jalapeno peppers, salt and water, he proceeded to make biscuits to put in the Dutch oven. There's a secret to making the perfect biscuits in a Dutch oven and this ole cook had it down to a science. His south Texas technique was to place the Dutch oven on top of hot coals and then place hot coals on top of the Dutch oven, thus spreading the heat evenly and baking every biscuit to the desired equal perfection.

Then Cooky, as the ranch hands affectionately called him, sliced up a large salted down pork belly slab into thick slices of bacon to fry in one of his large iron skillets.

The enticing aromas of coffee boiling and the bacon frying began waking up the cowboys one-by-one. Their orders from Jesse were to be up by 4:15 a.m. and begin brushing down and saddling up their horses before breakfast, and that's exactly what they did on this early momentous morning.

Ole Cooky observed the cowboys with a keen eye and timed his next two duties perfectly; making red-eye gravy for the biscuits and throwing a large chunk of lard in his second iron skillet to fry up some fresh eggs, which would become a scarcity in the days and weeks to follow.

Cooky was proud of his recipe for red-eye gravy, which was handed down to him from his Mexican padre. The red-eye gravy was used as a dip for his baked to perfection golden brown, light and fluffy biscuits. It was a sauce that the ranchers affectionately referred to as poor man's gravy. However, Cooky preferred to call it "bottom sop".

His secret recipe was a simple one. When the bacon was finished frying, he would remove the bacon and then pour the grease into another pot. Then he would take black coffee and pour it into the iron skillet he used to fry the bacon, deglazing the skillet. The next step was to take a separate bowl and pour the coffee from the skillet and the bacon grease from the pot together in a one-to-one ratio. The water-based coffee would sink to the bottom and the grease would rise to the top creating what would appear to be a large red-eye, thus the name red-eye gravy. On occasion, he would also make red-eye gravy with the grease from fried salted country ham.

The way the cowboys would use the red-eye gravy was classic. They would cut their biscuits in half and dip the inner side of the biscuits in the gravy adding moisture and flavor to their "biscuit and bacon" or "biscuit and country ham" sandwiches.

When the meal was prepared and the eating utensils and tin coffee cups were laid out, the cook held up his oversized steel triangle and struck it with a metal rod on the inside shouting "Come and get it!" The triangle was so big, it was jokingly speculated by the cowpokes that the loud clanging sound could be heard ten miles south of the Rio Grande.

It should be noted here that the sound of the triangular dinner bell did not spook the cattle since the ranch cook desensitized them to it due to its daily use.

The clanging sound of the so called dinner bell cued the cowboys to line up with their tin coffee cups and plates while Cooky served the grub for a hearty breakfast. It was a welcome start to the beginning of the drive because today the goal was to travel sixteen miles by sundown, which would be a huge challenge and a grueling start for both the cowboys and the livestock.

After the cowboys ate breakfast and while the cook cleaned up and repacked the cooking utensils, etc., the cowboys and vaqueros rounded up the longhorn steers and horses respectively.

The anticipation was really building now. Everyone took their place in regards to where they would be positioned in relationship to the herd.

The cattle would take the lead and the horses would follow directly behind. Horses tend to move faster than cattle so it was wise to have them trail the longhorn steers. In addition, positioning the horses in the rear would aid in pushing the cattle forward and up the trail.

Caldwell took the point (the front of the herd) and two of the greenhorns took the drag (the back of the herd). Those two greenhorns had the hardest and the dirtiest job since they would be eating dust all the way to Sedalia. They above all would require the use of their cowboy kerchiefs or bandannas using them as dust masks. But the bandanna had many more uses out on the trail. For example, it could be used as a potholder, as protection from sunburn on the neck, a washcloth, a tourniquet in case of an injury and even earmuffs in cold weather. A cowboy would never begin a cattle drive without his bandanna.

The covered supply wagons were positioned in the midpoint of the herd, one on either side, and then the men were positioned equally on either side of the herd as well.

Caldwell was informed by previous drovers that cattle would follow the lead steer better if the herd was stretched out long-ways which meant that the width of the passel would be quite narrow as they headed up the trail. This technique of course made for a longer stretch of cattle. In fact, Caldwell's herd stretched out as far as three-fourths of a mile long. However, controlling the herd would be much easier and that would be a welcome occurrence on this two to three month long arduous adventure.

Caldwell rode the prettiest horse in the territory. It was a golden palomino quarter horse that stood 16 hands tall and had a silky white mane and a long flowing white tail.

When everyone was in place and the cattle and horses were still, Caldwell stood up in his stirrups and looked backwards toward the herd and his drovers. His foreman Jack was about 50 yards behind him on the right side of the herd. He then shouted to Jack, "Take them to Missouri!", and that they did. With hats being waved high in the air, cowboys whooping and hollering, cattle bellowing and horses neighing, they began their long awaited journey up the old Shawnee Trail.

The guns were noticeably silent though because Caldwell gave direct orders not to fire their pistols in the air during the drive in fear of starting a dreaded stampede which had the immense potential of catastrophic consequences harming and even killing both cattle and cowboys alike.

So on a cool clear March morning, Jesse Caldwell's first of many cattle drives to the railheads of the north began. His herd was one of the first out after the Civil War but over 250,000 longhorn steers and over 100 drives would subsequently follow the same path up the Shawnee Trail that spring with Sedalia, Missouri being their final destination.

Week 1 of the drive – 100 miles to Waco

Caldwell's objective of reaching Waco in six days was aggressive but achievable. They would have to travel about sixteen miles each day to accomplish their goal. During the first week of the drive there were really no disasters. Everything went fairly smooth. Oh there were a few saddle blisters and some stiff backs developing from riding all day in the saddle, but nothing serious. The days were still fairly cool, likewise as were the nights and the weather was dry with no rain. They had plenty of food to eat at breakfast, lunch, and dinner and water and coffee supplies were still plentiful.

Week 2 of the drive - 96 miles to Dallas

This stretch of the drive was not as pleasant as the first. The drovers ran into two days of solid rain and another day of "off and on" rain. It was cold, wet, muddy and miserable and now for the first time all of the cowboys knew that this trip would not be the glamorous cakewalk they had perceived.

Several of the nights were cold and stormy with lightning strikes and clashing thunder and morning seemed to never come. The cowboys all attempted to sleep and stay dry under canopy tents that were trenched around the perimeter to keep water from flowing in. But even with that, and the fact that they wore their slickers to bed, they still could not stay dry because the north wind was blowing the chilling rain under and through their partial shelters.

Even more miserable and weary were the slicker clad cowboys watching over the herd during the night wondering if a bolt of lightning followed by the deafening clap of thunder would be the catalyst for a precarious stampede.

On a normal night the two cowboys on horseback, who would watch the bunched up herd, would be singing out loud for two reasons; first, to calm the herd and secondly, so that the two cowboys knew where each other was located. However, on this dark and stormy night, the overriding concern of a stampede had the songbirds as quiet as a bobcat sneaking up on its unsuspecting prey.

They would also normally be tightly grasping their night latch, a piece of thick leather attached to the front of their saddles to hold onto, in case they fell asleep while riding. Falling off your horse while sleeping was not the "cowboy way". However, the anxiety of a stampede that night gave the cowboys the same effect as if they had drunk a pot of thick black coffee with a double dose of caffeine. So there was no worry about drifting off that dreadful night.

Well, they made it through the ungodly stormy night in good fashion without an incident and at the end of the second week, they safely reached the outskirts of Dallas where they took a much needed day off and loaded up on more supplies from town.

Weeks 3 and 4 of the drive – Heading north to Denison, Texas and camping on the southern banks of the Red River

The blistering cold front from the north had blown through and was replaced with accolades for a high-pressure system, which brought clear skies and cool but pleasant temperatures for the first part of the week and then warming to the high sixties later in the following week during this leg of their already exhausting long journey.

The rain, which plagued the cowboys during the second week, actually was a blessing for the third and fourth weeks because it literally dampened the trail thus knocking down the dust, which was a drovers' menace during most of the journey. During these weeks, the bandannas did not have to be worn to cover their faces.

The temperatures during the days were in the high sixties and during the nights were in the fifties, which was typical for mid-to-late March in northern Texas. With the days warming into the sixties the cowboys had to be alert at all times for diamond back rattlers which were sunbathing along the trail.

Although the cowboys weren't up to it every night, it was often a welcome event when sitting around the large campfire on a cool starlit night to have one of the cowboys named Josh begin playing a few songs on his harmonica (a wind instrument which was developed in Europe in the early 19th century). The popular songs of the day were songs played and sung during the Civil War. The harmonica player made it his business to learn as many of those songs as possible and enjoyed playing those inspirational tunes on his harmonica while one of the other cowboys joined in with his mouth harp. Those who knew the words would happily sing along with the melody.

There were four favorite songs Josh loved to play and they were the drovers' favorites as well.

They were:

Aura Lee
Published in 1861
Music by George R. Pouton
Lyrics by W. W. Fosdick

This was a song about a lovely maiden with blue eyes and golden hair. When listening to the song sung around the campfires during the Civil War, it reminded the soldiers of their sweethearts they left behind and longed to be with when the War would end.

When Johnny Comes Marching Home
Published in 1863
Music by Louis Lambert
Lyrics by Patrick Gilmore

Both sides in the Civil War sang this song. However, Patrick Gilmore actually wrote the song for his sister Annie who continually prayed for the safe return of her fiancé, John O'Rourke, a Union Artillery Captain in the Civil War.

I Wish I was in Dixie
Published in 1860
Lyrics and music by Daniel Decatur Emmett

This song was played on February 18, 1861 at Jefferson Davis' inauguration when he became President of the Confederate States of America. It was after this that the song spread like wildfire throughout the South and became the unofficial national anthem of the Confederate States of America. It was the most recognizable song during this time period.

Even though Caldwell was a Unionist, he had no problem with his drovers playing and singing the song. He felt it kept their attitude upbeat during the drive.

The Yellow Rose of Texas
Published in 1858
The writer is unknown

This was the Texans' favorite song and had a special place in Caldwell's heart because of his father's involvement in aiding Sam Houston in defeating Santa Anna at The Battle of San Jacinto.

Here is the legend that is associated with this song.

It seems that a woman by the name of Emily West (a.k.a. Emily Morgan) was captured by Mexican soldiers in Galveston. She was a mulatto who was said to have yellowish skin, hence the reference to the Yellow Rose of Texas. She supposedly seduced Santa Anna at San Jacinto lowering the guard of the Mexican Army and Santa Anna, facilitating Sam Houston's victory over Santa Anna's Army. Being totally surprised by Sam Houston and being preoccupied with Emily, Santa Anna was not aware of Houston's surprise attack until it was too late. Santa Anna fled without a weapon or armor and was easily captured the next day. This seduction legend may or may not be historically factual.

However, this song became popular with the Texas Confederate troops in the latter part of the Civil War.

Weeks 5 and 6 of the drive – Crossing the Red River and heading toward Fort Gibson

River crossings were always one of the most dangerous parts of a cattle drive. Many of the cowboys did not know how to swim and back in the 1800's these rivers were full of the most aggressive pit viper in North America, the water moccasin better known in the South as the cottonmouth snake.

After breakfast and when everyone was ready to hit the trail, Caldwell gave instructions on how to cross the river safely. He warned the drovers that disturbing the waters like they were about to do would probably stir up some water moccasins. He also warned them that if they were attacked by the water moccasins, they probably would not survive the bite. So the instructions were, "Do your best to stay on your horse, no matter what."

Caldwell could easily see the bottom of the swift flowing river through the crystal clear water and it appeared to be about 3-1/2 feet deep where they elected to cross. The plan was to send the two wagons across first. Going down the steep bank would have been very dangerous if it weren't for the deeply grooved path created by previous cattle drives.

Caldwell demonstrated his knack for leadership by deciding to show the way. So he lightly spurred his horse to move forward down the precarious, slippery, 30-degree slope of the riverbank. As he entered the slope, his horse suddenly stumbled forward, nearly throwing him directly over his horse's head. However, holding onto the saddle horn tightly for dear life, enabled him to maintain his balance and remain in the saddle.

Everyone looked on with horror and momentarily held their breath as they watched their trail boss almost fall into the snake infested river, which was the ultimate fear of every drover on this cattle drive.

Caldwell quickly collected himself, stood up in his stirrups leaning to one side to straighten his saddle, and confidently galloped across the entire river. Then he turned around and trotted back to the middle of the river and waved the wagons forward, hoping all the while that the wagons would not hit a large rock on the riverbed which could potentially collapse a wooden wagon wheel.

The teamsters grabbed the reins, whipped them across the horses' hindquarters, yelled "yeehaa!" and slid down the bank into the river. Luckily, both wagons crossed in good fashion.

Caldwell then had two cowboys spread out in the middle of the river to create a narrow corridor for the cattle to go through as they crossed the waters of the Red River. And so it was, 2,000 cattle strong and over 40 trotting horses slid down the banks of the Mississippi tributary that separates Texas from what was later to be known as Oklahoma. Some cattle strayed out of the corridor but were quickly rounded up.

When about 1,500 head had crossed and everyone assumed that there would be no more incidents, one of the cowboys yelled out, "water moccasins!" There they were, about seven of them swimming from the banks toward the steers. One of the cowboys took out his gun and began shooting. Another cowboy joined in as one of the moccasins opened his mouth widely and clamped down on the foreman's boot. Jack frantically took his foot out of the stirrup and shook it relentlessly until the snake let go at which point he drew his gun and unloaded the whole chamber into the water missing with every shot.

By now the cattle were stampeding across the river. Four of the three-foot long cottonmouths latched onto one of the steers with their poisonous fangs and kept biting away. Caldwell saw what was happening and drew his pistol and sacrificed the steer knowing that it had no chance of surviving and hoping that the snakes would concentrate on the steer and none of the horses or drovers. The steer sank and the swift current took both it and the poisonous water moccasins downstream.

After all the cattle crossed, the vaqueros quickly rushed the horses across the river with no incidents although you could see the trepidation in the wideness of the horses' eyes.

In the meantime, several cowboys were in front of the cattle as they crossed and were able to calm the longhorns down as the herd came out of the water and moved forward up the Shawnee Trail.

When the last longhorn steers crossed, everyone scurried to get back along side of the herd to retain calmness and full control of the drive.

As was predicted, the crossing of the Red River was the biggest and most dangerous challenge to date. Luckily, no one was injured or bitten and they only lost one steer, which was quite a remarkable occurrence given the hazardous risk that existed with a cattle drive river crossing.

It took about two hours to cross the river and the stress factor wore heavily on the drovers. Jack saw the tension and nervousness in not only the eyes of the cowboys but also in the eyes and the behavior of the livestock. So he galloped over to Caldwell and suggested that they make this a short day and let the drovers take the rest of the day off.

Caldwell immediately agreed because he knew that there could be even greater challenges lurking ahead in the form of hostile bands of Cherokees, Apaches, Comanches, or other Native Americans who abandoned their reservations to rustle cattle and horses and raid peaceful settlements. He knew that it was important that everyone have their full wits about them on this next leg of the journey because of the more than likely event of an Indian attack.

So they stopped the herd in a location where there was plenty of grass for the horses and cattle to graze and they set up camp before traversing the potentially precarious lands known as the Indian Territory.

Because of the possible danger from hostiles, Caldwell had four instead of two men ride guard watching over the herd in four-hour shifts. The others caught a much-needed afternoon siesta while the cook received permission from Caldwell to butcher a small 800-pound steer to cook up steaks for dinner that night. The rest of the meat would be salted down and wrapped for the next day and some would be made into sausage and beef jerky.

Cooky had been soaking pinto beans for 24 hours to cook up for supper and he made corn bread biscuits, which went great with the pinto beans and steak. At 5:30 p.m. sharp he rang the dinner bell and everyone stood in the cook's line for what was to be one of his best dinners on the drive.

As was an every evening occurrence on the trail before eating, Caldwell, a devout Christian, led the group in a prayer of thanksgiving and asked for protection on this long and dangerous journey. Every night he would change up the prayer and make it relevant to what they would be facing the next couple of days. This was his prayer this evening,

Dear Father in heaven, we thank you for all of our gifts which we are about to eat and ask you to bless this evening's food. As we begin our journey into the Nations, we ask for your protection against the hostiles, which may try to bring their wrath down upon us. Give us the strength and awareness required to keep us safe from harm. And Father, if it pleases you, please bless us with the good fortune of pleasant weather as we travel to Fort Gibson these next ten to twelve days. We ask this in Jesus' name, Amen.

All the drovers then repeated, "Amen".

"Now let's eat this New York style supper," Caldwell jokingly said, as they all dug in.

It was an excellent dinner arranged by ole Cooky. Everyone crammed their bellies to capacity with the opportunity to eat two steaks each, if they so desired.

As the sun departed and reddened the western sky, four drovers rode out to the herd to guard the cattle from night raiders and such. The others stayed in the camp: some played cards while others just laid around using their saddles as their pillows listening to the harmonica player knock out a few of those Civil War melodies while the coyotes seemed to join in with their chilling shrieking howls in the background out on the open prairie.

At 1:00 a.m. the four night guards came in and switched places with four other cowboys. This was an every night occurrence during the cattle drive. These last four cowboys had the worst job on the drive because they came in the next morning in time for breakfast and then they immediately hit the trail as the cattle drive moved northward. It was common for these cowboys to fall asleep in the mid-afternoon heat on their quasi-rocking, slow-moving quarter horses, holding on tightly to their night latches which prevented them from falling off and being the laughing stock of the cattle drive.

On the fourth morning after the crossing of the Red River, one of the cowboys on the west side of the herd glanced over to his left and saw twelve Indians in the distance riding in a single line parallel to their herd. The cowboy quickly trotted up to inform Caldwell of his sighting. Caldwell told the cowboy that he noticed the Indians following them for about an hour now and told him to go back to his position alongside of the herd and stay alert in case the Indians made a move. Caldwell did not show it, but he was very concerned because he noticed that the Indians were armed with rifles and if they were to come in firing, they could start a dreaded stampede.

After giving it great thought, Caldwell went on the hopeful assumption that the Indians only wanted cattle for food. So he waved up two of his cowboys and told them to ride to the back of the herd and cut out ten head of longhorns and push them over to the Indians and then quickly ride back trying to avert an incident.

"I don't want any gunfire that could start a stampede, understood?" he asked in a commanding voice.

They both shook their heads "yes" and then the two cowboys spurred their horses and galloped as quickly as they could to the back of the herd. By now, all the other cowboys and the vaqueros had seen the Indians and had a pretty good idea of what was happening because they remembered that Caldwell had told them that they would probably run across Indians who would try to rustle cattle for food. Everyone watched with trepidation while the two cowboys cut the ten head out of the herd and steered them toward the Indians.

When the cowboys were about 100 yards out from the herd, the Indians trotted over toward them whooping and hollering. The cowboys quickly turned their horses around and swiftly rode back to the herd while the Indians gathered the ten longhorns and drove the cattle off to their Indian village.

All the drovers gave a huge sigh of relief because if guns and rifles were fired, it could prove to be catastrophic in so many ways.

The balance of the drive to Fort Gibson was not as tense as the beginning of this leg of the journey. Although, the days were still long and the nights seemed extremely short.

Being on the trail now for several weeks, the long horseback rides were taking their toll on the aching backs of the worn down drovers. They were also filthy, dusty, and unshaven and without a doubt needed a bath. Tempers were starting to flare up during meal times and Caldwell could see that attitudes were turning for the worse.

About ten miles from Fort Gibson, the drovers came across a clear stream where they decided to bed down for the night. Caldwell thought it was time to give the guys a day off since he could see that the drive was creating negative attitudes, which could eventually affect the success of the drive.

So after dinner, he gathered everyone together and jokingly said, "You cowpokes are the dirtiest, smelliest and grubbiest looking Texans I have ever been around. So, I'm gonna make a deal with you guys. I'll give you tomorrow off on one condition. I want each of you to take a dive into that stream over there and take a bath using "real" soap. Cooky bought some fancy eastern soap in Dallas, which will make you guys smell sweeter than a San Francisco whore. Then I want you to shave and put on clean clothes all the way down to your long handles so that me and the cattle don't have to suffer and smell you all the way up to Sedalia. Are you in?"

They all laughed and shouted and welcomed a day off. Immediately Caldwell could see the positive effect his decision had on the attitudes of the drovers and he knew that his assessment was right on the money. This was just another example of Caldwell demonstrating his natural leadership ability.

Since the drive was just a few miles south of Fort Gibson and they hadn't seen any hostiles for a couple of days, Caldwell and Jack agreed that it wasn't necessary for four men to ride guard over the herd so they only sent two out that night while the rest of the men just sat around camp and began talking about what was awaiting them at the end of the trail in Sedalia, Missouri.

When morning arrived, even the cook slept in. He normally awoke at 3:30 a.m. each day, well before sunup, but today he slept in until 5:00 a.m. while most of the cowboys slept in until seven o'clock.

Cooky took some mesquite wood out of the wagon and built a new campfire to heat the coffee. Then he went through his morning ritual of making biscuits in the Dutch oven, frying country ham, making red-eye gravy, and preparing a pot of hominy grits. It was a beautiful morning with the temperature in the mid-fifties, partly cloudy, and very low humidity, which made it a great morning to just loaf around and enjoy the day off.

When the sun was straight up in the sky and the temperature warmed to seventy, Caldwell set the example for his crew. He grabbed a bar of that fancy smelling soap, headed to the stream, stripped down to his long handles, jumped in the water and shouted to everyone, "Take your bath or go back to work!"

So whooping and hollering and running toward the water half-naked with a bar of fancy smelling soap in their hands, they all did the same and jumped into the water when they reached the bank of the small but swift flowing stream. The cattle and horses were also wallowing in the water so the cowboys bathed upstream from the herd for obvious reasons. They soaked and splashed around for about an hour before they all got out, shaved, got dressed in clean clothes and enjoyed the rest of the afternoon.

At about 4:00 p.m. reality set in when three riders slowly rode into camp. One was badly beaten and the other two showed signs of exhaustion. At this point the mood became somber.

All the cowboys gathered around and helped the three get off their horses. Then they all walked over to the campfire where coffee was boiling.

Caldwell told them to sit down while he introduced himself to the three. In the meantime, Cooky poured each of them a cup of coffee.

Then the three introduced themselves to the group. The first one was Johnny Wilson from San Antonio, the second one was Bobby Sherwood from Dallas and the third one who was badly beaten said, "My name is James Nettle, where are you taking your cattle to?"

Jack said, "To Sedalia."

"Are you aware of what's going on up there with the Jayhawkers and the vigilante groups?" Nettle asked.

"No, fill us in," Caldwell anxiously insisted.

"Well we drove about 400 head of my longhorns up from Texas. It was really more than the few of us could handle. Just as we were about to enter Baxter Springs, Kansas, we were approached by a group of vigilantes. They ordered us to turn our herd around and head back to Texas."

"Why did they do that?" Jack asked.

"Because they claimed Texas cattle carried some type of disease which killed their local herds plus they claimed that the cattle drives before us had trampled all over their fields and crops and caused them to lose food and income. I offered to pay a small sum to go around the field but they refused to let us through. One of my good friends on the drive lost his temper, drew his pistol and was shot and killed instantaneously by two of the vigilantes. One bullet hit him in the head and the other, right in his gut. Then while they held guns on Johnny and Bobby, two others pulled me off my horse and beat the living daylights out of me. Then they scattered our herd and told us if they ever saw us again they would kill us and all of our cattle too. My cook took the chuck wagon and drove off after the first shot was fired. He's probably halfway back to Texas by now, I suppose."

Nettle then took a sip of coffee while Caldwell continued to question him. At this point you could see the serious concern in the drovers' eyes as they stood in a circle listening in disbelief. Caldwell had mentioned to his group before the drive that they could possibly run into trouble like this up along the Kansas/Missouri border but no one really thought it would come to killings.

"What did you do then?" Caldwell asked.

"Well when they left us be, we were able to gather up about 150 of our steers and herd them to Fort Scott in Kansas along the Missouri border. They gave us pretty good money for the steers and I guess we did OK considering the circumstances. I heard that a vigilante group also caused trouble with another cattle drive which was led by a guy named Daugherty out of Texas." At this point Nettle paused, looked down to the ground and said, "I'm just really saddened that I lost a good friend in the process."

Jack looked over at Caldwell and asked with a concerned look on his face, "Well Jesse, what now?"

As he pulled his pistol from his holster and twirled the cylinder making sure it was fully loaded, Caldwell said, "We continue to head north to Sedalia. Nobody, and I mean nobody is stopping this drive."

The immediate reaction was that everybody else drew their sidearm as in a defiant gesture against the vigilantes and mimicked Caldwell by checking their cylinders to make sure their pistols were also fully loaded.

Nettle stayed in camp with his two partners that night and then headed back to Texas the next morning at sunup after eating breakfast with Caldwell's men.

Week 7 of the drive – The encounter at Baxter Springs, Kansas

When the cowboys broke camp, they had a whole new outlook of the probable dangerous challenges they would encounter the next several weeks. They passed Fort Gibson later that afternoon and were once again warned, this time by some of the cavalry soldiers they met along the trail, of the possible serious trouble lying ahead.

What Caldwell had going for him though was that his herd was much larger than Nettle's plus he had more men on his drive, as well. The other positive thing going for Caldwell was that he and his men knew how to effectively defend themselves with their pistols and rifles. They were quick on the draw and straight shooters too. Caldwell himself was a sharpshooter with both his pistols and his Henry rifle. In his mind he knew that gunplay would be his last resort. However, make no mistake about it, Caldwell wasn't about to allow anyone to scatter or turn his herd around, not on this cattle drive or any other future ones for that matter. For Caldwell always carried with him the memory of and respect for his father's bravery who was willing to give up everything to join Sam Houston to fight for the independence of Texas. His father set the example of leadership and bravery for his family and Caldwell knew that he had to do the same for his men.

After about four days of travel from the Fort Gibson area, the drive approached Baxter Springs. Caldwell had warned his men the night before to stay alert as they moved toward the Kansas border. When the cattle began crossing into Kansas, Caldwell who was riding the point with Jack, spotted five men on horseback facing them lined up as if to form a blockade.

Caldwell stopped, stood up in his stirrups, looked back, and waved for three cowboys to ride up and join him and Jack. Then the three Mexican vaqueros rode up as well.

Caldwell and his seven men then stopped the herd and rode up to the five vigilantes, shoulder to shoulder in cavalry style. They came to a halt about ten feet from the group of vigilantes. You could feel the tension in the air.

Then Caldwell spoke, "Can I help you gentlemen?"

"Yes, you can turn your dang herd around and head back where you Johnny Rebs came from," demanded one of the vigilantes.

Well that type of talk did not sit well with Caldwell and he responded in an angry voice, "Move out of our way right now or be prepared to suffer the consequences."

Then one of the vigilantes cocked his rifle. In a split second and in one fluid motion, Caldwell and his seven men drew, cocked their pistols, and pointed them at the heads of every vigilante, daring them with their eyes to make a move.

The vigilantes were stunned at the speed of the draws and sat there in shock with their eyes wide open looking down the barrels of "eight" six shooters. The vigilante with the cocked rifle put it up to his shoulder aiming it as if to get ready to shoot. Caldwell immediately shot it right out of his hand and shouted, "The next one goes into someone's head!"

Then Caldwell looked them straight in the eyes and with the cadence of a brigadier general said in a stern voice to the group of vigilantes, "My name is Jesse Caldwell, these are my drovers and we are taking my cattle to Sedalia. If there are any other objections, speak or act now."

The vigilantes stared momentarily and then swiftly turned their horses around and galloped away in a cloud of dust leaving the rifle lie on the ground. Then one of the vaqueros looked at Caldwell and said, "Senor, you are one tough gringo."

"Gratias mi amigo and so are you guys," Caldwell laughingly replied.

"Now guys, let's finish this drive."

"What about the rifle senor Caldwell?"

"Leave it lay."

Jesse once again demonstrated his leadership skills with his quick thinking and firm hand and once again averted unnecessary bloodshed on the trail.

The vigilantes spread the word quickly that it was not wise to mess with the Caldwell cattle drive. They told everyone that

Caldwell hired a bunch of gunslingers to protect him and his cattle. Even though that was not the case and an unknowingly fallacious assumption, Caldwell and his men were as fast and accurate as any hired gun in the territory and their reputation spread like wildfire throughout the cattle towns in Missouri and Kansas over the next few years.

Weeks 8 and 9 of the drive -The home stretch

With about 120 miles or so to travel and ten days left on the trail, tensions were still running high after the incident at Baxter Springs, Kansas. Rumors were surfacing that there could be more vigilante groups to deal with on the way to Sedalia. However, what they weren't aware of was the fact that their reputation preceded them, which gave them an edge when it came to realizing a successful and a relatively easy last leg of the trip.

As they traversed through the more wooded areas of the Missouri Ozarks, they discovered that they had a better choice of wild game for their meals. They were able to harvest plenty of whitetail deer, squirrel, wild turkey and rabbits along the way. Caldwell enjoyed using his Henry rifle for a morning or late afternoon hunt when the drovers desired something different for dinner that night or breakfast the next morning.

It always gave their attitudes a boost when variety was offered during one of the meals.

The drovers hit a few of those dangerous midwestern spring rainstorms along the way, which on occasion scattered the herd. Luckily, in most cases, they were able to round up the strays and lose only just a few.

When they were about two miles outside of Sedalia, Missouri, the drovers pitched camp while Caldwell and Jack rode into town. They found a more positive attitude amongst many of the townspeople than what they had expected based on the resistance they encountered from local farmers and ranchers along the drive.

Most of the businessmen enthusiastically welcomed the cowboys and their cattle because it meant an income boost to their businesses. The railroad men and cattle buyers were also elated to see the drovers because it was money in their pockets as well.

It was about eleven o'clock in the morning when Caldwell and Jack arrived in Sedalia. The cattle buyers from Chicago, who had contracts with a Chicago slaughterhouse, along with a few railroad men from the Missouri Pacific Railroad, knew about Caldwell's drive coming up from Texas. So they were in town staying at the Cattlemen's Hotel but doing their business out of a small office near the railroad spur and the stockyards. They were anxiously waiting to finalize a deal with Caldwell and start shipping "beef on the hoof" to the East.

When Caldwell and Jack entered the town, they noticed that the stockyards next to the railroad were empty. They looked at each other and you could see the concern in their eyes. Then they saw a sign on a small building near the stockyards that read "Cattle Bought Here". Jack and Caldwell dismounted from their horses in front of the building, tied their reins to the hitching rail and walked into the office.

There were three men in the office, two cattle buyers and one railroad man. They introduced themselves to each other and proceeded to do business.

Caldwell said, "Gentlemen, I have about 2,000 head of cattle five miles outside of town and we came from Texas to sell them."

The buyers and the railroad man smiled and one of the cattle buyers said, "Mister, you came to the right place." Well that brought a smile of relief to Caldwell and Jack's faces as the cattle buyers asked them both to sit down.

"Did you have any trouble along the way?" one of the buyers asked.

"Nothing that we couldn't handle," Jack said.

Then the railroad man spoke, "We heard you put the fear of God into some vigilantes in Baxter Springs. It was wise to hire professional gunmen to help you get through the Kansas/Missouri border."

Jack and Caldwell looked at each other knowing that the rumor was false but decided that it was best for their drovers to let the rumor stand. So they remained quiet.

"Well we want to buy your whole herd," a buyer said. "What do you want per head?"

Caldwell, not really knowing what the market price was, said, "Offer me a price and I'll tell you if it's any good or not."

The buyer responded, "We are able to offer you $30 per head. That should let you make a profit and it will allow us to make a little money too when we ship them on the railroad cars and sell them to the slaughterhouse we do business with in Chicago. Is it a deal?"

Jack and Caldwell looked at each other. Caldwell saw a slight smile on Jack's face and knew he approved so the answer was, "Yes, you have a deal."

All of the gentlemen then shook hands.

"When are you bringing them in?" the railroad man asked.

"Tomorrow morning," Caldwell replied.

"Well then we'll have the railroad cars waiting for you. They're due to arrive this afternoon. I ordered them ahead anticipating your arrival," the railroad man responded.

Then one of the cattle buyers said, "We'll get a count tomorrow as you load the cattle into the cars and then we'll walk over to the bank together and you'll get your money."

"Fair enough," Caldwell agreed.

They then shook hands again and Caldwell and Jack left the small office, mounted up and rode out of town grinning from ear to ear because they were about to see more money in one day than they had seen in their lifetimes.

When they arrived into camp, all the men were standing up waiting and wondering if Caldwell and Jack had good news.

Both got off of their horses looking a little coy. They walked over to the campfire where Cooky just boiled a fresh pot of coffee. They didn't even have to ask. Cooky brought over two tin cups and poured them a cup of coffee each as all the drovers surrounded them. Jack and Caldwell sat down with their poker faces on. By now the rest of the drovers began thinking that there was a problem.

"Well, let's have it," one of the drovers demanded.

Caldwell took a long sip from his coffee cup, looked up at the drovers and said, "Gentlemen, you earned yourselves a $150 paycheck plus a $100 bonus."

"Yeehaa!" came the shouts from the drovers as Jack and Caldwell broke out with laughter.

It took about ten minutes for the crew to settle down since they were overwhelmed with elation.

Then Cooky asked as everyone else looked on, "When do we take these doggies in?"

"First thing after breakfast," Caldwell said. "We'll take them to the stockyard and then load them into the cars. The buyers will have men stationed at each car doing a count. We'll try to get our own count too when we drive them into the corrals at the stockyard.

After that, I want everyone to hang around the cattle buyers' office. I'll walk over to the bank with the buyers and as soon as I get paid for the cattle, you'll get your wages. Then you're on your own for three days before we head back to Texas. And let me make this clear, I don't want anyone in this crew breaking any laws and gettin' thrown into jail. You can have fun as long as it's legal or sanctioned by the town. I am dead serious about that. Anybody who breaks the law and gets thrown into jail will be on their own, understood?"

Everyone said "yes" and could hear the seriousness in Caldwell's voice.

"In the meantime," Caldwell said, "take the rest of the day off." And so they did

Caldwell had four men watch the herd during the night because he did not want anything to go wrong being this close to the end of the trail. Most of the drovers felt a calmness come over them that evening because they realized that the stress of the drive was just about to come to an end. They also knew that they had three full days of rest and relaxation in Sedalia and looked forward to buying new boots and clothes and especially taking a much-needed hot bath.

Cooky was so excited about the drive coming to an end that he had problems sleeping that night. He was up by three o'clock the next morning and began his early morning duties of grinding roasted coffee beans, putting out the utensils, and building a couple of camp fires; one for the coffee pot and the Dutch oven and one for cooking breakfast.

On the menu this morning was fried rabbits he and another drover shot the day before, biscuits baked in the Dutch oven, fried cured country ham, hominy grits and of course his classic red-eye gravy.

The drovers woke up at 4:30 a.m. just before sunrise. You could see the extra excitement in their attitude by the way they moved. This was their big day. The drive was just about over and the good times awaited them in Sedalia.

Cooky struck the triangle dinner bell loudly at five o'clock sharp and the drovers didn't waste a minute forming a serving line.

In fact, they ate twice as fast as they normally would because they couldn't wait to get the show on the road.

When the men had finished eating, Cooky cleaned up and packed everything away. All the men saddled up and took their positions alongside of the herd, as did the two wagons as well.

Caldwell assumed his position at the point and this time Jack took the drag with the two greenhorns. For the last time on this drive, Caldwell stood up in his stirrups, turned around, looked back to his drovers and shouted "Let's take these doggies to Sedalia!"

And so they drove the herd northward up the final leg of the Shawnee Trail and eventually straight down Main Street. Onlookers were hooting and hollering, waving their hats in the air as if it was the start up of the County Fair. This was one of the first of many large cattle drives after the Civil War and the town was ready to resume a boom in business.

The drovers felt like they were heroes or men of importance because of the reception they were receiving. The businessmen and town politicians were elated because of the extra money that would be spent by the drovers. Even "ladies of the street" waved to the drovers from their balcony.

Caldwell led the cattle to the stockyard next to the railroad spur. As promised, the train was in place and the cattle railroad cars were open and ready for loading. The drovers proceeded to herd all the cattle into the stockyard. It took about ninety minutes to complete.

The noise of the longhorns bellowing in defiance was deafening at times but to the drovers, the buyers and the railroad men, this was like the beautiful music of gold coins dropping in a cash drawer.

The buyers' men and some of the drovers took their positions at the side doors of the railroad cars to count the cattle while the rest of the men drove the steers up the ramps and into the railroad cars.

It took about two long arduous hours to finish the loading but by four o'clock that afternoon, the job was completed. Then the drovers did what Caldwell had told them to do the day before; they all walked over to the cattle buyers' office, sat down, and waited.

Caldwell and the buyers spent about thirty minutes adding up the totals. They came to an agreement that there were 1,948 head of cattle loaded on the train. That meant that Caldwell's gross income was a whopping $58,440.

Caldwell and the buyers walked over to the bank. The banker opened up an account for Caldwell and transferred the money from the buyers' to Caldwell's account. Then Caldwell drew out enough money to pay his men the wages plus the promised bonus. The total was $250 per man, a handsome well earned sum.

When the men received their money, the party began. They all went over and signed into a hotel. Then they all scattered. Some men took baths and got a shave, others went directly to the saloon, while some went to the general store to buy new clothes and new boots. However, all met that night at one of the dance halls/gaming houses and rightly celebrated the success of their first cattle drive. Even Caldwell joined in on the fun.

During the next couple of days, while the drovers partied and spent their money all around town, Jesse Caldwell talked to the cattle buyers, railroad men, businessmen and politicians about future cattle drives.

He discovered the growing animosity that townspeople and local farmers had toward Texas cattle drives. He also heard more about the fact that local cattlemen were blaming the Texas cattle for the disease that was killing their local herds.

The valuable information he learned those few days while in Sedalia was that he would have to find another railhead farther west to drive his cattle to.

That railhead would be Abilene, Kansas at the end of the Chisholm Trail.

When the party was over, the men packed up their gear to head back to Texas. Cooky loaded one of the wagons with food and other supplies and they planned to load up the other wagon with firewood they would find on the trail. The drovers spent $100 to $150 of their hard earned money on the hotel bill, drinking, gambling, women, and new clothes but were smart enough to take some back to Texas with them.

Caldwell did not want to leave his money in the bank in Sedalia, Missouri so he took a huge risk by taking the cash back with him to deposit in a bank in Austin. He figured that they were all good enough with their guns to withstand any robbery attempts.

It took about five weeks to return back home and they made it without incident. Caldwell told his men that they would make their next drive in two years and then every other year after that. In the meantime, they would continue expanding Caldwell's herd and make improvements on the ranch using some of the money that was earned on the cattle drive to Sedalia.

As the years went by, men on Caldwell's ranch came and went. Most of them were only good for up to three cattle drives. For some, just one was enough. Over the next several years, Caldwell took his cattle to Abilene, Wichita, Hays City, Ellsworth, and just about every cattle town in Kansas, always receiving top dollar for his herds thus expanding his wealth significantly. By the late 1870's he was one of the wealthiest and most famous cattlemen in the country.

But as he grew older, he became increasingly weary and tired of the cattle business and especially those long trips to the north. Even though he remained true to his principles over the years, the difficult cattle drives and dealings with border raiders, vigilantes and Indians along the trails made him more callous and forced him to use his pistols and his rifle to protect himself and the lives of his drovers.

In 1879, he made plans for his last cattle drive. It was to be the most promising of all. He had a whopping 2,800 head to drive north and this time he would take the Western Trail to the Queen of the Cow Towns, Dodge City, Kansas.

Over the years he partnered with the husbands of his two sisters and they became very wealthy as well. One day he called for a family meeting and surprised everyone with his announcement and proposal. He told them that he was making his last cattle drive and it would be to Dodge City. The shocker came when he told them he was not returning to Texas and wanted to sell his share of the ranch to his two sisters' families.

He gave no real reason for not wanting to return to Texas other than it was time for him to move on and find new adventures to hang his hat onto. He was always interested in entering politics and he even thought he might head to Washington, D.C. to evaluate that possibility. As a congressman who would have experienced life on the New Frontier, he felt he could legitimately represent the people out West and convey their needs to the politicians in Washington. At this stage in his life, he was wealthy enough to afford anything he desired to do.

Caldwell made a deal with his two brothers-in-law and sold his share of the Caldwell ranch to them. He then put his plans together for his last big cattle drive to the north, which would leave in early April. However, about a week before the beginning of the drive, Caldwell was bucked off a horse and sustained a compound fracture in his left leg. He was bedridden for several weeks and did not fully heal until late May.

Still determined to drive his cattle to the north, he hired twelve drovers and promised to pay them extra wages because they were leaving later in the year and would run into some very hot weather along the trail. Jack was still part of his crew as were one of his brothers-in-law, and the three original vaqueros along with Cooky. Everyone else was new. Caldwell always made sure that a prerequisite to working for him was that his new hires had to be very good with a gun because of the dangers along the way.

All of the drovers, except for Caldwell, had plans to return to Texas after the drive.

It was now late June, 1879. The horses and cattle were corralled for the trip. Cooky had all of the supplies bought and firewood gathered and loaded into the wagons.

After saying his final goodbyes to his sisters, he stood up in his stirrups for the very last time, turned around to look at his drovers and shouted, "Let's take these doggies to Dodge!"

And Caldwell's final cattle drive commenced. Leaving as late as he did in June, he knew that they would not arrive in Dodge City until sometime around the first week of October.

He assumed that since his cattle drive would probably be the last one to arrive in Dodge City that year, the town would be quite peaceful and orderly.

However, he was to find out that his assumption was inaccurate and just the opposite would be true.

CHAPTER SIX:

The Night of the Comanche Moon

On July 10, 1879, the Thomas O'Brien family made a bold move by packing up all of their belongings into two covered wagons and departing from Scott County, Kentucky for a newly established western town named Dodge City, Kansas. Thomas had aspirations to be part of the great cattle boom in Dodge City and eventually wanted to be a cattle buyer for one of Chicago's famous slaughterhouses. The cattle business was in his blood since he was raised on a cattle farm in rural Pennsylvania.

He wasn't a tall man but a man of average height, about 5' 10" and had an average build. He wore a thin moustache which made his rounded face seem even fuller than what it really was. Thomas had a wife whose name was Elizabeth Bannister O'Brien. Together they had three children; a fourteen-year-old son named Josh, and twin nine-year-old daughters named Jeanie and Jennie.

As they were passing through Evansville, Indiana on their way to St. Louis, they came across and joined several families traveling in a small wagon train headed toward St. Louis as well. The difference was that the wagon train's final destination was Hermann, Missouri, just west of St. Louis while the O'Briens were traveling on to Dodge City, Kansas.

When the wagon train stopped in Mt. Vernon, Illinois one evening, the wagons were driven to form a circle to corral the horses. Several campfires were built and every family prepared their own supper. Many sat on logs and others removed wooden chairs from their wagons to sit on. After supper, they all sat around a large campfire and socialized. One of the travelers asked Thomas where he was from. Thomas replied,

"I'm originally from Pennsylvania but ended up in Scott County, Kentucky."

"How did that happen?"

"Well, it's a long story; do you really care to hear about it?"

"We have the whole night ahead of us and everyone here already has told their story to the group so sure, we would like to hear about it," the stranger replied.

"OK," Thomas said.

He began his story as a youngster growing up on a farm in Pennsylvania, continuing with his joining the Union Army in Ohio during the Civil War in October of 1861, and how he participated in the Battle of Shiloh also known as the Battle of Pittsburg

Landing. After that he told the group how he met his lovely wife, Elizabeth.

"My ma and pa were immigrants from Ireland and purchased a small cattle farm just outside of Philadelphia. I had a brother and a sister growing up. I was very close to my sister but my brother and I never got along. He seemed to have different values than me and he was always getting into trouble. He left the family at an early age and honestly, that did not bother me a bit. I've seen him a few times since then but lost track of him the last couple of years. Knowing how he was, it would not surprise me if he were in some kind of trouble and on the run from the law; anyway, enough about him."

Then one of the strangers butted in and asked Thomas in a somewhat joking manner,

"What's your brother's name just in case I run into him some day?"

"His name is Danny, and if you ever come across him, I would certainly keep your distance," Thomas responded with a very sober tone in his voice which had the traveler looking at him in a strange way.

Then Thomas quickly changed the subject.

"I really enjoyed helping my pa take care of the cattle on the farm. In fact, that's why we are headed to Dodge City, Kansas. I have plans to get into the cattle business. They say a guy can make a decent living nowadays in that business. I aim to see if it's true.

In October of 1861, I joined the Union Army in Ohio. I was just seventeen years old but I was looking for adventure and didn't really know what I was getting myself into. I was pretty good with a gun because we had to shoot most of our food if we didn't want to starve to death.

My pa taught me how to use a pistol and a rifle at an early age. In fact, I have a Winchester '73 and absolutely love it. It'll give my family and me plenty of protection on the way to Dodge City.

Back in April of 1862, I fought under Major General Don Carlos Buell at the Battle of Shiloh in Hardin County, Tennessee. Some call it the Battle of Pittsburg Landing. Shiloh was a small log church there and the battle was named after it. The irony is that Shiloh in Hebrew means, "Place of peace" and it happened to be the scene of the bloodiest battle to that date in the Civil War. I heard that 1,754 were killed and 8,408 were wounded on the Union side and 1,728 were killed and 8,012 were wounded on the Confederate side.

I was wounded there too and it was a tough time in my life. However, they say that good things sometimes come out of bad. I believe that's true because if I weren't wounded in Shiloh, I would not have met my beautiful wife Elizabeth. I'll tell you how that came about in a few minutes.

I have heard so many different accounts of how we won the Battle of Shiloh that I don't know which is true and which is false. I only know what I know and that is that we won the battle and it was the worst experience of my life. I hope I never again have to shoot at another human being and of course, I hope I never get shot at again."

Just then one of the strangers interrupted and asked, "How long did the battle last?"

"It lasted only two days. My regiment arrived the evening of the first day of the battle along Pittsburg Landing on the Tennessee River. From what I heard, Grant and Sherman both refused to believe that the Confederates were close by so they had no idea that the Confederates were planning a sneak attack on them that day.

Grant's Army was better trained than the Confederates and they were also better armed with more modern firearms. When the Confederates attacked on the morning of April 6, 1862, it took the Union soldiers by surprise. The fighting was extremely intense and they said that the gunfire went on all day long. I don't think anyone really knew who was winning the battle. Although I later heard that General Beauregard of the Confederates sent President Davis a telegram later that day which proclaimed "A complete victory".

Beauregard thought that he had Grant where he wanted him and thought that he could defeat Grant the next day. I don't think Beauregard knew that Buell's troops were arriving that evening. About 15,000 Union soldiers arrived from 6:30 that evening till 4:00 the next morning. If Beauregard would have pressed on before we arrived, he might have defeated Grant. But he didn't and that was probably the fatal mistake of the battle by the Rebs.

Anyway it was getting dark when we arrived. When we settled in during the night, we heard sounds from that day's battlefield, which haunt me to this very day. You could hear the wounded on both sides moaning, groaning, crying, and screaming for help. It was both eerie and horrible. The sad thing was that no one did anything about it. Those poor souls just laid out there all night long and most of them died before sunup. I also remember that we had thunderstorms that night, which made things even more dreadful and lonely for the wounded. I heard some single gunshots on the battlefield and assumed it was soldiers taking their own lives."

The strangers could see that Thomas was visibly shaken by his memory of the events. He paused for a few minutes while everyone else remained silent. Tears came to Elizabeth's eyes because she knew what Thomas went through the next day of the battle and the weeks to follow.

Then Thomas collected himself and went on with the story. "By the second day, we outnumbered the Confederates 45,000 men to 20,000, some say 28,000.

Beauregard was unaware that he was outnumbered so badly. His plan was to attack and drive Grant into the Tennessee River. However, we began to move forward in a massive counterattack and surprised the Confederates with our numbers.

Some of us met the enemy and engaged in bayonet fighting. It was at the place they called the Hornet's Nest where a group of us soldiers charged the enemy. As I thrusted my bayonet into a Southern soldier, the one next to him turned and stuck his bayonet into my side. As I was falling to the ground, a slug from a pistol went through my shoulder and knocked me down to the ground onto my back. I figured I was a goner.

I laid there bleeding while fighting was going on all around me. I had never heard so many gunshots in all my life. It was continuous and seemed to be never ending. One shot after another. People yelling and screaming like madmen. It went on and on and on. Then a peace came over me as I accepted the fact that I was probably going to die that afternoon and I just laid there and closed my eyes. I could feel the warm sun beating down on my face, as I went in and out of consciousness. I was even too weak to finish the Lord's Prayer as I lay dying.

After awhile, the gunfire and noise seemed to fade and move away from me. To my surprise, I was still alive. As I opened my eyes and turned my head in my weakened state, I could see that there was a Union doctor checking out the wounded to see if any of us were still alive. I struggled in pain to roll over on my side and then my belly. Then I tried to kneel by pushing myself up with my hands.

Just then, the Union doctor who was wearing a white apron over his uniform, put his arm around me and said, "Son, you're going to be all right now." He yelled for a stretcher and shouted, "Here's one that's still alive, bring the stretcher over here!" I was in so much pain it was unbearable. According to the doctor, the bayonet went through my oblique muscle but didn't hit any organs. The bullet went right through my shoulder and fractured my collarbone.

I was put in a wagon and driven to the hospital tent where I was treated, bandaged, and given medicine to ease the ungodly pain I was suffering."

"Wow, that is quite a story," one of the strangers remarked. "It was miraculous that you survived those wounds."

"Yes it was," Thomas responded.

"Where did you go to recuperate?" asked one of the strangers.

"I was shipped to a hospital in Cincinnati, Ohio by way of the Tennessee River and the Ohio River. I recouped in the hospital for several weeks after that hoping and praying that an infection would not set in. Luckily it didn't and I was released from the hospital in June."

By now his three children were sitting there in a quasi-state of shock and utter disbelief. Both of his daughters were actually crying as he told the story of accepting that he was going to die. They had no idea that their daddy had gone through so much grief during the Civil War. Thomas always preferred to wipe that memory completely out of his mind and was disappointed that he got caught up in the trap of reliving the horror of that battle once again.

Then he continued his story. However, this part had a much happier feel about it.

"Once I was released from the hospital, I received an honorable discharge from the Army because of my wounds. Even after I left the hospital, I continued to experience a lot of pain.

I was still very young and didn't really have any long-term plans for myself. My first order of business was to find a temporary job and earn some quick money. I got wind of a tobacco farmer who was hiring in northern Kentucky and was paying pretty good wages. So I headed south to the Bannister Plantation in Scott County, Kentucky.

I applied for the job with Mr. Bannister himself. He was a very nice soft spoken, silver haired gentleman, and I was really excited when he hired me that very same day. I moved into the plantation workers' bunkhouse. They actually had two bunkhouses, one for the white folks and one for the black folks even though we worked side by side with each other.

I did everything on the plantation. I cultivated the ground, planted seed, cut the tobacco plants and hung them in the barn to cure. After about a year, Mr. Bannister invited me to dinner at his house one Sunday evening. That's when he asked me to be his foreman. I thought that was the best thing that had ever happened to me until he introduced me to his daughter Elizabeth who was the prettiest lady I ever laid eyes on."

At this point Elizabeth started to blush and their three kids began to giggle like young children do.

"I couldn't take my eyes off of her during dinner and I could see that she was somewhat embarrassed over it. That night when I fell asleep I actually dreamt of her. She didn't come outside much previous to that. I later found out that she read a lot, practiced playing the piano and she was tutored at home. I guess you could say she was being raised in a more eastern-style tradition and was well sheltered."

Elizabeth nodded her head yes as the group looked at her and smiled.

Then one of the strangers commented to Elizabeth, "Beings that you were raised the way you were, I'm a little bit surprised that you are moving to the more uncivilized West."

Elizabeth responded in a soft voice, "Well, I'm afraid that Thomas didn't really leave me much of a choice. I must be honest, I'm not the traveling, nor the adventurous type of person that my husband is. I said I would go along and hoped that I would grow accustomed to the new life."

Elizabeth said that because she knew in her own mind that this move, the traveling, and living in a more uncivilized fashion, would be quite challenging for her. In her heart she really didn't know if she was cut out to do this sort of thing. She was also worried about the safety of her children traveling and living out West. She was concerned about their education, as well.

"She'll get used to it. She'll have to," Thomas said.

Elizabeth looked on with displeasure when she heard that comment.

One of the strangers jumped in right away and asked Thomas to continue his story. So he did.

"Well, one Friday evening I asked Mr. Bannister if I could take Elizabeth on a Sunday afternoon picnic. He said yes and I was thrilled. Then I asked Elizabeth if she would join me and she said yes also. So we made our plans. Since I only had a horse, I asked to borrow Mr. Bannister's buggy. Elizabeth's mother offered to make the meal for the picnic. She made southern fried chicken, pinto beans and rice, greens and corn bread. She was a great cook.

On Saturday evening, Elizabeth asked me if I would go to church service with them on Sunday morning. I said I would love to; not because I was a church going person mind you, but it just gave me another opportunity to be with Elizabeth again.

The service was in a small Baptist church in town. I was so impressed with Pastor Walker's sermon that morning that I went back every Sunday after that for more inspiration and teachings. I actually became a church going Christian because of Pastor Walker. He even gave me my very own Bible, which I still carry with me to this day.

At about 1:00 p.m. on Sunday, I arrived at the front door of the Bannister house. My heart was beating as fast as a racehorse after a quarter mile sprint, and my knees were knocking louder than a blacksmith's hammer hitting a steel rod over his anvil. I was scared to death.

I knocked on the door and Mr. Bannister answered and told me to come on in. It was a beautiful two-story plantation house with a lavish partially carpeted stairway going up to the second floor. Mr. Bannister called for Elizabeth who was upstairs at the time. Then I heard a door open and then shut and I looked up.

There she was. It was Elizabeth. She looked radiant. She was wearing a beautiful long flowing white dress, and her hair was golden yellow with a flower in it. As she walked slowly down the steps holding onto the rail, I could not take my eyes off of her. She looked at me and I at her and we both smiled ear to ear. It was like I was watching an angel, all-a-glow, descending from heaven."

"My word," Elizabeth interrupted, "you're embarrassing me, Thomas. Hush now."

Everyone laughed, including the O'Brien's three children.

"It's true," Thomas insisted, "you were so beautiful, and by the way, you still are."

Thomas continued, "Just about the time Elizabeth reached the bottom step, her mother came out of the kitchen with the picnic basket filled with our picnic dinner. I can still smell the aroma of that freshly made fried chicken. Wow, it was terrific.

Then we left the house, got into the buggy and rode down the dirt road a bit to the large lake on the plantation. We put down a couple of blankets on the ground under a large willow tree next to the lake and just talked for a while. Elizabeth didn't know it at the time, but I was determined to not leave that day without kissing her.

Anyway, we talked for about an hour before we ate. We found out that we had many things in common but we differed in a few. We both wanted a family with children and someday have our own land where we could raise cotton, tobacco or cattle. Actually, I was the one who wanted to raise cattle. I wanted to move west to be part of the cattle boom in Missouri and Kansas but Elizabeth's heart was really in Kentucky where she grew up. You see, I'm a little more adventurous and I guess I always see greener pastures on the other side of the hill. Even at that young age I thought about being a cattle buyer in Missouri for the Chicago slaughterhouses. I guess you could say if cattle were involved, I wanted in.

Then we ate our meal, packed up and went back to the house. I was too bashful to kiss her at the time, so I waited for our next picnic.

Anyway, to make a long story short, we married in 1864 and had our first child, a son in 1865. Our two girls were born in 1870. We lived in the Bannister's house all of that time, while I worked for my father-in-law on the plantation and saved enough money to move to Kansas where we plan on starting a new life for ourselves. By the way, where are all of you going to?" Thomas asked.

One of the strangers who had remained quiet up to now jumped in and spoke with a German accent, "We are headed to St. Louis and from there, we are traveling west to Hermann, Missouri. We are German immigrants and wine making has been in our families for years. We are planning to buy land and plant vineyards and start up a wine business. We have relatives in that area now who have vineyards and wine making facilities and we are looking forward to joining them."

Elizabeth who was very educated and kept up on current events said, "You know, if it weren't for the Eads Bridge in St. Louis, we may have not risked crossing the Mississippi River on a ferry. That seems very frightening to me."

"We heard about the new bridge but don't know much about it," one of the strangers said.

"Well, I just know what I read about it and it's an amazing engineering feat," Elizabeth said. "It was named after the man who designed the bridge, James B. Eads. It was built with two decks, the lower being for railroad traffic and the top being for foot and wagon traffic. It is the first bridge to cross the Mississippi River and it has now connected the East to the West.

I read that the bridge was completed in 1874 and is about 6,442 feet long and about 46 feet wide. There's a funny story about when the bridge was completed. They say a guy named John Robinson led a test elephant across the bridge on June 14, 1874."

"Whatever for?" One of the wives of a stranger asked.

"They say that elephants can sense when a structure is unsafe. The elephant felt comfortable when it crossed so the first thought was that everything was OK.

Well, I think Eads needed more proof than that so they say that he sent fourteen locomotives back and forth across the bridge at one time. Everything seemed to be great so they opened the bridge on July 4th and celebrated with a parade in the streets of St. Louis that stretched out fifteen miles long.

That's about all I know about it. We are really looking forward to seeing it and crossing it."

Well, the group didn't do much talking after that. It was getting late and the plan was to get up early the next morning, eat breakfast and continue their travels through southern Illinois to St. Louis, Missouri.

Since it was late July, the Midwest was experiencing its normal hot and humid summer. It really wasn't the best time of the year to be traveling.

It took three days to reach the Mississippi River from Mt. Vernon and they did so on the evening of July 29th. They camped out in East St. Louis on the riverbank and gazed at the fast flowing river and the Eads Bridge all night long anxiously waiting to cross the next morning. Thomas promised his family that they could stay one day in St. Louis and shop some of the fancy boutiques to buy new clothes but he made the point that they needed to cross the state of Missouri by the end of August and be in Dodge by the first week in October. He wanted for sure to be in Dodge City, Kansas when the last cattle drives from Texas arrived.

The strangers who the O'Briens were traveling with decided not to spend a day in St. Louis. Instead they continued to travel on to Hermann, Missouri the next morning actually leaving camp about an hour before the O'Briens. Because of the blistering summer heat, they wanted to get an early start.

The O'Brien family packed up and crossed the bridge at about 8:00 a.m. The kids were as excited as if they were going to a county fair. They actually walked across the bridge looking down at the river while Elizabeth and Thomas each drove a wagon across the bridge looking upstream and downstream at the mighty Mississippi.

Elizabeth and the girls spent the day shopping for new dresses, shoes and hats while Thomas and his son shopped for new boots and visited some of the trading posts and general stores along the streets adjacent to the riverfront. They even watched some of the steamboats unload on the riverbank. It was quite an event for this family. The city was really buzzing and had a flair of the eastern culture about it but still hanging onto some of the early western cultures as well.

While walking around the riverfront with his son, Thomas spotted a poster, which was an advertisement for a melodrama, which was playing on the showboat that was docked in St. Louis that week. The poster boasted a dinner and a show. The name of the showboat was the Water Queen.

The first showboat is credited to a British-born actor by the name of William Chapman, Sr. His boat was named the "Floating Theater". He created the concept in Pittsburgh in 1831. Chapman, his family of nine, along with two other people lived on the boat and performed plays, musicals and dances along the waterways. In 1836, his family was able to upgrade their boat and then they subsequently changed its name to the "Steamboat Theater". William Chapman died on board his showboat in 1841.

During the Civil War, showboat entertainment ceased to exist because the waterways became means of transporting supplies for troops and in some places, the waters became places of fierce battles.

The showboat era came back to life once more in the year of 1878 and was said to focus on melodrama and vaudeville. Four of the major showboats of the era were the New Sensation, the New Era, the Water Queen and the Princess.

Well when Thomas saw the poster, he thought that his wife Elizabeth and his children would really enjoy spending time on the showboat that evening. So he caught up with her and his two daughters, and they signed into a local hotel. They freshened up the best they could, and attended the dinner show on the Water Queen that evening. Everyone had a wonderful time.

Elizabeth was quite surprised at how much she enjoyed St. Louis. She was thinking in her mind that maybe this adventure would not be the disappointment she expected. However, what she didn't know at the time was that the farther west they traveled, the more uncivilized things would become. Certain events would force her to wonder if she had made a huge mistake leaving Kentucky.

The next morning, the O'Brien family got an early start. Before hitting the trail, they sat down to a wonderful breakfast in the café of the hotel at which they were staying. They were in a great mood and the girls talked a lot about how they enjoyed shopping the stores in St. Louis. They also spent a good portion of the time during their breakfast discussing the fun they had attending their first melodrama on the showboat.

After breakfast they went back up to their room, packed up their clothes, signed out, and walked to their two wagons, which were left behind the hotel. One of the covered wagons was filled with some small furniture and belongings they brought with them from Kentucky while the other wagon was filled with food and camping supplies.

Elizabeth climbed into the driver's seat of one of the wagons with her son while Thomas climbed into the driver's seat of the other wagon with their two daughters. When they were about ready to ride out, one of the daughters looked back into the wagon and innocently asked Thomas, "Daddy, where's our food?"

"What?"

"Our food, daddy, it's gone."

"My word," Thomas said in disgust, "somebody stole our food."

He then climbed down from his wagon and walked over to Elizabeth to inform her about the robbery knowing that this ill-timed incident would really shake her up. He was right, it did. She began crying and asked Thomas, "Now what do we do?"

He said that he would notify the local police and then they would restock the wagon with food from the general store. So that's what they did and two hours later they were able to begin their journey once again.

The trip across the state of Missouri was long, difficult, and dusty. It was August now and the hottest time of the year in the Midwest as they traversed the state in the sweltering heat of the seemingly endless and tiring dog days of summer. But traveling across Missouri in August is not just about being miserable due to the heat and dust; it's also about ticks, chiggers, gnats and snakes. During the night you're swatting those annoying vectors of diseases, the mosquitoes, and during the day, you're pulling off other bloodsucking insects, like ticks. Even the horses are miserable due to nuisances like face flies and horseflies. Those large horseflies breed this time of the year and bite and suck blood from their hosts. They literally drive the horses crazy especially when the horseflies land just above the horses' tails making it practically impossible for a horse to swat them away. At this point horses become virtually impossible to control and even become dangerous at times.

These were the traveling conditions which Elizabeth had no idea that she would be facing. "Is this how living out West would be during the summer months?" she despondently wondered. As the dust kicked up from the wagon in front of her and the hot August afternoon sun began draining her energy, her mind began to take her back to the good times of her life on her father's plantation, sitting on a swing on the front porch with a glass of lemonade, in the cool breezes of the northern Kentucky evenings. But those times were gone now.

The route the O'Briens traveled was a path just south of the Missouri River. They crossed the Gasconade River on a ferry near Mount Sterling, Missouri and camped on the west bank for the night.

Thomas was becoming concerned that they were just a few days outside of the Missouri and Kansas border and he was keenly aware of all the horror stories about the border gangs, vigilante groups, Jayhawkers, Red Legs, and outlaws. Although, some of these groups had long dispersed, he wasn't taking any chances.

Thomas had acquired a Winchester '73 while working on the Bannister Plantation in Kentucky. He became quite a sharpshooter with it, practicing quite often in an open field near the tobacco curing barn. Elizabeth despised guns and everything they stood for. Where she grew up on her father's plantation in Kentucky, there was no need for guns so she really wasn't exposed to them like many others were during that time period; not until Thomas acquired his Winchester rifle and began his target shooting every chance he got.

While the O'Briens were camped out along the Gasconade riverbank, Thomas was preparing to do some target shooting with his son. However, just before unpacking his rifle, he spotted two jackrabbits hiding in the brush. So he hurriedly grabbed his rifle and as fast as you could say "muleskinner" he put a slug in one of the rabbits with his Winchester from 20 yards away. In just a few minutes after reloading and following the path that the other rabbit took, he spotted it in some brush and bagged it as well.

That evening his family had a real treat for dinner, jackrabbits roasted on an open fire seasoned with Elizabeth's special herbs and spices she brought with her from the plantation. She also made corn bread in the Dutch oven and cooked up some delicious pinto beans.

After dinner, while Elizabeth and the girls cleaned the cooking and eating utensils, Thomas and his son took a walk down the riverbank and did some target shooting, taking potshots at floating debris in the steady but slowly moving current of the Gasconade River. Thomas taught his son how to shoot a rifle at an early age when they lived in Kentucky and his son was becoming quite a marksman for being so young.

Because Josh seemed to be mature beyond his years, Thomas knew that he would be procuring a new rifle for Josh in the near future. However, rather than waiting until they arrived in Dodge City to do so, he made a decision to surprise Josh with a new rifle and purchase it during their next stop which would be Sedalia, Missouri.

The O'Briens got an early start the next morning knowing that their daytime travel would be hindered during the heat of the day. Elizabeth and Thomas both woke up at 4:30 a.m. Thomas built a small campfire, placed coffee grounds and water in the coffee pot and hung it on the tripod above the fire. This was their daily every-morning routine. Thomas, Elizabeth and even Josh were all early morning coffee drinkers.

Elizabeth then prepared biscuits in the Dutch oven. She brought with her several mason jars of homemade strawberry preserves from Kentucky, which the girls loved to spread on their warm freshly baked biscuits in the early morning. When they were in St. Louis, Elizabeth took a chance on buying a couple dozen of eggs and they still seemed to be fresh so she fried up some sunny side up eggs in the iron skillet after she fried up a few slices of country ham. This breakfast was as good as it gets out on the trail.

The temperature was around 68 degrees but the humidity was very high making it incredibly miserable so early in the morning. A high-pressure system was lingering over the Midwest causing it to become another cloudless day, which would allow the temperature to rise that afternoon into the unbearable triple digit category just like the day before. Since the O'Briens suspected that this day would be another scorcher, they did their best to get an early start. Their goal was to arrive in Sedalia by early afternoon and then spend the rest of the day in town resting both themselves and the horses during the mid-afternoon heat.

So while the girls took care of cleaning up after breakfast and packing up the bedrolls and utensils, Thomas and Josh brushed down the horses and hitched them up to the two covered wagons.

Elizabeth asked the twin girls to take a few minutes before they left and gather up some campfire wood since there were plenty of small branches scattered throughout the campsite. They kept a stockpile of campfire wood in one of the wagons at all times to ensure that they always had enough to build a fire for meals.

Jeanie went in one direction and Jennie in the other. It seemed to be a normal day with everyone performing his and her daily morning chores before heading out on the lonesome wagon trail. It was fairly quiet and you could hear the birds singing while a gentle summer morning breeze rustled the leaves of the giant white oaks nearby.

Then, like the deafening yell of a bobcat with a steel trap clamping down on its leg, Jeanie screamed and yelled, "I've been bit!"

Everyone stopped what he or she was doing and looked Jeanie's way as she was screaming and crying hysterically while shaking her hand frantically up and down. Then Thomas ran to her as fast as he could and grabbed her.

"What's wrong?" he yelled.

"I've been bitten!" she screamed while still shaking her hand frantically.

"Let's see, let's see," Thomas said in a panicky voice.

"It hurts daddy, it hurts real bad!"

"Oh my God," he shouted to Elizabeth, "She's been bitten by a snake."

Josh ran over to the area where she was bitten and saw the snake. It was a venomous copperhead. He ran back to the wagon and grabbed a shovel to kill it. In the meantime, Jeanie's hand had swollen up, nearly doubling in size and turned black and blue.

"Am I going to die, daddy?"

"No honey, we're going to get you to a doctor as quickly as we can."

"It hurts daddy, it hurts real bad," Jeanie yelled while crying.

"Elizabeth, put some water on a towel and wrap Jeanie's hand in it!" Thomas shouted.

Then he yelled, "Josh and Jennie, get up in the food wagon and Josh, you drive!"

Once Elizabeth had Jeanie's hand wrapped up, Elizabeth climbed into the back of the other covered wagon and Thomas picked up Jeanie and placed her there too.

Elizabeth asked, "Where are we going?"

Thomas responded hurriedly, "We're going to Jefferson City; it's only about twenty-five miles away."

Then he ran to the front of the wagon, climbed up into the driver's seat, looked back at Elizabeth and shouted, "Hang on," as he whipped the reins on the horses as hard as he could yelling, "Heeyah!" at the top of his lungs.

Both wagons took off at blinding speeds with the horses at a full gallop kicking up a cloud of dust while both Josh and Thomas continued to whip the reins across the horses' backs demanding even greater speed from their galloping Morgans.

Jeanie's hand continued to swell as did her wrist and her forearm. Elizabeth kept checking her for a fever while she tried to keep Jeanie's hand cool with a wet towel.

Thomas and Josh could not keep the horses at a full gallop for the 25 miles otherwise the horses would surely die from exhaustion. So they had to slow down to a trot and sometimes a walk for several miles.

Getting to Jefferson City seemed like a lifetime. Jeanie was now sleeping and had a slight fever. The swelling did not progress beyond her forearm but was not abating either.

Then just as they thought they were making good progress toward Jefferson City, they approached another river. It was the Osage River, a tributary of the Missouri River and one of the larger rivers in the state. Thomas did not have this river on his map and was visibly shaken when they came upon it.

They encountered a few strangers on horseback near the river and asked them how to cross. The strangers told Thomas that there was a ferry about two miles downstream which would take them across, and Jefferson City was about eight miles from that crossing.

So now once again, Thomas and Josh whipped their horses with the reins and forced them into a full gallop. Jeanie was waking up now and began crying again because the pain was excruciating. As Elizabeth cradled her nine-year-old daughter she consoled Jeanie by telling her that it wouldn't be long before they arrived in Jefferson City.

When they reached the site of the ferry crossing, they were in luck. The ferry had just arrived from the other side of the river. So they drove both wagons onto the ferry and immediately headed across the Osage River.

While they were crossing the river, Thomas asked the ferry owner where the doctor was located in Jefferson City. He told Thomas that the doc was on the east side of town located on Main Street. His name was Dr. Williamson.

It took about twenty minutes to cross the river and then it was another hour to Jefferson City. They rushed into town and found the doctor's office quite easily. He had a large sign on the outside of his building which read "George Williamson, MD".

The O'Briens parked both of their covered wagons in front of the doctor's office. Thomas jumped off and ran to the back of the wagon, opened up the tailgate and asked Jeanie to crawl into his arms. At this point, Jeanie was very lethargic but gathering as much strength as she could, she crawled over to her daddy.

Thomas picked her up and swiftly carried her into the doctor's office. The whole family followed behind Thomas. Fortunately, no one else was waiting to see the good doctor so Dr. Williamson could attend to Jeanie immediately.

Thomas set Jeanie on what appeared to be an operating table and began telling the doctor the story of the ill-fated event. Dr. Williamson then asked Thomas, "Do you know what species of snake bit her?"

Thomas replied, "My son said it was a copperhead."

"Is he sure it was a copperhead?" Dr. Williamson asked.

"Josh can identify the different species of pit vipers so I would say yes, it was a copperhead. Is that good or bad doctor?"

Everybody anxiously waited for the doctor's response. You could see the worried look in Jeanie's eyes. She was afraid of the doctor's answer, as was everyone else.

The doctor put his hand on Jeanie's head and said, "Honey, today is your lucky day. We are not aware of anyone who has ever died from a copperhead's bite." He then smiled and said, "If I had to be bitten by a snake, I would pray it would be a copperhead too." Jeanie smiled for the first time since she was bitten.

Then the doctor told Elizabeth and Thomas about Missouri's venomous snakes while working on Jeanie's wound.

"Missouri has several venomous snakes, which are members of the pit viper family: the copperhead, cottonmouth, western pygmy rattlesnake, massasauga rattlesnake and the timber rattlesnake. The most common pit viper in Missouri is the copperhead and it's probably the least deadly.

It's easy to identify a venomous pit viper. They have a pit located between the eye and the nostril on both sides of their head. Also, their pupils appear as slits within the eyes as opposed to having round eyeballs. And of course, they have a pair of well-developed fangs as your daughter is well aware."

Well you could see the relief on everyone's face as the doctor once again told them that she was going to be all right.

Elizabeth then walked out into the waiting room, sat on a chair, placed her face in her cupped hands and began sobbing uncontrollably. It was a cry caused by both relief and exhaustion.

While the doctor worked on Jeanie's wound, Thomas and his other two children joined Elizabeth in the waiting room.

Thomas saw Elizabeth crying and assured her that everything would be OK.

Elizabeth looked up at Thomas with an anguished and frustrated look on her face and asked, "Thomas, what are we doing? Why did we leave the good life that we had in Kentucky? Please tell me what we are gaining by dragging our family across the country and jeopardizing their lives? I don't understand. What is it all for?"

Then with her head down and wiping the tears from her eyes with her handkerchief, she slowly stood up and walked outside, while Jennie followed directly behind her. Thomas was speechless and felt that it was wise to say nothing and just leave Elizabeth be. Josh was confused because it was the first time that he had ever witnessed any kind of conflict between his ma and pa. Not knowing exactly how to react, Josh decided to go back into the room where the doctor was treating Jeanie. Thomas just sat there befuddled and pondered whether he had made the right decision by taking his family westward.

The struggles, both physically and mentally, were now bearing down strongly on this entire family and they all were experiencing a multitude of emotions.

While Thomas was sitting in the waiting room, the doctor came out to update Thomas and Elizabeth on Jeanie. Thomas went outside and asked Elizabeth to come back inside to hear what the doctor had to say.

"How is she?" Elizabeth asked the doctor.

"She's going to be all right. However, she went through a lot of trauma with this bite and her hand is still swollen some. I treated the wound with medication to prevent infection. That's what I am really concerned about at this point. I know you are heading out west but I must insist that you stay in town for a couple of days so she can rest and so I can monitor her progress to make sure an infection does not set in. I'll give you something for the pain to take with you as well.

There's a hotel down the street you can sign into. They also have a couple of rooms designated for baths that you can use to wash up. You can park your wagons at the livery stable that's about fifty feet north of the hotel. I would like for you to bring Jeanie back in at about two o'clock tomorrow afternoon so I can check and re-bandage her wounds. Like I said before, I believe she's gonna be just fine."

Well, the good doctor's prognosis was a welcome relief to the family.

After the doctor spoke, Elizabeth looked at Thomas and said with an uncharacteristically demanding tone in her voice, "As soon as we sign into the hotel, we all need to clean up, take a bath, put on clean clothes and eat a good home cooked meal this evening at a nice family restaurant. I want this evening to be as normal tonight as if we were eating dinner back in our own home on the plantation in Kentucky." They all agreed and that's exactly what they did.

There wasn't much said at dinner that evening. However, Thomas made it clear that their family was still heading west to Dodge City and that this incident would not change their original plans. He also warned them that they would probably be facing other challenges along the way but if they stuck together as a strong family unit during those hard times, they would make it through.

The next morning after breakfast, Thomas made a visit to the local gun shop. He had decided to purchase a new Henry rifle for himself and give his Winchester '73 to his son. He had no desire to make a big deal of it but he feared that there was a good possibility of running into some undesirables along the Missouri/Kansas border and he felt that even though Josh was only fourteen, his shooting skills might be a plus to the family in case they ran into trouble. Josh was used to shooting the Winchester so Thomas' plan made good sense.

Two days came and went quickly. Elizabeth enjoyed staying at the hotel and dreaded hitting the trail once again. Conversely, Thomas was anxious to begin their trip westward. Getting to Dodge City could not come quick enough for him. Jeanie was feeling much better and the doctor gave her a clean bill of health. So at midmorning on a very humid August day, the O'Briens once again loaded up their wagons with their belongings and more food and supplies and headed west toward Kansas. Their plan was to make Sedalia, Missouri by nightfall. If they could accomplish that goal, Thomas would once again sign his family into a hotel room. He knew that would suit Elizabeth just fine.

Traveling the trail once again was brutal. The temperature this scorching hot August summer day was topping 101 degrees and the high humidity made it feel like it was 108 degrees. The heat was not only taking everything out of the O'Briens but even the horses were struggling and dragging along with their heads down while they sweated profusely losing precious body salt. Several times along the trail they stopped to water the horses from small creeks and then rested them under the shade of large oak trees which were very common in those parts of Missouri.

After a very tiring and exhausting day, the O'Briens finally arrived in Sedalia around 9:30 p.m. The town was fairly quiet and they were fortunate to find a room at a hotel in the main part of town. They also found a café which was still open where they could get a bite to eat before calling it a day.

Their next stop was Blue Springs, Missouri, one and a half days from Sedalia. Blue Springs was a little township that was not incorporated until 1880. It was located just nineteen miles east of Kansas City, Missouri in Jackson County. It was a great stopover location for people heading west because of its supply posts and most importantly, the availability of its fresh clean water. The water from the spring of the Little Blue River was famous for being cool and clean. It was this beautiful flowing spring which was the source of the name of the town, Blue Springs.

They also had a brand new hotel in town that was built in 1878 named The Chicago & Alton Hotel, which was located on Main Street, just west of the railroad tracks. This was a perfect place for the O'Briens to spend the night. Obviously, Elizabeth would rather spend the night in a hotel versus sleeping outside. It was more comfortable and definitely much safer.

However, the night before they reached Blue Springs, they would have to sleep outside underneath the stars. It was that night that changed the life of one of the O'Briens and would haunt him the rest of his life.

At ten o'clock that evening they kicked dirt on the campfire to put out the flame and bedded down for the night. Josh decided to sleep in one of the covered wagons (he went to bed earlier than the rest because the sun and the heat wore him down that day) while the two girls slept on one side of the campfire and Elizabeth and Thomas bedded down on the other side.

This was a night of a Comanche moon, so named because the Comanche Indians would raid homesteaders during a night with a full moon. Well this night it wasn't the Comanche's lurking in the shadows waiting until everyone fell asleep. Rather, it was two outlaws on the prowl who were aware that there was one good looking young woman in camp and a couple of young kids being escorted by just one man.

They were determined to rob the family, kidnap the woman, have their way with her somewhere down the road and then leave her for dead. If it was necessary, they would have no problem killing anyone who interfered with their plan, no matter the gender or age of the person.

These two scumbag outlaws were no good murdering thieves who created havoc along the Missouri/Kansas border for two years. They were never caught and were wanted "Dead or Alive" with a reward on their heads of $2,000 each.

At about eleven o'clock, they made their move when everyone in camp had fallen asleep.

Both of them removed their pistols from their holsters and quietly moved toward Elizabeth and Thomas. They felt that there was no danger to them from the kids, so they went directly for the parents.

One of the outlaws snuck up on Elizabeth's side while the other crept up on Thomas' side. In unison, they both cocked their single action six-shooters and pressed the barrels of their pistols up against the heads of Thomas and Elizabeth. The outlaw next to Elizabeth anticipated a scream so at the same time he pressed the barrel against her head, he placed his other hand over her mouth. That didn't do any good. She shook her head away from the outlaw's hand while screaming and instantaneously, the outlaw slapped her across the face and told her to "shut up". The other outlaw expected a reaction from Thomas and immediately said to him, "If you so much as lift a finger, you're dead along with your entire family."

At this point the two girls woke up and began screaming. One of the outlaws pointed his gun toward them and shouted, "If you don't shut up now, your ma and pa will be shot right here in front of you, now shut up you two!"

While all of this was going on, Josh who had decided to sleep in one of the covered wagons laid low trying to figure out what to do. The outlaws were not aware of Josh being in camp at this point.

Then one of the gunmen spoke, "OK, here's what we want. We wanna know where all of your money is and then if you don't start any trouble, we'll leave. Leave of course with your wife," he said to Thomas.

The girls yelled, "No, don't take our momma!"

"Shut your mouths!" One of the bandits yelled.

Thomas was trying to figure out what to do. He had an idea and decided in a split second to take the gamble of his life, hoping it would work.

The outlaw holding his gun on Thomas demanded to know where their money was.

Thomas pleaded, "I'll tell you but please let my family alone."

The outlaw then shouted, "This is the last time I'm asking you, where's your money?"

Thomas pointed to one of the wagons and said, "It's in there."

Elizabeth looked at Thomas in disbelief while one of the bandits walked over to the wagon Thomas had pointed to.

As the bandit began climbing into the back of the wagon, a loud gunshot rang out echoing across the countryside and a bullet from a Winchester '73 went right through the bandit's head.

At that moment, Thomas turned around and knocked the gun out of the other outlaw's hand and wrestled him to the ground. Elizabeth saw the pistol hit the ground and ran over and picked it up. Josh jumped out of the wagon and grabbed the pistol from his ma.

When Thomas kicked the bandit off of him, Josh took aim with the pistol and unloaded all six bullets into the outlaw's chest and continued to pull the trigger even though there were no more bullets left in the gun. Thomas ran over to Josh and took the pistol away from Josh and said "It's over son, it's over, calm down, calm down now. You saved our family, now calm down."

Thomas hugged Josh while Elizabeth ran over to the twins and hugged them both.

"It's over. Everything is going to be OK now girls," Elizabeth said.

Then the twins walked over to Josh and hugged him and Jennie said, "Josh, you are my hero." Josh smiled but he had mixed emotions, because he just took the lives of two men. However, he had no other choice.

Elizabeth then asked Thomas, "What do we do now?"

Thomas thought about it for a few seconds and then said, "Well, there is no way that any of us will be able to get back to sleep. Let's do this. Josh and I will move the bodies over to the side. Josh, you then go find their horses. Elizabeth, you restart the fire and make some coffee. We'll have something to eat, drink some coffee and then we'll hitch up the team of horses to the wagons and take these two outlaws to Blue Springs. Who knows, there might even be a reward on their heads."

The moonlight from the Comanche moon lit up the campsite enough that Josh was able to find the horses quite easily. He brought them into camp and then tied them to the back of one of the wagons.

While the coffee was boiling, Thomas rolled up the bedrolls and packed them into a wagon. Then the family sat around the campfire, drank their coffee and had some leftover corn bread from dinner earlier in the evening. Obviously none of them were very hungry but they knew they needed to eat something because they had a long night facing them. They were all anxious to get on the trail so they didn't waste any time. After their quick meal, Elizabeth and the girls cleaned up and put out the fire.

Thomas and Josh lifted the two men onto their horses and placed them both in a "dead man" position tying their hands and feet to the stirrups on either side of the saddles.

Thomas and the girls took the lead wagon while Elizabeth and Josh followed behind them with the outlaws' horses tied to their wagon. Thomas and Josh both kept their loaded rifles up front with them not taking any chances on the trail to Blue Springs.

The trail was easy to follow because of the full moon and they arrived in Blue Springs about an hour before sunup. They drove into the heart of town and located the sheriff's office where they parked the wagons and waited for the sheriff to arrive. As the townspeople began moving about town, they started to gather around the wagons and the dead men.

The O'Briens were tired from their lack of sleep and riding all night so they just stayed in their wagons as more and more people gathered to see who the dead men were. Josh and the twin girls were sleeping in the wagons. It had been a very emotional night and they were exhausted. Then out of nowhere, at about 7:00 a.m., the sheriff, a soft spoken weathered face man in his late fifties, walked up to Thomas and said, "I'm sure you are here to see me, come on in." He was carrying a pot of coffee in his hand that he routinely picked up every morning at the café across the street from his office.

Thomas and Elizabeth both climbed down from their wagons and went inside with the sheriff. After the sheriff poured himself a cup of coffee, he offered a cup to Elizabeth and Thomas. They both declined because they had enough coffee in their systems to last them for two days.

The sheriff then lazily sat in his chair behind his desk, took a sip of his steaming hot black coffee and asked Thomas and Elizabeth to have a seat. After introductions, the sheriff asked in a nonchalant tone, "Well, tell me what happened and the events that led to those men's demise."

So Thomas told the entire story just as it had occurred.

When Thomas finished describing the events of last night, Josh walked into the sheriff's office not knowing what to expect. Thomas looked at Josh who seemed a bit weary and frightened and then Thomas looked at the sheriff and said, "Sheriff, this is my brave son, Josh. He's the one who did what he had to do to save the lives of everyone in our family. He became a man last night."

The sheriff stood up and walked over to Josh, shook his hand and said, "Josh, it's a pleasure to meet such a brave young man. I don't think you are aware of who those men are out there. Before I asked your pa to come in, I checked them out. Josh, you and your family just brought in two brothers who are the most ruthless murdering border outlaws and gunslingers on the Missouri/Kansas border. They are cousins to the Dalton Gang. Their names are Cole and Hank Dempsey. You will also be happy to hear that there is a reward out on their heads for $2,000 each."

"Holy smokes!" Josh shouted, "We're rich!"

Everyone smiled.

The sheriff then said to Josh, "You and your father's bravery did this community a real service young man, and we will always be grateful to the O'Brien family for that."

Then the sheriff looked at Elizabeth and Thomas and said, "The reward for the capture or death of these two outlaws was put up by the Union Pacific Railroad. The mayors of the towns along the Missouri and Kansas borders have the right to offer the rewards from their banks if they have enough money on hand to do so. The protocol is to then notify the Union Pacific Railroad and they will reimburse the bank. We won't be incorporated until next year but our township did vote for a person who is our acting mayor. So as far as Blue Springs, Missouri is concerned, he's legal," the sheriff said as he grinned ever so slightly.

"I know for a fact that we have enough cash on hand right now so if you want to, I'll take a few minutes, get the paperwork together, and we'll walk over to the bank. By the way, if you decide to stay in town tonight, we have a brand new hotel named The Chicago & Alton Hotel. It's right plush for a small country town. You probably saw it when you rode down Main Street this morning."

"Yes, we did," Thomas confirmed.

While the sheriff finished up the paperwork and his deputy took care of the two bodies, Thomas said that he and his family would first go across the street to the café for a hot breakfast and talk about their plans for the rest of the day and that night. So they did, leaving their wagons parked in front of the sheriff's office.

During breakfast, Elizabeth reconfirmed and "demanded" that they spend the night in the new hotel in town. After the ordeal she and her family had been through, there was no need for discussion on that topic.

After breakfast, Josh took each wagon over to the livery stable while Elizabeth walked down the street with the girls and signed into the hotel. Thomas went back over to the sheriff's office to collect the reward.

Before they walked over to the bank, the sheriff asked Thomas to sit down and join him for a cup of coffee. Then the sheriff asked Thomas where they were headed. Thomas answered,

"We are on our way to Dodge City, Kansas."

"Whatever for?" the sheriff asked.

"I'm getting into the cattle business to become a cattle buyer and I figure Dodge City is the place I need to go. The cattle business is really booming there now and I want to be a part of it."

"Your wife seems more like an Easterner. How does she feel about the move?"

"Not real crazy about it," Thomas admitted.

Then the sheriff said in a very serious tone, "Young man, you are about to take your beautiful family through one of the most uncivilized territories in this country. There are outlaw gangs all over Kansas who are thieves and murderers. They have no values and certainly no respect for the law much less someone's life. They'll cheat, rob and kill at a blink of an eye and show no remorse. I just hope you know what you're getting your family into."

"Sheriff, we've been exposed to that already all the way from St. Louis. I appreciate your concern but I promise you, we'll make it to Dodge City one way or another."

"Yes son, I believe you will," the sheriff said in a sincere voice. "Now what do you say we take a walk over to the bank? It's time to collect your reward."

And so they did. Thomas received $4,000 bounty for bringing the Dempsey brothers in. The bank owner, being concerned about Thomas carrying around so much cash, gave Thomas a money belt to conceal his stash.

Then Thomas shook the sheriff's hand and headed to the hotel. Not sleeping at all the night before, they all napped until about 5:00 p.m. They ate dinner that evening and then went back to their hotel room to make plans for the balance of the trip.

They figured they still had about 330 to 350 miles to go. Their planned route was to travel to Kansas City, then proceed to Lawrence, Kansas, onto Topeka, Abilene, Salina, Great Bend, and finally to Dodge City.

Several of those towns were notable cow towns. It was in those towns where Thomas learned more about the conflicts between the farmers and townspeople, and the drovers and cowboys from Texas. He also educated himself on the so-called Texas fever, which earned an infamous reputation around western Missouri, and eastern and central Kansas.

However, what pleased him the most were the stories he heard about the great financial rewards which were available to anyone who understood and was willing to work hard in the cattle business. Texas still had thousands of cattle to bring to the Kansas railheads and the demand for beef continued to grow in the eastern parts of the United States.

Driving their wagons across Kansas during the month of September was not as exhausting and dangerous, weather-wise, as was August in Missouri. Since they felt that they were ahead of schedule, the O'Briens stayed a few extra days in some of the famous cow towns like Abilene and Salina to learn more about the cattle business.

Elizabeth didn't mind that one bit since she was able to spend more nights in a soft feather bed with clean sheets, and a roof over her head. She didn't miss seeing the sights of the bright stars shining in the moonless sky or hearing the creepy sounds of the howling and barking coyotes on the lonesome prairie; no sir, not at all.

The O'Brien family camped northeast of Dodge City, just a few miles from Fort Dodge the night before arriving at their destination. It was October 3rd and they were so proud of themselves because they had traveled across several states, ran into quite a few obstacles, but through all the trials, tribulations, turmoils, and tragedies, they would arrive at their destination (the Queen of the Cow Towns) as planned.

It was a cool rainy October night just outside of Dodge City, Kansas. The O'Briens were gathered in one of their covered wagons, eating a light meal, and reminiscing about their long arduous trip across the precarious midwestern states.

Tomorrow would be the culmination of their onerous but memorable journey to the city of their dreams and the wonderful future they set out to attain.

What Thomas, Elizabeth, Josh, Jeanie and Jennie were totally oblivious to was the fact that the events of the next couple of days in Dodge City would change their lives and their family's plans forever.

CHAPTER SEVEN:

Retired Texas Ranger Meets Wyatt

He was the grandson of a Scottish immigrant and the son of Mathew Johnson and Anna Hurley Johnson. He was born on a cool and cloudy misty morning on September 15, 1846 in a sod house on a small family ranch just outside of an area they now call Fort Worth, Texas. His name was Scott Johnson.

Mathew and Anna Johnson were pioneers and moved to Texas from Springfield, Missouri in 1844. Mathew, a hard working burley type man, was the town's blacksmith in Springfield, Missouri. He and his wife moved his craft to the Fort Worth, Texas area in 1844 and acquired a small 175-acre ranch there.

He opened up his own blacksmith shop, in the small community, which over time became very successful. During the days of the Old West, blacksmiths were some of the most important people in their communities. Many people assumed that all that blacksmiths knew how to do was to shoe horses. Nothing could be further from the truth. Back then there were no hardware stores. A blacksmith was capable of making just about anything you could find in a hardware store today. They made tools, nails, spikes, wagon parts, branding irons, door hinges, hooks for hanging things, horseshoes, knives, swords, and even shackles for prisoners. On occasion they also made jailhouse bars for jail cells. A town could not function without the presence of a skilled blacksmith.

Fort Worth was a small community until it became a stopping off point for cattle drives along the Chisholm Trail. It eventually grew to be one of the most successful cattle towns in the Old West. It earned its name the "Queen City of the Prairies".

In Scott's early years he worked in his father's blacksmith shop doing simple jobs like starting the forge fires and throwing air on the fire by pumping the large bellows. The forge is a container for the fire and is positioned at a convenient height to suit the blacksmith. It also contains an opening which air is pumped into by the bellows to raise the temperature of the fire to the desired heat, which enables the blacksmith to bend or shape steel.

Forges can be made out of sheet steel, cast iron, stone or brick. Mathew's forge was made out of stone found around the banks of the Trinity River, which bordered Fort Worth, Texas. However, his pride and joy and the workhorse of his blacksmith's shop was his 150 pound steel anvil which was fastened to a black walnut stump he brought with him from Missouri.

Being the big man that he was, Mathew was able to do his entire blacksmith hammering with a heavy three-pound sledgehammer, which he used to pound steel over the anvil with authority.

As Scott grew into his mid-teens, his pa taught him how to bend and shape steel. Scott's first real blacksmithing job was to craft 10 inch long hunting knives for some of the cowboys on ranches nearby and for some of the Texans who were joining the Confederate Army at the beginning of the Civil War. He became a very skillful craftsman and his knives became the preferred blade by many in Fort Worth.

Scott loved to work with steel and felt great satisfaction in crafting useful things out of pieces of scrap metal. He also became interested in handguns since his pa loved to spend his spare time target shooting with him using his .44 caliber, Third Model Dragoon revolver, with an attachable shoulder stock, carried by cavalry troops in the pre-Civil War West. Scott's pa traded work on a covered wagon for the Dragoon revolver which was owned by a retired U.S Army cavalryman who scouted for the U.S. Army in Apache territory in New Mexico.

In 1863, at the young age of seventeen, Scott left Fort Worth for Austin and joined up with the Texas Confederate Army. He was enlisted and on active duty until the end of the War but saw no real action.

After the War, he went back home to Fort Worth only to find a struggling economy with money, food and supply shortages due to the effects of the Civil War.

During the War he was exposed to many types of guns and pistols and developed aspirations to some day become a gunsmith in a booming town and earn the same type of respect that his pa had from the townspeople. He knew for a fact that being a respected gunsmith was what he wanted out of life.

He put a lot of thought into it and figured that he could best learn the gunsmith trade by working in a gun manufacturing plant actually assembling guns from scratch. Through months of research, he learned about the Smith & Wesson Company located in the East.

The Smith & Wesson Company was founded in 1852 by Horace Smith (October 28, 1808 - January 15, 1893, lived to age

84) and Daniel B. Wesson (May 18, 1825 – August 4, 1906, lived to age 81) and was headquartered in Springfield, Massachusetts.

Scott was seeking employment with the company just when the Smith & Wesson Company would begin a global sales campaign introducing its revolvers and ammunition to new markets, such as Russia and European countries. This campaign would establish the Smith & Wesson Company as one of the world's premier manufacturers of firearms.

Scott did not want to spend the time nor the money making a trip to Massachusetts on the hope that he might get a job with the Smith & Wesson Company. So instead, he composed the following letter, while sitting at the kitchen table next to the fireplace, which kept the sod house toasty warm on this cold and cloudy January winter morning.

Smith & Wesson Company
Springfield, Massachusetts

Dear Sirs,

My name is Scott Johnson. I am the son of Mathew Johnson and Anna Hurley Johnson of Fort Worth, Texas. My father is the blacksmith in town and I was his apprentice for several years before I enlisted in the Texas infantry.

I have always loved working with metal and have aspirations to be a gunsmith someday. However, at present, I have a desire to work for one of the largest gun manufacturers in the East.

I would deem it a privilege and an honor to be employed by your company. I can assure you that I will be an honorable, trustworthy, and hardworking skilled laborer whom you would be proud to employ.

Thank you for your serious consideration and I hope to hear from you in the near future.

Yours truly,
Scott Johnson
Fort Worth, Texas

After completing the letter, Scott saddled up his horse and rode to town and dropped off the letter at the telegraph office before showing up for work at his pa's blacksmith shop.

He had no idea how long it would take to get a response from the Smith & Wesson Company. Everyday he would ride on horseback alongside of his pa to help out at the blacksmith shop. On his lunch breaks and directly after work he would walk over to the telegraph office to see if there was any response to his letter.

Three weeks went by and still no response. By now, Scott was about to give up all hope of getting hired and much less even hearing from the Smith & Wesson Company.

However, during the fourth week of anxiously waiting for a reply, at about 10 o'clock on a Tuesday morning, the telegraph office manager came running down the street kicking up dust on the dry dirt road waving a telegram in his hand above his head yelling, "Scott, Scott, your answer came, your answer came!"

Scott looked up, saw and heard the telegraph operator, dropped his hammer and ran to meet the telegraph manager in the middle of Main Street. "Scott, this is the telegram you've been waiting for," the telegraph manager said while trying to catch his breath.

"Let me see," Scott anxiously demanded as he grabbed the letter faster than a duck snatching up a June bug.

Before he read the telegram, he knew it must have been good news because of the way Ed, the telegraph manager, was smiling. By this time, Scott's pa had caught up to him.

"Read it out loud," Ed encouraged.

"Yeah," Scott's pa insisted.

"OK, I will. It says:"

Dear Scott Johnson,
Fort Worth, Texas

We are impressed with your desire to seek employment with our great company and be part of producing the best firearms in the U.S.

We are anxious to talk to you very soon as we are increasing our workforce due to the increased number of orders we are receiving around the country and the world.

Please inform us at your earliest convenience when you will be able to arrive in Springfield, Massachusetts. I would like to meet with you personally and I am certain we will have a position open for your immediate employment.

Looking forward to hearing from you soon.

> *Sincerely,*
> *Daniel Wesson*
> *Smith & Wesson Company*

"Gosh darn!" Scott shouted, "I'm going to Massachusetts!"

Scott's pa put his arm around Scott and congratulated him, "I am proud of you son. It looks like your dream has come true. Your ma and I are going to miss you but there comes a time in everyone's life when you have to move on and follow your own dream," Scott's pa said with some obvious sadness in his voice. However, this would not be the first time Scott would have left home, since he was gone for two years during the Civil War.

"Why don't you take the rest of the day off and ride home to the ranch and inform your ma of your good fortune," Scott's father suggested.

And so he did. Scott's ma knew this day would come sooner or later so she had been preparing herself for this moment for several weeks.

At dinner that night Scott told his ma and pa that he would be responding to Daniel Wesson's telegram the next morning and that he would be leaving for Massachusetts within a week.

His plan was to buy two horses and a wagon in town for his trip to St. Louis where he would take a ferry across the Mississippi River, and pick up a train in Terre Haute, Indiana. That train would carry him all the way to Springfield, Massachusetts. Since he had hoped to eventually receive a positive response from Smith & Wesson, he had been working on this itinerary for a couple of weeks.

So in early March of 1866, Scott packed up his clothes and some of his personal belongings, said goodbye to his ma and pa, and headed northeast to St. Louis, Missouri in a buckboard wagon pulled by two beautiful Belgium draft horses. He carried $850 with him, which was plenty of money to allow him to stay in small hotels and boarding houses along the way, pay for his train ticket in Terre Haute, and pay rent for a small house in Springfield, Massachusetts, until he began earning a salary with the Smith & Wesson Company.

Scott took a longer route to St. Louis, in order to circumvent the Indian Territory just north of Texas. His route took him from Fort Worth to Dallas, Texas, and onward to Texarkana, Little Rock, and to West Memphis, Arkansas. He then traveled north along the west banks of the Mississippi River to St. Louis. It was a grueling 800-mile trip, which took him a little over a month and a half to travel. After he crossed the Mississippi River, he still had about ten days to travel before he could board his train in Indiana.

On May 14, 1866, Scott finally arrived in Terre Haute. He made it in good fashion experiencing no trouble along the way that this determined young Texan couldn't handle.

Before he caught a train eastward, he had a few chores to take care of in Terre Haute. Obviously, the first thing he did was to buy his train ticket to Springfield, Massachusetts. Then he sold his buckboard and horses to the livery stable. Once he did that, he took that money from his sale and used it to buy a new suit, coat, new pants, shirts, an eastern style top hat and a brand new pair of boots. He wanted to be sure that he made a good first impression when he met Mr. Daniel Wesson.

The very next day he boarded the train for Springfield, Massachusetts. This would be one of the best parts of the trip because this next and last leg of his journey would prove to be much easier than the first. He'd be able to rest on the train and collect his thoughts before his all-important interview that would change his life forever.

His train trip took him through Ohio, Pennsylvania, New York and then to Massachusetts. This young man from the economically poor town of Fort Worth, Texas witnessed new parts of the country the likes of which he never knew existed.

He quickly realized how much more civilized the East was than the Western territory he grew up in. Buildings stood stalwart and were made of bricks, and many houses were two stories tall. Horse buggies were fancier, and the clothes people wore were more pristine. Soon he would discover that the people would seem to be more educated, refined and polite.

"Wow, I could get used to this part of the country," he thought as he peered out of the passenger car window traveling through New York just before entering Massachusetts.

Scott's train arrived in Springfield on the afternoon of May 21st. When he stepped off the train with a suitcase in either hand, he stopped, smiled, took a deep breath, looked skyward and gave out a good old fashioned Fort Worth "Yeeha!" before he realized he was not out West anymore. Everyone around him looked his way as he smiled, turned red in the face from embarrassment and quietly, underneath his breath said, "Sorry".

Within minutes, he forgot about his embarrassing entrance into Springfield and quickly asked directions to the nearest hotel. Wasting no time, he walked quickly down the street to the hotel and signed in immediately and asked the hotel clerk for directions to the Smith & Wesson Company. He was elated to discover that the Smith & Wesson Company was in walking distance and only two blocks away. This was perfect since he could stay at the hotel until he found a house to rent.

Not aware of the eastern procedure of making an appointment in advance of a visit, Scott arrived at the office of Daniel Wesson at 9 o'clock the next morning. Wesson knew that Scott was from the small western town of Fort Worth so he overlooked the fact that Scott didn't follow proper business protocol.

Scott sat in the reception room for fifteen minutes before he stood up and began pacing the floor. At about 9:25 a.m., an elderly gray haired lady opened the door to the main office and came out into the reception room.

"Are you Scott Johnson?" she asked.

Scott stood up and holding his new hat in front of him said, "Yes madam, I am."

"Well then, Mr. Wesson is ready to see you young man."

With his heart beating twice its normal rate and nervous perspiration dripping from his forehead, he followed the elderly lady into the main office. He immediately saw two doors with frosted glass windows. One window had the name Horace Smith on it and the other door window was stenciled with the name Daniel B. Wesson. Scott looked at both doors and then the door on the right opened up and a man about six foot tall, wearing a dark pinstriped suit and a full face beard, walked out, extended his arm for a handshake and said, "You must be Scott Johnson, I'm Daniel Wesson. It's a pleasure to meet you."

"It's a real pleasure to meet you sir."

"Come on into my office and let's talk."

They both sat down, Wesson behind his large bulky oak desk and Scott on a leather covered chair in front of Wesson's desk.

"Would you like a cigar?" Wesson smiled and asked Scott.

"No sir, I don't smoke."

"Well then, let me light up mine and we'll get started with the interview."

"Suits me just fine; I mean yes sir," Scott corrected himself with a look of embarrassment on his face.

Wesson smiled, struck a match and lit up his large, expensive Columbian cigar, taking several puffs on it and blowing the smoke in the air with an obvious look of great pleasure on his face.

"Now Scott, you said you were looking for a job and someday wanted to be a gunsmith. Well, you're in luck young man. I'm looking for good men who have a desire to learn all they can about the business of making firearms. I figure if you have an interest in your job and a desire to learn the business, you're probably going to be a good employee.

You indicated in your telegram that you had worked with metal in Fort Worth. Well that's a good start because in this trade you have to possess skills as a metalworker, a mechanic, a machinist, a woodworker, and an artisan. Your training will consist of shop mathematics, ballistics, and chemistry and above all, you must be capable of working accurately and precisely.

One of the most important technical responsibilities of a gunsmith is to ensure that the firearms which you make function safely. So we inspect every gun we manufacture for improper assembly, missing parts, cracks, bore obstructions, safety mechanisms, firing pins, balance and more. We even test fire random samples.

Are you still with me?" Wesson asked with a smile.

"Yes sir," Scott responded with an overwhelmingly degree of enthusiasm.

"Good, there's more. We'll teach you about finishing with various chemical processes like parkerization, which is a method of protecting a steel surface from corrosion and increasing its resistance to wear; and blueing, browning and more.

We'll show you how to carve gunstocks from wood. We have a woodshed out back full of high quality wood like walnut, birch, maple, and even apple wood. When you make the stocks, you'll be using tools like saws, chisels, gouges, rasps, and files. And then you will learn sanding, staining, oiling, and lacquering. We'll even train you how to engrave designs in wood and metal."

By now Scott was overwhelmed but energized at the same time. He knew that he came to the right place to become exposed to the intricacies of being a gunsmith.

"Well Scott, that gives you a pretty good idea of what you will be learning and doing while working here at Smith & Wesson. Do you still think it's what you want to do?"

"Yes sir, it's exactly what I want to do."

"Then I want you to be here Monday morning at 8:00 sharp. My partner Mr. Smith is out of town now but he'll be back on Monday. I'll introduce you to him then."

Well that day was the beginning of Scott's dream coming true and the beginning of a seven-year career with the Smith & Wesson Company. But most important of all, he was now on the path to becoming a gunsmith, which was his ultimate goal.

Scott would be with the company during some of the best years that the Smith & Wesson Company experienced. Notably, he was employed when the company manufactured one of its most important model pistols of the Old West, the Smith & Wesson Model 3. This was a single action, cartridge-firing, top-breaking revolver which began production in 1870. It was originally chambered for a .44 but was later produced in an assortment of calibers including .44-40, .32-44, .38-44, the .44 Henry Rimfire, and the .45 Schofield.

The Model 3 was produced in several variations and sub-variations of which the three most popular were the "Russian Model", the "American Model" and the "Schofield".

Scott would work on the Russian Model and the American Model but would leave Smith & Wesson before the Schofield Model went into production.

The Russian Model was so named because of the fact that in 1871, the Imperial Russian Army ordered 20,000 No. 3's in the .44 caliber.

In 1870, the U.S. Army made the .44 caliber American Model 3 its first standard-issue cartridge firing revolver in the U.S. Service. This was a much improved and more reliable pistol than the black powder cap and ball revolver, which would misfire on many occasions during wet weather conditions.

Smith & Wesson eventually received a contract from the U.S. Ordnance Board to outfit the military with the Schofield Model, which was a Model 3 revolver that was redesigned by Major George W. Schofield. As was true about other Model 3's, these revolvers were popular with both lawmen and criminals alike. These are just a few of the other users of the various Model 3's;

Wyatt Earp, Virgil Earp, Pat Garrett, Jesse James, John Wesley Hardin, Theodore Roosevelt, Billy the Kid, and the Royal Canadian Mounted Police.

Scott was fortunate to be with Smith & Wesson during the booming Model 3 production years because it would certainly help him in the future when he became a gunsmith out West where this revolver was the revered revolver of many.

In February of 1870 Scott's friend and co-worker Todd Smith and his wife Madeline introduced Scott to a young lady named Martha Shrewsbury at a church social. Martha and Scott discovered that they had a lot in common and were attracted to each other. Both were young, single, and very gregarious and loquacious and both possessed an adventurous spirit, which was evident by the subject matter they spent time talking about.

Soon after that mutually auspicious encounter, Scott began to court Martha during the next eighteen months. In June of 1872 Scott and Martha were married. People who knew the couple said that this marriage was truly a match made in heaven.

The newlyweds bought a small ornate Victorian style house with a white picket fence just on the outskirts of town where they had plans to start a family. Scott was earning a good salary with the Smith & Wesson Company and was rapidly progressing up the ladder on the organizational chart because of his intelligence and his ability to learn quickly. Both Smith and Wesson were also impressed with Scott's craftsman skills and actually had plans to place Scott in a key management position in the company.

However, Scott's personal aspirations never changed. His desire remained the same, that is, to go into business for himself as a gunsmith in a booming western town. He had a longing to move back West sometime in the future where he knew his craft would be much more appreciated than in the East. This would mean a greater degree of financial success and rewards for his entrepreneurial spirit. His wife Martha was also anxious to move out West as well. She was ready for new adventures in her life and to see for herself the exciting life of the West, which she had only read and heard about.

One evening in early September when Scott came home from work and walked through the front door, he was greeted by the aroma of a beef pot roast cooking on the wood-burning stove in the kitchen. As he turned and looked toward his left into the small dining room, he saw that the table was set with the couple's best China dinnerware, which was a wedding gift from Martha's parents. Also on the table were a bottle of imported French champagne and two long lit white candles in sterling silver candleholders. It had the appearance of a setting for a royal family. At least, that's how Scott perceived it.

Scott walked into the kitchen, gave his wife a kiss and asked, "What's the big occasion dear?"

Martha said, "I'll let you in on a secret, as soon as I'm finished cooking dinner. Now go and change out of your work clothes and sit on the porch until dinner is ready."

Scott was visibly excited about Martha's little secret and couldn't wait to hear what it was. After waiting on the front porch for about 35 minutes, Martha told Scott to come into the house. She walked with him into the dining room, put her arms around Scott and said, "Honey, are you ready for my good news?"

"You bet Martha, what is it?"

"Well dear, I am expecting a baby sometime in April of next year."

"Praise the Lord!" Scott shouted as he hugged Martha, sweeping her off her feet and twirling her around. "That is the best news of my life," Scott said with a great big grin on his face.

Then when Scott set Martha down, Martha said, "Let's celebrate with a toast of champagne. I picked it up at the store today after I received the news from the doctor."

So Scott popped the cork and they toasted to the upcoming birth of their first child, which they hoped would be the first of many.

The winter of 1873 and early 1874 was a hard one with many weeks in the low teens and numerous days with the ground covered with snow due to an unusual number of snow storms that particular winter.

Even with the inclement weather, Scott looked forward to going to work because he enjoyed learning something new everyday and continued to look forward to honing his gunsmith skills. And what made things even more interesting for him was the fact that Scott was now in charge of test firing rifles and pistols, which came off the rudimentary assembly lines. Test firing became one of his favorite things to do.

The Smith & Wesson plant had an attached building set up as a gun range, which was used to test fire random firearms before shipment. This job was given to a person who was a skilled marksman and an accomplished craftsman who was able to discover, analyze and correct a defect in a single firearm or identify a flaw in the engineering design of a pistol or rifle.

The firing range was also available for the personal use of employees on their off hours, meaning they could access it on their lunch hours, after work hours, and even on weekends. Scott often took advantage of this opportunity because he never ceased to enjoy the recreational sport of target shooting, which was a delightful part of his life growing up in Fort Worth, Texas.

In October of 1873, Scott and Martha's best friends, Todd and Madeline Smith moved to Pensacola, Florida to be close to Madeline's aging parents. It was a sad episode in the Johnson's life. The two couples spent many hours together at church socials, attending local plays, enjoying dinners at quaint and sometimes lavish restaurants and even going on weekend trips together. It was extremely hard for the two couples to say goodbye to each other. However, they did promise to stay in touch and to make it a practice to visit on occasion. Scott promised that directly after their child's first birthday, they would ride a train down to Florida to visit the Smiths for a week-long vacation.

During the day of February 6, 1874, the weather turned for the worse. It was just cold and cloudy when Scott hitched up his horse to his buggy and headed for work. However, around 11 o'clock, freezing rain fell from the dark clouds for about two hours and the freezing rain then turned to snow. It was a virtual blizzard outside with 3 inches of snow falling every hour right on top of the half-inch layer of ice making for a very dangerous situation. The wind was howling and blowing at a clip of 40 miles per hour. It was your textbook Nor'easter.

As the temperature continued to fall throughout the afternoon hours, Martha, who was close to being 7 months pregnant now, could feel the temperature in the house dropping to a very uncomfortable level. The fire in the fireplace was low and the wood pile was depleted inside the house. Unfortunately, the firewood shed was behind the house. Martha knew that the flame would go out soon so she had to go outside in the blizzard and carry in at least three logs to keep the fire burning until Scott arrived home. She was anticipating Scott to leave work early because of the dangerous winter storm.

So Martha put on a shawl and a heavy coat to fetch three logs for the fire. When she went out on the back porch, she was not aware that there was a layer of ice underneath the snow. The events that followed were sheer horror. Martha slipped on the very first step and slid down five steps, falling directly onto a ceramic flower pot near the bottom step, cracking a rib and puncturing a lung.

She was in incredible pain and had problems catching her breath. She lay there immobile and feared the worst for her unborn baby. Martha then tried to get up but every move she made came with unbearable pain. She suffered in the cold snowy blizzard for a long forty-five minutes hurting, moaning, and crying before Scott finally came home.

When Scott walked in the front door, he sensed something was wrong. The fire was out in the fireplace and the house was extremely cold.

"Martha," he called out. "Martha where are you?" He ran from room to room and couldn't find her. Then he noticed that the back door was cracked open. He opened the door, looked down the steps and shouted, "No, oh my God, Martha, Martha!" He held on to the banister and ran down the steps as fast as he could.

There was Martha lying on the ground, covered with fresh fallen snow, shivering and moaning and nearly unconscious. Scott had no idea how bad she was hurt. So he picked her up and gingerly carried her up the steps. Every little move made Martha scream in pain. After he took her coat off, he laid her in bed, and covered her with as many blankets as he could find. Then he ran to his neighbor's house and asked him to ride into town and bring the doctor back as quickly as possible.

Two hours went by and still no doctor. The blizzard outside continued to get worse with every passing hour. There were already ten inches of snow on the ground and drifts were almost two feet deep. Scott was helpless and could only hope and pray that Martha would be all right. Martha continued to moan in pain in a semi-conscious state.

Finally, after waiting three hours, Scott heard someone knocking on his front door. The doctor had finally arrived. Scott ran to the door, opened it up and led the doctor to Martha.

After Scott explained to the doctor how he found Martha, the doctor said, "Son, why don't you leave the room, close the door and make some coffee for us while I exam her. I'm sure everything will be all right."

So Scott did what the doctor asked, closed the door to the bedroom and the doctor began his examination. After making coffee, Scott restlessly paced the floor outside of the room praying for Martha's recovery. Then he got down on his knees and looked skyward, "Please dear Lord, I have never asked for much from you. Please, I beg of you, please don't take Martha away from me. She is all I have."

As he continued to pray, the doctor came out of the room with a very serious and worried look on his face.

"Scott, let's sit down and talk."

"How is she doc?" Scott asked with a very worried look on his face and tears filling his eyes.

"Son, it is not good," the doc responded.

"What about the baby, doc? Is the baby going to be alright?"

"It's too early to tell, Scott.

The best I can figure, she broke three ribs in the fall and I'm afraid one of those ribs punctured her left lung. She's having problems breathing. I am now worried about her catching pneumonia in the good lung. I gave her some laudanum for pain. Laudanum is a combination opium and alcohol solution, which will also help her rest easy. If you don't mind, I would like to stay here tonight and watch over her. I brought some extra clothes with me anticipating such, what with the storm and all."

"Sure doctor, that would make me feel better knowing you're here in case anything should happen during the night."

Scott pulled an upholstered chair next to Martha's bed for the good doctor to use and Scott laid on a couch in their living room. At about 2:00 a.m. the snow ceased to fall and the wind finally let up. The blizzard had moved on to the north.

Scott was so worn out that he fell into a deep sleep during the night. While he slept the doctor stayed up all night with Martha.

Then at about 5:00 a.m., Scott woke up to find the doctor sitting at the kitchen table drinking a cup of coffee. The bedroom door was closed.

"How's Martha this morning?" Scott asked.

The doctor stood up and faced Scott and put his hands on Scott's shoulders and quietly said with a quivering voice, "Scott, I am so sorry to say that your wife passed away in her sleep at 4 o'clock this morning. In fact, we lost them both."

"No!" Scott yelled, "It can't be!" as he turned around and ran into the bedroom where Martha was lying. He fell to his knees next to the bed and sunk his face into his hands and cried out loud. Scott was devastated as the doctor looked on, wiping the tears from his own eyes as he witnessed such great sorrow, pain, and misery pouring out of Scott's grieving heart.

That day, Scott's life changed forever. His dreams of growing old with his best friend and wife and raising a family of children vanished in the blink of an eye on that cold and snowy bleak wintry day in Springfield, Massachusetts.

Two months after the funeral of his wife, Scott felt that it was time to make a critical decision in his life. He no longer had any desire to remain in Massachusetts after his wife's untimely passing. He came to the realization that it was time for him to move on. He was satisfied that he had learned enough about his trade over the years at Smith & Wesson and he was now ready to start up his own business as a gunsmith in a town somewhere out West which would require and value his specialized skills.

Scott had not been back to Fort Worth since his first trip to Massachusetts and he felt it would be a good time to visit with his parents and then subsequently move on once again. However, instead of heading straight to Texas, he wanted to stop and visit with his good friends Todd and Madeline Smith in Pensacola first and inform them all about that dreadful day in February. After all, it was Todd and Madeline who introduced Scott to Martha four years prior in the same month Martha met her demise.

On May 1, 1874, Scott had a scheduled meeting with Daniel Wesson. It was then that Scott informed Wesson that he was resigning from the company and moving back to Texas. Wesson was not surprised by Scott's resignation because he always remembered that on the first day they met, Scott had informed Wesson that he had plans some day to open up his own gunsmith shop. Wesson also knew that the loss of Scott's wife had a devastating affect on Scott and he understood that Scott had to move on from a place that gave him intolerable sorrow.

"You were one of the most loyal and skilled employees in my company," Wesson said with a trace of emotion in his voice.

"You will truly be missed. But I am sure that you will meet with great success as you follow your dream and move on to your new endeavors."

Then Scott gratefully replied, "Mr. Wesson, I owe you a lot. I came here to learn a trade and I'm leaving here with much more knowledge about firearms and gunsmithing than I ever thought possible. I didn't know what I didn't know about firearms until I signed up with your company. You've given me every opportunity to learn the craft and I took advantage of that opportunity. You are a fair and good man and I really enjoyed working for you."

Wesson knew from gossip he had heard around the factory that Scott was close to resigning. So he had prepared a special gift for Scott and presented it to him on that very day.

With a smile on his face Wesson handed Scott a beautifully finished walnut wood box.

"What's this?" Scott asked.

"Open it," Wesson insisted.

Scott unhooked the small box latch and slowly opened the hinged lid. There they were. Lying in plush red velvet, were a pair of nickel-plated S & W Model 3 Schofield revolvers that were not even in production yet. They were also engraved with the initials S.J. for Scott Johnson. Scott was overwhelmed with gratitude and was speechless as Wesson looked on with a gentleman's smile. Scott would cherish those pistols for the rest of his life.

At that, the two men said their farewells. Scott sold his fully furnished house within the next couple of weeks and caught a train to Pensacola. After spending a week with his friends, he rode on horseback to Fort Worth, Texas. He had telegraphed his parents that he was on his way home and would probably arrive there sometime within the next three weeks. Scott's parents were extremely elated since they had not seen their son in years.

Little did Scott know that his life was about to take on a new twist.

Scott arrived home midmorning on June 22, 1874 and was greeted with great enthusiasm by his ma and pa. His pa was still the town's blacksmith and was well known for his excellent skills and work around, not only Fort Worth and Dallas, but as far south and east as San Antonio, Houston, Waco, and Austin. When you're the best at what you do, word travels fast and Scott was to witness for himself exactly how this was true for his own pa.

Scott rested that afternoon after the long trip from Pensacola while his ma prepared a large welcome home dinner. At 6:00 p.m. the three sat down at the dinner table, said grace and began eating. His ma made a wonderful southern meal with fried chicken, corn on the cob, fresh greens, pinto beans and corn bread. Since Scott had a family-inherited sweet tooth, she made a blue ribbon style peach cobbler with peaches they harvested from their own backyard peach tree. There was a lot of small talk around the dinner table that evening and nothing new and earthshaking was revealed among the three since Scott and his parents wrote many letters to each other while Scott was in Massachusetts. This was a common practice during that time period.

After dinner, Scott and his pa went out on the front porch. Then the subject matter became more serious and to the point.

His pa started the conversation, "It was a welcome sight to see you today son. I believe you are 28 years old now and in the prime of your life. Your ma and I are very proud of your accomplishments. Going off to Massachusetts on your own at such an early age was truly respectable. Experiencing such a family tragedy, which you did, was dreadful and too awful for such a young man to experience. I guess my question is, where do you go from here, son?"

"Pa, I went to Massachusetts to learn how to become a gunsmith so I could move up north or out west someday to one of those booming cow towns where there's plenty of excitement, where my skills are needed, and where I can make a good honest living. One thing I learned from you and ma is that if you put in an honest day's work, you'll receive an honest day's pay. I always respected you two. You never asked for anything from anybody. You worked for what you have and I have always tried to model my life after your fine examples. As I grew older, I also became more aware of why you took time doing what you did, whether it was building a covered wagon, making hinges for doors and windows or shodding horses. You took the time to do those things to the best of your ability and demanded perfection from yourself. Well, your example has shaped the way I feel about things. I have always taken pride in my work and produced some of the finest firearms on the market today with the S & W name on them. Now I want to take that experience and put it to work."

"Well son, something has come up which I want to talk to you about. You see, I have this friend from Waco. He doesn't live there now; he lives in the governor's mansion in Austin."

Scott looked over at his pa and asked with a sense of astonishment on his face and in his voice, "You know the governor pa?"

"That's right son."

"What's his name?"

"It's Governor Richard Coke. We've been friends for a few years now."

"That's incredible. How did you meet him?"

"Well like we said before, when you do good work, the word gets around. Governor Coke learned about my work by word of mouth and during the last several years, I've been doing special blacksmith projects for him and some of his friends."

"Well how does the governor of Texas fit into this conversation, pa?"

"Here's the deal son. I told the governor all about you awhile back. He was impressed with your aspirations and experience and asked me to give you this proposal if and when you came back to Texas."

"What proposal?" Scott apprehensively asked. Scott was visibly taken aback by all of this and didn't know how this news would fit into his personal plans.

"Governor Coke is re-commissioning the Texas Rangers. You see, during the Reconstruction in 1870, the Rangers were disbanded and replaced by a Union-controlled version of the Rangers. They were called the Texas State Police. Well when Governor Coke took office, he and the Texas Legislature re-commissioned the Texas Rangers."

"That's great but what does that have to do with me?"

"Son, Governor Coke is looking for a good man like you not only to be a Ranger but also to manage and care for their firearms. This could be a great experience for you in several ways. You can work with your trade plus help establish law and order in Texas. You wouldn't have to make a career of it. You could do it for just a few years and then take your experience up north or out west or wherever you wanted to go. Son, look at you. What are you, about

6' tall now? You're lean, long legged, high facial cheek bones, like your mother's side of the family, dark brown hair and eyes and with that four inch long and thick moustache, well son, if you don't look like a lawman, I don't know who does." As they both laughed, Scott then said,

"Pa, do you mind if I sleep on this one? This all comes as a surprise to me and I really don't know what I think about it yet."

"I understand Scott," his pa said and with that, they took a walk down to their small lake and talked about old times. Scott took along his two Schofield revolvers and his newly purchased holsters and gun belt with him to do a little target shooting down by their lake before the sun totally disappeared from the long horizon of the Texas flat lands.

The Texas Rangers were based in Austin, the capital of Texas. They were a law enforcement agency which had statewide authority/jurisdiction. Stephen F. Austin (November 3, 1793 – December 27, 1836, lived to age 43) who Austin, Texas is named after, is known as the unofficial founder of the Texas Rangers because in 1823 he declared a "call-to-arms" to protect his new colony of 300 families he brought to Texas. These 300 families are known in Texas history as the "Old Three Hundred".

The Texas Rangers were formally constituted on October 17, 1835 by Daniel Parker (April 6, 1781 – December 3, 1844, lived to age 63). On November 28th of that same year, Robert McAlpin Williamson (1804? – December 22, 1859, lived to age 54/55) was chosen to be the first Major of the Texas Rangers. By 1837 the Rangers were made up of 300 men.

From 1837 to 1846 the Texas Rangers were involved in fighting the Cherokee and the Comanche Indians. They also fought in the Mexican – American War from 1846 to 1848. Largely disbanded after the Mexican – American War, the Rangers were once again commissioned in December of 1857 by the newly elected Governor Hardin Richard Runnels (August 30, 1820 – December 25, 1873 lived to age 53), (6th Governor of Texas, in office December 21, 1857 – December 21 1859). They then continued to fight the Comanches who were raiding settlements.

When the Civil War began, most of the Rangers enlisted to fight on the Confederate side and once again the Rangers were disbanded. After the Civil War and during the so-called Reconstruction era, specifically in 1870, the Union replaced the

Texas Rangers with their adaptation of the Rangers, which they called the "Texas State Police". However, they were abolished on April 2, 1873, only three years after their launch.

Now in 1873, Richard Coke (March 13, 1829 – May 14, 1897, lived to age 68) (15th Governor of Texas, January 15, 1874 to December 21, 1876) was elected governor of Texas and took office in 1874. He and the Texas Legislature reinstated the Texas Rangers once again.

Scott's father had sent a telegram to his friend the governor and told him that Scott was interested in joining up with the Texas Rangers. The governor sent the following telegram back to Scott's father.

Dear Mathew,

I am extremely elated to hear that your son Scott has chosen to join the Texas Rangers. We need good men to maintain law and order in Texas. I have plans to create two branches of the Texas Rangers, specifically the Frontier Battalion under the command of Major John B. Jones and a Special Force, which will be commanded by Leander H. McNelly. Initially, I will order Scott to be temporarily stationed in Austin where he will be in charge of the setup, organization, and coordination of the Rangers' blacksmith and gunsmith shops at our Ranger training camp. He will be paid a respectable sum for his specialized duties. The duration of this assignment will be about three months.

McNelly is signing up young men now here in Austin and I would like for Scott to enlist with McNelly. Eventually, your son will join McNelly's Special Force on McNelly's most critical border assignment.

I will personally inform McNelly about my intentions in regards to your son. I am certain that Scott will make us all proud.

Sincerely, your friend,
Richard Coke
Governor of Texas

After receiving the letter, Scott headed to Austin and signed up with the Rangers. During the first several months, the newly enlisted force spent most of their time training and performing small law enforcement duties in the surrounding 150-mile area.

During this time period, McNelly took sick for a while and went home to his cotton farm near Burton, Texas to recuperate. McNelly was suffering from tuberculosis, which would eventually take his life on September 4, 1877, one year after he was forced to retire due to his deteriorating health.

In April of 1875, Governor Coke finally ordered McNelly to put together the Special Force and head south to Nucces County to end the cattle rustling by Mexican bandits along the Rio Grande. McNelly and his force were financed by southern Texas cattlemen.

Scott went on several of the Mexican border missions and was not happy with the questionable methods that McNelly used to get the job done. McNelly instigated many illegal executions and used torture to acquire information and confessions from his prisoners. However, the Special Force's mission was successful from the standpoint that they were able to retrieve many of the stolen cattle and finally end the cattle rustling along the Texas – Mexico border.

During this time period, Scott became friends with the second in command to McNelly, a man by the name of John Barclay Armstrong (January 1, 1850 – May 1, 1913, lived to age 63). Under McNelly, Armstrong, being McNelly's right hand man, earned the rank of sergeant and the nickname "McNelly's Bulldog". Scott did not always agree with Armstrong's sometimes seemingly lawless tactics but as a co-Ranger, Scott got along with him very well and he respected Armstrong's bravery and fighting spirit.

With the retirement of McNelly in 1876, the Special Force branch of the Texas Rangers was brought into the Frontier Battalion branch and Armstrong was promoted to lieutenant.

Scott was enjoying his tenure with the Rangers and loved the excitement it brought to his life. He was always willing to go on dangerous assignments and he always demonstrated great courage and bravery under fire. During his time with the Rangers, he continued to tote his two nickel-plated Model 3 Schofields and always wore them in a "cavalry style", drawing the left gun with his right hand and the right gun with his left hand.

In July of 1877, Armstrong approached Scott and asked Scott to join him on a dangerous mission in an attempt to capture John Wesley Hardin (May 26, 1853 – August 19, 1896, lived to age 43). John Wesley Hardin was an outlaw, gunslinger and murderer, killing his first of many men at the age of 15.

Hardin broke the law many times in Texas and was present when Brown County Deputy Sheriff Charles Webb was shot and killed by Hardin's gang in a saloon. Hardin escaped and shortly after was suspected of horse thieving with a new partner, Mac Young.

Fed up with all of Hardin's criminal activities, the Texas Legislature, on January 20, 1877 authorized Governor Richard B. Hubbard (November 1, 1832 – July 12, 1901, lived to age 68) (16th Governor of Texas, December 21, 1876 – January 21, 1879) to offer a $4,000 reward for the apprehension of John Wesley Hardin. Hardin went into hiding on the Alabama / Florida border and lived under the alias of James W. Swain.

After an undercover agent named Jack Duncan intercepted a letter from Hardin giving away his whereabouts, Armstrong asked Scott to join him in capturing Hardin. Scott was enthusiastic about this assignment because this was a chance to catch and bring to justice one of the most wanted criminals in Texas' history.

On their arrival in Pensacola, Florida, Scott Johnson and John B. Armstrong met with the authorities and formulated a plan to capture Hardin. Hardin and four of his men had boarded a train in Pensacola. Armstrong, Scott and the local authorities knew Hardin was on the train with his gang. So on August 24, 1877, with guns drawn, they boarded the train. Hardin saw the lawmen and yelled out to his gang, "Texas by God!" Then Hardin drew his gun but it got caught up in his suspenders. Armstrong quickly ran over and hit Hardin on the head with his pistol and knocked him out cold. Several shots were then fired. A bullet pierced Armstrong's hat but he was uninjured. Armstrong instinctively swung his gun hand to the right and shot and killed that gang member while Scott yelled at the top of his lungs to the other gang members, "Throw down your guns right now!" They did and were immediately arrested. There was a lot of tension on the train that day but once again, Armstrong and Scott proved that they both had nerves of steel and could look danger and even death in its face with abandon.

Scott was hoping to be able to spend time with his friends the Smiths in Florida but Armstrong needed help transporting Hardin and his gang back to Texas. So his planned visit needed to be postponed.

Hardin was tried for murder in Texas and was convicted. He was sentenced to 25 years in prison. However, seventeen years later, Hardin was pardoned by then Governor James Stephen "Big Jim" Hogg (March 24, 1851 – March 3, 1906, lived to age 54), (20th Governor of Texas, January 13, 1891 – January 15, 1895) and released from prison in early 1894. But on August 19, 1896, John Selman, Sr. in the Acme Saloon in El Paso, Texas, murdered John Wesley Hardin. Like they say, "If you live by the sword, you die by the sword".

At the age of thirty-two, Scott decided to turn in his badge and retire from the Texas Rangers. He was honored for his dedication and his bravery as a Texas Ranger at his retirement party in December of 1878.

He had already made up his mind to move north to one of the booming cow towns where his skills and his profession as a gunsmith would be put to good use. He did his research and discovered that the cow town that was enjoying present-day success was Dodge City, Kansas.

So on April 21, 1879, after spending three and a half months living with his parents and helping his pa in his blacksmith shop, Scott hitched up his newly purchased team of horses to his buckboard and headed north to Dodge City following the Western Trail.

The trail was easy to negotiate because it was well beaten down by the thousands of cattle that had traversed the trail in previous years.

On the way up the trail he came across several herds of longhorns, which were also on their way to the railhead in Dodge City. On occasion he would camp out with a group of drovers and pay to eat dinner and breakfast with them before heading out again on his own. He enjoyed spending time with the cowboys, if they seemed to be decent people. However, he really preferred to stay in hotels and sleep under a roof and in a nice soft feather bed which he had become accustomed to while living at home with his parents and while living in Massachusetts.

After traveling the lonely dusty cow trail for several weeks, Scott arrived in Dodge City on May 30, 1879 tired and worn down from the long journey. Even though he was healthy and in good physical condition, he lost about fifteen pounds due to the long grueling trip. Scott always kept himself in good shape and was "lean and mean" at six foot tall weighing 150-pounds. He had that traditional lawman appearance about him so reminiscent of guys like Wyatt and Virgil Earp.

His first impression of Dodge City was even better than he expected. It was a booming cow town with stores, saloons, hotels, dance halls, gambling houses and more. The streets were full of townspeople and cowboys and appeared to be quite orderly. He had heard about the reputation of the lawmen in Dodge City and surrounding areas. The names of the Earp brothers and the Mastersons were no strangers to Scott.

He could hear the cows bellowing across town and the shriek of the high pitched train whistle blowing as a steam engine was backing its cattle cars out of the railroad spur onto the main tracks to begin its long journey eastward across Kansas and Missouri to the Chicago slaughterhouses in Illinois.

On the way up from Texas he had a lot of time to think about his future. He was ready to begin looking for a young lady to court and to start a family all over again. The more he observed that day, the more he knew he made the right decision to choose to settle down in Dodge City.

After arriving in Dodge, he rode up and down the streets in his buckboard wagon just to get an idea of what types of businesses were in town and where they were located. Specifically, he was interested to search out a hotel, the marshal's office, the bank, and he looked around to see if he could spot a gunsmith shop in town.

The first building he spotted that was on his list was the marshal's office. Being a retired Texas Ranger and lawman, he felt that it would be easy to strike up an immediate rapport with the local marshal and his deputies. So that was the first stop he made in Dodge City.

When he opened the door to the marshal's office, it was like entering the "Who's Who of Lawmen" building of the Old West. Behind the desk doing paperwork was Charlie Bassett, the town's marshal. Over in the corner to the left, sitting around a small round table playing cards were Assistant Marshal James Masterson (Bat's brother), and Deputy Marshals Wyatt Earp, and James Earp. Scott was briefly overwhelmed being in the presence of these exceptional lawmen. Masterson and the Earps briefly glanced up when Scott walked through the door then immediately continued their card playing.

Scott walked over to Charlie Bassett and started the conversation, "Howdy sir, I'm looking for the marshal."

"You're looking at him mister," Charlie said with a nonchalant attitude.

Then Scott introduced himself and extended his arm for a handshake, "I'm Scott Johnson, a retired Texas Ranger from Fort Worth, Texas and I came to Dodge City to settle down."

Well at the point when Scott said, "a retired Texas Ranger", Wyatt, James Earp and James Masterson, all looked up at the same time, set their cards down on the table, and walked over to greet Scott with handshakes.

"I'm Wyatt Earp and this is my brother James Earp."

"I'm Scott Johnson and it's a real pleasure to meet you," Scott said with a big smile on his face.

"Hey there, I'm James Masterson, the real lawman around here," James said jokingly.

Scott laughed and said, "It's a pleasure to meet you too sir."

"Can I get you a cup of coffee?" Charlie asked.

"You bet," Scott replied without hesitation.

As Charlie was pouring the coffee for all five of them, he looked over at Scott and inquired, "Scott, what do you plan to do here in Dodge City?"

"Well sir, like I said before, I retired from the Texas Rangers late last year. Before I became a Ranger, I worked seven years for Smith & Wesson in Springfield, Massachusetts to learn how to become a gunsmith. I always wanted to open up and be the proprietor of my own gunsmith shop. When I was a Ranger I did a lot of gunsmith work for the force during my tenure. I figured a town like Dodge City would have a lot of business for me."

"You know Scott, you might be in luck," Wyatt said. "We have a gunsmith here in town who's about 70 years old and has been talking about selling his business in about a year or so. His name is "Pops" McCarthy. He knows which end the bullet comes out of the pistol and that's about all," Wyatt jokingly said. "We could sure use a good gunsmith in town who knows what he's doing."

Then James Earp said, "Wyatt, don't you have a Smith & Wesson pistol you're having trouble with?"

"That's right. It's my second gun. I think there's something wrong with the trigger mechanism. I quit using it before it gets me killed someday."

"What model is it?" Scott asked.

"It's a modified version of the Model 3."

"I'm very familiar with that revolver," Scott said. "I made and test fired hundreds of them."

Wyatt put an uncommon smile on his face and said, "Ranger Scott, I'm glad you came to Dodge."

They all laughed and then Scott asked for directions to the best hotel in town and directions to the gunsmith shop as well. Minutes later, when he walked out of the marshal's office, it was obvious that he was happier than a pack mule with his head buried in a bucket of grain.

The first thing he did was to ride over to the hotel and sign in. Behind the counter was a cute little brunette, about five-foot-four inches tall and as skinny as a rail, probably in her late twenties and with no rings on her fingers. Scott flirted with her for a couple of minutes before asking for a room. Her name was Janice and she was the daughter of the owner of the hotel. She lived down the street in a small two-bedroom house just on the edge of town.

After he unpacked and changed into some clean clothes, he walked over to the barbershop to get a haircut, a face scrape and a hot bath. Then allowing no time for grass to grow underneath his feet, he swiftly walked over to the gunsmith shop to meet with "Pops" McCarthy.

Ole Pops was a rugged looking old codger; bent over at the shoulders and puffing on a black smoldering homemade corncob pipe, which he positioned in the space of his mouth where his three front teeth were noticeably missing.

"What can I do for you, sonny?" Pops asked.

Scott introduced himself, talked about his background and told Pops why he came to town and what his intentions were. Pops was immediately impressed and thought his prayers were answered.

"Son, I have about one more good year of work in me. My old bones ache me everyday. If it wasn't for my whiskey and my tobackie, I don't think I could make it through another moon.

I'm looking for someone who could help me out in this here shop right now and maybe buy me out when I call it quits. You just may be that rascal I'm looking for," Pops said.

"I believe I am," Scott quickly responded. "Can you take a couple of minutes and show me around your shop?"

"Sure sonny, follow me. By the way, you can see that I sell a few thingamajigs besides repairing guns."

They walked over to one side of the store where he had rifles in a locked sliding glass door display case. In just a few minutes Scott would realize that he had inaccurately prejudged Pops. The case held about fifteen rifles. Pops removed a set of keys from his pants' pocket, unlocked the case, and slid the glass doors to the side. Then he reached into the case and pulled out a rifle that was in pristine condition.

"Do you know what this is son?" Pops asked Scott.

"Tell me Pops."

"It's an original Henry rifle, one of the 900 that were produced between 1862 and 1864 during the Civil War. It was mostly used by Union troops. The Confederates called it the "damned Yankee rifle that they load on Sunday and shoot the rest of the week".

Those dang redskins, the Sioux and Cheyenne Indians used this rifle against the 7th Cavalry at the Little Bighorn. Some say Custer was defeated because the odds were stacked against him. On the day of that massacre at Little Bighorn, it was the hostiles' Henry repeating rifles, against the 7th Cavalry's single shot '73 Springfields. Lookie here son, I have three of those Henry beauties for sale, and one Springfield '73 that I can't give away to save my soul."

By now Scott figured that this old codger was really a lot smarter than what Wyatt made him out to be.

Then Pops took out another rifle from the case. It was the famous Winchester '73, the gun with the reputation that won the West. He talked about that rifle with authority for ten minutes. And then he showed Scott his 1866 and 1876 model Winchesters and spent another ten minutes on the history of those two rifles. The point was that ole Pops was no novice or amateur when it came to knowing his firearms. He was extremely astute on the history and workings of some of the most famous and popular rifles of their time.

Pops proceeded in showing Scott all of the revolvers he had for sale along with his inventory of cartridges. Then he took Scott over to his worktable where Pops worked on and repaired both rifles and pistols. This was right up Scott's alley. Pops asked Scott a few questions about the repair of a couple of the pistols. Scott knew that Pops was testing his knowledge. Pops soon discovered that, when it came to repairing handguns and rifles, Scott was the "Real McCoy", a real pro.

With that, Pops offered Scott a job and Scott accepted it faster that a longhorn steer could whip off a horn fly with the switch of its tail. Scott Johnson, the young man from Fort Worth, Texas was finally on his way to fulfilling and realizing a life-long dream.

After he accepted the job, and after stopping for a bite to eat at a small little café across from his hotel, he decided to go back to his room and rest awhile before visiting with the "Land Sales and Housing Company" in town. He was determined to find a house to rent first until he settled in. Then he would later search out a house to purchase.

When he entered the hotel, he was somewhat disappointed that Janice, the hotel clerk, was not at the sign-in counter. His room was on the second floor of the hotel. After walking up the red-carpeted flight of steps and down the long hallway to his room, he noticed that the door to his room was slightly cracked open. He stopped, with his left hand on the door handle, he reached for his pistol with his right hand but realized he wasn't wearing his Schofields. So he slowly opened the door, looked in but no one was in the room. He began to check his belongings to see if anything was stolen. Nothing was taken and what seemed to be a break-in, went unexplained.

It took about two weeks but Scott finally found a small house to live in right at the end of Main Street. It had been vacant for about a month and was up for sale but the owner agreed to rent it to Scott for six months. Scott would eventually have to make a decision whether to buy it or move out. The owner, who inherited the house from a recently deceased relative, wasn't interested in renting it any longer than six months; he wanted to sell it and be rid of it.

The summer of 1879 in Dodge City was hot, dry and dusty. Cattle were being driven in from Texas on the Western Trail everyday so the constant bellowing of those long-legged Texas longhorns echoed continuously throughout the streets of Dodge City. Steam locomotives with high pitched whistles blowing at a deafening sound arrived every other day pulling a combination of cattle cars and passenger cars.

Dance halls, gambling houses, saloons and brothels were buzzing with cowboys every night keeping the lawmen on edge at all times. This was the thrilling booming cow town Scott had always heard about and he savored every minute of it.

Scott was also happy with the amount of business they did in the gunsmith shop with locals and the cowboys and could envision a profitable outcome for years to come when he eventually bought the business from old man Pops. They did not only have many repairs to perform but also did a respectable gun sales business, as well.

In August, Scott and Janice began spending more time together but Scott was not yet ready to make a commitment. He wasn't sure if his friendship with Janice was just a fling or was something that could grow into becoming a long-term relationship. It was just too early to tell.

Law and order was in check in Dodge City by late summer and the Earp brothers were getting restless. One day Wyatt brought his Smith & Wesson Model 3 into the gunsmith shop for Scott to look at.

"Good morning Scott," Wyatt said.

"Hey Wyatt, to what do I owe the pleasure of your visit?" Scott asked.

"Well, back in June I told you I had this Model 3 revolver that misfires every once and awhile. This is it right here," Wyatt said as he handed the revolver to Scott.

As Scott was looking over the pistol, Wyatt asked Scott, "How do you like Dodge so far?"

"To be honest with you Wyatt, it's a lot more peaceful than what I expected."

"Yep, you're right Scott. It has become a right quiet town. That's why James and I are leaving this town in September. Our job is done in this town."

"Boy, I hate to hear that Wyatt. Where are you guys headed to?"

"We're traveling to a silver-mining boom town named Tombstone, Arizona and do a little gambling there. Maybe even go into business for ourselves. We're done with being lawmen. I have two other brothers who are gonna meet James and me there."

"What are their names?"

"Virgil and Morgan. Virgil is the one who wrote me about Tombstone."

While Wyatt was talking, Scott discovered that the spring mechanism for the trigger was broke. It was an easy fix and only took about ten minutes to repair.

In the meantime Scott asked about James Masterson, "Is Masterson staying on as the assistant marshal?"

"Yes, when he's around," Wyatt said with a sarcastic tone in his voice. "Masterson is out of town more than he's in town. He's always chasing after somebody. Say Scott, maybe you'll become the next deputy marshal when I leave."

"Not a chance," Scott quickly replied. "I have had enough of getting shot at as a Ranger. I like doing just what I'm doing, fixing and selling firearms."

"I don't blame you one bit," Wyatt said.

With that, Scott completed the repairs on Wyatt's Model 3 and Wyatt asked Scott to keep his departure from Dodge City a secret until Wyatt himself informed Charlie Bassett. Scott agreed to tell no one.

When September arrived, Wyatt, his common-law wife Mattie Blaylock, and James and his wife rode out of town together. They also had a friend join them who arrived in town just the day before their departure. His name was Doc Holliday (August 14, 1851 – November 8, 1887, lived to age 36). Holliday was also traveling with a lady friend named Big-Nose Kate, his loyal companion. The Earps and Holliday planned to make various gambling stops as they made their way to Tombstone. This untimely departure of the Earp brothers left a huge gap in the law enforcement ranks in Dodge City.

It was early October now. The cattle drives were coming to an end for this year. There was just one more herd of cattle arriving in town being driven up from Texas and it was Jesse Caldwell's drive. In fact, on this particular midmorning in early October, while sitting on a chair in front of the store taking a break, Scott could hear the loud and constant bellowing of the cattle as Caldwell and his drovers were arriving at the stockyards next to the railroad spur on the other side of town.

Everyone in town was happy that the cattle drive season was coming to an end because things would finally become quiet and settle down and the townspeople could get back to their normal lives.

While Scott was sitting on the porch, settlers in two covered wagons pulled up in front of his store to ask for information about the town. It was the O'Brien family; Thomas, Elizabeth, and their three children Josh, Jeanie, and Jennie. Thomas was driving one wagon and Elizabeth was driving the other. After traveling months on the trail, they had finally reached their destination, their new home, Dodge City, Kansas. Thomas jumped down from the wagon and walked up to Scott while the others stayed put.

"Hello there," he said, "I'm Thomas O'Brien."

Scott stood up, shook hands with O'Brien and said,

"Hi there, I'm Scott Johnson."

Scott could obviously see they were new in town and that they had been on the road for a while.

"Where are you from?" Scott asked.

"We came all the way from Kentucky to start a new life here in Dodge City. It was a tough trip across the Midwest. Oh, we ran into some trouble along the way but we were able to handle all of the problems that plagued us. The good Lord took care of my family in good fashion."

"What was the magnet that brought your family all the way to Dodge City?"

"I'm getting into the cattle business."

"Surely you aren't planning on going on cattle drives are you?" Scott asked.

"Heavens no, I'm aiming to try to get into the buying and selling side of the business."

"Well you're in luck friend. The last cattle drive up from Texas is coming in right now. From the sounds of things, it seems like it's a pretty sizable herd too. The train is due tomorrow which will pick up the cattle and take them to Chicago. Maybe you'll be able to meet with the trail boss of the drive between now and then."

"I hope so Scott," Thomas said eagerly. "That would be great. In the meantime can you direct me to the nearest hotel; one that is fit for a family with three young children?"

"You bet, it's just down the road here toward the end of Main Street. It's the largest one in town. That's where the cowboys from

Texas generally stay too, so you might run into the trail boss there."

"Thank you, you have been very kind, Scott. I'll see you again soon I'm sure," O'Brien said as he climbed back onto his wagon.

Then they rode off as all the kids peered in curiosity at Scott from the back of the wagons.

After the O'Briens signed into their room and unpacked, they went for a walk to familiarize themselves with the town. Elizabeth took the two girls to the general store while Thomas and Josh walked down the street heading toward the Dodge City Cattle Office, which was adjacent to the stockyards. He once again passed Scott who was standing in the doorway of the gunsmith shop and he invited Scott to join him and his son for a walk down to the stockyards. Scott yelled into Pops and told him he would be back in about an hour. It was about time for his lunch break anyway. Pops mumbled something just under his breath like he usually did while Scott walked away smiling. The three, Scott, Thomas and his son Josh, headed to the stockyards.

The drovers were busy running the weary thin longhorns into the corrals next to the tracks while the trail boss, Jesse Caldwell, rode over to the cattle office to discuss price with the cattle buyers from Chicago at the Dodge City Cattle Office.

Scott was acquainted with the two men at the Cattle Office because he had sold revolvers to both of them. On occasion, Scott would go down to shoot the breeze with them and the drovers when the drovers came up from Texas. He always enjoyed talking to the cowboys from his home state.

When the three arrived at the Cattle Office, Jesse Caldwell was already sitting in a chair and had negotiated a price per head. All that was left to do now was to count the cattle as they were loaded into the railroad cars tomorrow.

Scott Johnson introduced himself to Caldwell and then introduced O'Brien to Caldwell and the two cattle buyers from Chicago as well. Then they all sat down for a good hour drinking coffee and getting acquainted with each other.

Scott Johnson from Texas, Thomas O'Brien from Kentucky, and Jesse Caldwell from Texas seemed to strike up a good rapport and enjoyed talking and listening to each other's background stories. It was like they had been old friends for a long time.

As the conversation was coming to a close, O'Brien asked the Chicago buyers, "What time do you expect the train to arrive tomorrow?"

"It should arrive on time at about 1:00 p.m. We were told that there will be ten cattle cars on that train and two passenger cars. Don't know if we can cram all of Caldwell's cattle on those ten cars but we'll try."

"Sometime while you're loading them tomorrow, I intend to come down and just observe things," O'Brien said.

With that, Johnson, O'Brien and his son Josh walked back to Pop's gun shop and Caldwell and his drovers signed into the hotel. The cowboys spent the night whooping it up in town but were more orderly than most cowboys from Texas.

There was a sense of relief and tranquility coming over the town since tomorrow would be the end of the Texas cattle drives to Dodge City for the season, and the town would settle down into a more quiet state, at least until next spring.

Little did anyone know that tomorrow, October 5th, would become a literal nightmare that the townspeople of Dodge City, Kansas would never forget.

CHAPTER EIGHT:

Bloody Kansas

The morning of October 5, 1879, was like any other fall morning; the leaves around the countryside were beginning to turn their brilliant fall colors of orange, red and yellow.

The air was cool and crisp and you could hear the honking of geese flying overhead making their long journey south for the winter.

People were up and about, many visiting the several cafés in town for their morning coffee and country style flapjacks, eggs and bacon. Everyone seemed to be in good spirits. Today was the day the townspeople were waiting for, the end of the 1879 Texas cattle drive season. No more rowdy Texas cowboys until next year. Like other Kansas cow towns farther east, the townspeople were getting fed up with the noise through the nights: the gunfire, sounds of the cattle bellowing all day and all night, the train whistles blowing and the hustle and bustle of the saloons, gaming houses and brothels.

The morning seemed peaceful enough. Marshal Bassett arrived at the café at 7:00 a.m. as he did every morning. His Assistant Marshal, James Masterson, had left town the day before chasing after two outlaws who held up a local saloon in town. James was hot on their trail and felt that he could catch up with them in a day or two. Chasing after outlaws and eventually catching them and bringing them to justice was James Masterson's specialty.

This morning, Scott Johnson the gunsmith and Jesse Caldwell the Texas trail boss arrived at the café at about the same time, just minutes after the marshal, and decided to have breakfast together. Marshal Bassett asked if he could join the two. They said yes and they all sat down at the same small square table. Bassett was not acquainted with Caldwell, so Scott Johnson did the introductions.

"So, this morning I'm having breakfast with two Texans," Marshal Bassett jokingly said.

"That's right marshal," Caldwell responded. "But don't worry, we won't make you eat grits today."

When the waitress came over to pour coffee and to take their orders, Johnson glanced outside through the plate glass café window and saw two buckboard wagons go by, each being pulled by two horses. It appeared that they were heading in the direction toward the stockyards down by the tracks. Johnson could see that one of the drivers was wearing an eye patch and had a full black beard. Their eyes came in contact momentarily as the one-eyed man peered through the window of the café. At the time, Johnson didn't think much of it. He thought it was just a couple of guys passing through town.

However, the reality was that it was the two members of Mick Stonehill's gang, the Forty-Fours, Bobby "Whiskers" McFarland and Tex Mex, each driving a get-away-wagon. They arrived one mile east of town the day before, on October 4th as planned, in preparation for the greatest train robbery this country has ever known. Their responsibility the day before the robbery was to build a dirt ramp over the railroad tracks one mile east of Dodge. This ramp would be their escape path making it easy for the two wagons to cross the tracks and head north with the gold. It was an essential part of the gang's plan.

On October 4th, the day before the robbery, the remaining members of the gang arrived at their destination, one mile west of town. This location was the fuel and water stop for trains traveling both east and west.

There was just one main building on this location owned by the railroad and watched by one Dodge City resident, who was on the railroad's payroll.

He wasn't really a guard because there was nothing of value in that location. It was merely his responsibility to greet the train and make sure that the water tower was full of water for the steam engines and that there was plenty of wood available for fuel. He used the telegraph office in Dodge City to communicate with the railroad regarding water and wood supplies.

When Mick and his gang rode within sight of the building, they spotted a horse hitched up in front of the small structure. Mick held up his hand to stop the gang's forward movement toward the fueling station and said,

"Look guys, I don't know who's in that building and whether he's armed or not. One thing I know for sure though is I don't want any gunshots today, which could be heard by someone and possibly screw up this mission. So, Lance, since you're carrying that big ole Arkansas toothpick, I want you to take him out quietly and pull his body behind the building. Leave your revolver here with me so you can't do anything stupid. Wave to us to come in, when the coast is clear."

With that, Lance Carter, half Apache and half white man and raised by the Apaches, rode up to the building. When he reached the front of the building, a young man came out to greet him. His name was Stevie Cain. He was only twenty-two years old, single and an upright citizen of Dodge City.

Stevie spoke first, "Howdy stranger, what can I do for you?"

"Do you have any coffee in there friend? I haven't had a cup in a few days and I could sure go for one now."

"Sure, come on in. My name is Stevie Cain, what's yours?"

Lance got off of his horse and tied it to the hitching post.

"I'm Lance Carter."

After they walked into the building over to the wood burning stove where the pot of coffee was being kept warm, Stevie asked as he poured a cup of coffee with his back turned toward Lance, "Where are you headed?"

Just then, Lance pulled out his Arkansas toothpick with a twelve inch blade and said,

"None of your business," as he thrust the knife into Stevie's back severing his spinal cord and killing him straight away with a cowardly brutal attack from behind. The body slumped to the floor instantly. After wiping the blood off of his knife on the dead man's shirt, Lance poured a cup of coffee for himself, took a sip from the cup, spit out the coffee, tossed the cup into the corner of the room and said, "You make terrible coffee for a white man, Stevie."

Then Lance went outside and waved for Mick and the gang to ride in. In the meantime, Lance dragged the dead body by the feet out the backdoor and stowed it behind the building and threw some firewood on top of it so buzzards wouldn't start circling around the next two days.

Mick and the gang rode up to the building, tied their horses to the hitching rail and walked inside to case it out. There was a reason why Mick was the leader of the gang. It was because he always thought two steps ahead of everyone else. The first thing he did when he entered the building was to look for a bed. If he found a bed in the building, he could be pretty sure that the railroad worker lived in the building and nobody was expecting him back in town that night. Mick felt relieved when he spotted an unmade bed.

It was now evening and there wasn't much light left in the day. So Mick and the gang decided to go outside to check out the area where the train would stop and they would most likely get on board. It was easy to figure out where it would stop because they knew that the engine would have to be refilled with water by the elevated water tank.

Then Mick took a few minutes to plan where everyone would hide based on their responsibilities and the cars they were to board as the train approached and eventually came to a stop.

There were plenty of places to hide because there were four small woodsheds filled with firewood scattered near the tracks plus the main building was also only about thirty feet away. Mick felt very confident that they could easily board the train unnoticed from those vantage points and eliminate the soldiers quickly as planned.

At nightfall, one of the men lit a kerosene lantern and they nibbled on some jerky they carried in their saddlebags. They also cut open a few cans of beans they found on the shelves. Coming down from Wyoming, one of the wagons carried some of their food plus they ate in small towns along the way. However, on this night, the wagons were on the east side of town where Tex and Whiskers were camped out.

Mick went over the plans one more time after they finished grabbing a bite to eat. Most of the men were still concerned with being able to break into the freight car where the gold was stashed. Mick reassured them that he could get in from the top of the car and they would do that when they got to Dodge City.

Mick was an arrogant cuss and continued to insist that they would steal the gold in Dodge City to prove to everyone that the Forty-Fours were the most famous and ruthless outlaw gang that this country had ever known. His attitude had changed from previous years, as he now wanted his gang to be more talked about than the James-Younger Gang. Mick's desire for notoriety continued to grow as the train robbery came closer and closer to fruition.

When it was time to get some shut-eye, they went outside and unsaddled their horses and used their saddles as pillows on the inside of the building where they slept on the floor that night. Mick slept on the bed of course.

Instead of going to sleep right away, most laid there in the dark of the night with their eyes wide open wondering what tomorrow would bring. They all knew that they signed on to an extremely dangerous adventure. They also knew that lives would be lost tomorrow, but whose? A few of them felt that their planning and repetitive drills would make the difference. Many felt that if they could take out the soldiers as planned, they would be home free. Hours went by with most of them staring into the darkness.

Then Lance quietly asked Johnny, "Hey Johnny, what are you gonna to do with your hundred grand?"

"I've been thinking about that ever since we left Wyoming. I'm going back to Vicksburg, Mississippi and rebuild my family's plantation and home which that dang Yankee General Grant burnt down during the Civil War. How about you, Lance?"

"I'm gonna build me a big fancy trading post in Santa Fe, New Mexico and go straight unless Mick finds another million dollar train car to rob."

Everyone sort of chuckled at Lance's remark.

"I'm going to buy me a fancy saloon in St. Louis, Missouri and hire me a bunch of good lookin gals to run the place for me. I think I'll marry three of them," Jay jokingly said.

Then Danny O'Brien asked, "Mick, how about you, what are you going to do with your money?"

Mick paused a minute then shocked everyone with his answer. "I belong to an organization that I really don't want to talk about. I'm giving all of my gold to them and that's all I'm going to say. Now shut your traps and get some sleep."

With that, quiet filled the dark room once again as they began drifting off, one by one.

It is now the morning of October 5th. Caldwell, Johnson and Marshal Bassett are having breakfast in the café as Whiskers and Tex Mex just drove their wagons by while Johnson looked on unaware of their significance.

Thomas O'Brien, his wife and three children are getting dressed to go to breakfast as well.

The drovers from Texas are hung over from the night before and sleeping-in on this brisk October morning.

The soldiers on the train who are part of *Operation Last Spike* have become complacent and feel that since they are out of Indian Territory, things will now go smoothly.

The outlaws are up and about and scrounging around for some food for breakfast in the railroad building they slept in last night.

The train is due to arrive at the water and fuel station at 11:00 a.m. It was scheduled to be a one-hour stop.

At 10:00 a.m., the outlaws hid their horses behind the building.

At 10:30 a.m. the outlaws took their positions behind the woodsheds along the tracks and the waiting game began.

Hearts were pounding, blood pressures were rising, and most were perspiring profusely while they waited for the arrival of the train and wondered what their fate would be on this cool October morn. Mick tried to convince his gang that the element of surprise gave them the edge and that would make the difference this morning.

The two wagons in town driven by Whiskers and Tex were now in place, on the east side of the stockyards adjacent to the tracks. They had to pretend that they were waiting for a freight shipment of ranch supplies. Only they knew that this shipment was worth much more.

As the outlaws nervously waited, Mick became more confident by the minute that his leadership and planning would be the catalyst that would make this robbery the most daring and successful train robbery of all times.

And then they heard it, about one mile away, the shrieking sound of the train whistle. Everyone checked their revolvers one more time to make sure they were fully loaded. Each outlaw carried two .44's. Then Mick shouted out to his gang, "Remember men, board the train before it comes to a complete stop; watch my lead!"

The whistle became louder and louder as the train advanced closer and closer. Now they could see it approaching as it came around the bend about a half a mile down the tracks; a big black powerful mountain of steel pulling all the cars behind it. Then the engineer began slowing up the train and engaging the brakes as the sound of steel against steel, wheels against rail began squealing louder and louder as it approached. Then the hissing sound of the steam being released escaped from the engine. The sound was almost deafening as the locomotive came to a slow roll just before coming to a complete stop.

"Now, men!" Mick shouted as he jumped onto the locomotive sticking a gun in the engineer's rib. The engineer's assistant, Timothy Day, reached for a rifle that was standing up in the corner and Mick drilled him with two shots to the chest, killing him instantly. Mick then threw Timothy's body overboard.

Simultaneously, all the outlaws boarded the train and the barrage of gunfire began. The passengers were in a state of panic yelling and screaming and instinctively ducked down in their seats for cover.

Frank Rickets and Jay Johnson entered the second passenger car from the back with both of their .44's drawn. The six soldiers were right where they were supposed to be. Jay was on the right and Frank on the left. The soldiers were like sitting ducks and not prepared. Their rifles were underneath their seats and their Schofields were holstered. Frank and Jay began unloading their six shooters into the bodies of the six soldiers. None of them had a chance. They were all killed instantly. Then they told the passengers to stay seated and shut up while they both quickly reloaded as six officers of the U.S. Army lay slumped in their seats brutally murdered. They were Captains Shultz, Blaylock, and Fuller and Majors Trent, Kranes and Thomas. Never in history had six Army officers been killed in such a manner. Jay then ran up to eliminate the soldier who was sitting in the first row of the first car.

While this was going on, Danny O'Brien broke into the mail/payroll car and found Sergeant Snider just waking up and O'Brien put three slugs into him.

Lance and Johnny Reb surprised the confused Sergeants Maloney and Patrick in the caboose when they stormed through the front and back doors of the caboose. Once again, the soldiers were unprepared for the attack as Lance and Johnny unloaded their pistols into the two soldiers.

Gun smoke, blood and death filled the cars as passengers looked on in horror. It was the worst bloodbath ever recorded in the history of the railroad.

After Jay took out his three, he simultaneously reloaded his pistols while running up the aisle and through the door and then into the first passenger car to take out the soldier who was supposed to be seated in the first row. While he made his way to the front of the car with his arms outstretched and pointing both guns forward, he yelled to the passengers to shut up and stay seated.

What Jay wasn't aware of was that Corporal Jesse Taylor, at the first sound of gunfire, ran out of the front door of the passenger car and hid in the fuel car behind and underneath the firewood which he had quickly stacked on top of himself for cover.

His first instinct was to hide and survive. Then he would eventually figure out what to do. Since Jay did not see the soldier there, he assumed that Mick's information was incorrect and that there was no guard stationed in the first passenger car.

Colonel Jeffrey and the two Corporals, Jackson and Wilcox, could hear the volley of gunshots and knew that the train was being held up. Their only hope was that they would not be discovered in the freight car. They also hoped that the bandits were just after the payroll. Nevertheless they kept their guns drawn and waited for someone to try to break in. Jeffrey told the two corporals to remain calm and keep quiet.

When the gunshots came to a halt and the air cleared of gun smoke, the gang, except for Mick, escorted the passengers off the train on the building side while a couple of the bandits dragged the bodies of the limp and lifeless soldiers off the train.

The passengers were told to empty their pockets. Mick's gang had no interest in the passengers' valuables. They just wanted to be sure that no one was toting any firearms, which could be turned against them.

After everyone unloaded their pockets, they then told the passengers to walk about one hundred feet from the train and lay down on their bellies.

"If anyone gets up while the train is still in sight, I promise, we'll be back to kill every one of you!" Danny O'Brien threatened.

Then Mick asked the engineer if there was enough water in the boiler to get them to Dodge City. The engineer answered, "Yeah, I think so."

Mick said, "Well then stoke up the fire and let's get this train to Dodge City."

The outlaws mounted up. Jay ponied Mick's horse behind him while Mick rode with the engineer. Mick was also hoping that the gunshots were not heard in Dodge. They were fortunate that there was a strong wind that morning blowing to the west meaning that a cold front and a low pressure system was moving in. This was lucky for Mick's gang because the sound of gunfire would not travel toward Dodge City.

As the train rolled slowly toward Dodge City and Mick's gang rode beside it, the gang became increasingly confident that the most dangerous part of their criminal adventure was behind them.

It was now about 1:00 p.m. as the train pulled into the spur section of the tracks next to the stockyards. Whiskers had switched the tracks to make the train travel onto the spur instead of to the depot. There were no passengers getting off the train which the depot manager thought was strange although he didn't question it at the time. The cattle were due to be loaded at three o'clock that afternoon and the train was scheduled to leave at 6:00 p.m. that evening.

Everyone in town thought that it was business as usual in Dodge City. The train had just arrived, the cattle were in the stockyards and ready to be loaded and a few passengers were to board at 5:00 p.m.

The only difference this time was that the train was full of the blood of U.S. Army soldiers and there was $1,000,000 in gold bullion belonging to the government that was about to be stolen.

As the engine passed the stockyards and before it came to a complete stop, Corporal Jesse Taylor jumped out of the fuel car of the train unnoticed and began running down Main Street as fast as his legs could carry him. Jesse Caldwell, the trail boss, had just finished lunch and was riding on his palomino down the street toward the stockyards when he saw a soldier racing toward him in complete panic.

The soldier stopped Caldwell and yelled incoherently, "They were all killed!

They were all killed! It was a massacre, a massacre I tell you! Where's the marshal's office, where's the marshal's office?"

"What are you talking about, soldier?" Caldwell yelled back.

"Just tell me where the marshal's office is," the soldier demanded.

"Give me your hand, soldier," Caldwell suggested as he also took his left foot out of the stirrup. The soldier grabbed Caldwell's hand and put his left foot into the empty stirrup while Caldwell pulled him up behind him and they galloped down the street to the marshal's office.

Thomas O'Brien had just parked his wagon and was walking down Main Street with his son and overheard the conversation between the soldier and Caldwell, as did many others. However, having fighting experience in the Civil War, he was anxious to be part of the gunplay if it came to that while the rest of the town would run for cover. He told his son to run back to the hotel and tell his family to stay there until the smoke cleared.

O'Brien then ran over to the gunsmith shop where Scott Johnson was working and informed Johnson of what he heard and saw. He knew Johnson was an ex-Texas Ranger and would be a valuable help in a gunfight.

Thomas O'Brien wasn't carrying a gun at the time so he asked Johnson for a Henry rifle and a revolver. Johnson put his two-holster gun belt on and loaded up both of his .45 Schofields and grabbed a Henry rifle too.

O'Brien had his wagon parked on the street so they both ran to the wagon, jumped in it and rode down to the marshal's office.

When they went inside, the marshal was loading his rifle and tossed a rifle to the soldier. The marshal had been standing outside his office and saw the panic-stricken soldier and knew that trouble was brewing. Johnson asked the marshal where Masterson was. "Out of town," the marshal replied. "It's just us assuming that you three will help me and the soldier."

"You bet we will," the three answered.

"Great, now soldier, explain to me, Caldwell, Johnson, and O'Brien what we have here and do it quickly before we run off into a deadly gunfight."

"OK, there's a million dollars in gold bullion on that train."

"What?" Marshal Bassett asked in shock.

"I said, there's a million dollars in gold bullion on that train. Me and twelve other soldiers were guarding it from San Francisco to Philadelphia," Corporal Taylor hurriedly replied.

"Whose gold is it?" Johnson asked.

"It belongs to the government. Secretary of Treasury Sherman is in charge of the mission," the corporal responded. "The gold is in the freight car which is locked from the inside with two corporals and our officer in command, Colonel Jeffrey. They may be in grave danger if we don't get down there quickly."

"How many outlaws are there?" Marshal Bassett asked.

"I don't know for sure but there are probably a dozen based on the shooting I heard when we switched to the Santa Fe line and stopped west of Dodge for fuel and water."

"OK then, if everyone is fully loaded, let's go get us some outlaws," Bassett said.

Johnson then asked the marshal as they were leaving the marshal's office, "What's your plan marshal?"

"I don't know until we get there."

Bassett and Caldwell mounted their horses, while Johnson, O'Brien and the corporal jumped into O'Brien's wagon. As they rode down Main Street, Bassett stopped in front of the telegraph office and yelled for Joseph to come out. Joseph, the telegraph operator came running outside and said, "What's up marshal?"

Bassett said, "Send a telegram to the Secretary of Treasury in Washington, D.C. and tell him his gold train is being held up in Dodge City."

"What?" the telegraph operator asked in disbelief.

"You heard me!" Bassett yelled as he pulled the reins, turned his horse to the left, and galloped down the street.

As they approached the tracks, Corporal Taylor jumped out of the back of the wagon while it was still moving. He ran over to the freight car as fast as he could since he noticed the door was still closed.

Bassett and Caldwell jumped off of their horses while Johnson and O'Brien leapt out of the wagon. All four peered around the caboose on the stockyard side of the train to see what was going on.

In the meantime, Corporal Taylor haphazardly ran over to the freight car, frantically pounding on the side door yelling out as loud as he could, "Colonel Jeffrey, Colonel Jeffrey, are you all right? Open up, the other soldiers are all dead!"

Then the door slid open. Taylor was shocked that he could see clear through the freight car because the door was wide open on the other side and the outlaws were loading the gold into a wagon. Mick Stonehill was one of the outlaws standing next to Colonel Jeffrey. Taylor was stunned when he then spotted the two other corporals on the floor lying in pools of blood.

Then Corporal Taylor looked up at Jeffrey with a bewildered look on his face while Colonel Jeffrey pointed his pistol at Corporal Taylor's head and said, "Sorry about this corporal," as he pulled the trigger and shot Corporal Taylor between the eyes. Unbeknownst to everyone, Colonel Jeffrey was Mick Stonehill's cousin and the one who gave Sherman's entire plan to Mick.

After the yellow-bellied traitor Colonel Jeffrey shot Corporal Taylor, he jumped into the first wagon with Whiskers and they hurriedly raced eastward along the tracks. Mick stayed behind to manage the loading of the second wagon. At this point, Mick was not aware that Corporal Taylor had warned Marshal Bassett of the robbery. Mick thought he was home free.

However, Bassett was closing in along with three men who were newly acquainted and who had no skin in the game except that they were good courageous men and believed in right over wrong. They were: a trail boss on his last cattle drive (Jesse Caldwell), a retired Texas Ranger now a gunsmith (Scott Johnson), and a Civil War hero now a family man (Thomas O'Brien). They were the "Three" who could make the difference.

As the four peered around the back of the train on the stockyard side they could see the first wagon riding off. Two men were in the driver's seat. They noticed that one was a U.S. Army soldier wearing an officer's hat.

The second wagon had just backed into place and several outlaws began loading the gold into that wagon. Bassett shouted, "These guys aren't getting away!"

Bassett directed O'Brien and Johnson to run behind the stockyard and approach them from the front of the wagon. Bassett ran to the freight car on the town side of the train while Caldwell climbed on top of a cattle car to get a vantage point. The only shot fired so far was the one by Colonel Jeffrey so the better part of the town wasn't cued in yet on the robbery.

Then Mick looked out the side door of the freight car and saw the marshal running his way. Mick took several shots but missed. Then Caldwell, O'Brien and Johnson began firing their Henry rifles, one shot after another. Now several of the outlaws were firing back. Mayhem broke out on both sides of the tracks. Bullets were flying everywhere. Gun smoke filled the air. Townspeople were screaming and running for shelter. Mothers were picking up their kids off the street and running into buildings. Bullets were ricocheting off of the train cars and splintering the wood on the stockyard corrals while the Texas longhorns were panicking, pushing, and some even jumping over the corral fences and running down Main Street. The battle was fierce.

The other outlaws were no longer loading the gold but joined the gunfight instead. Tex, Frank and Jay jumped to the ground on the east side of the wagon using the wagon as cover and were shooting wildly at Caldwell, O'Brien and Johnson.

Mick Stonehill and Lance Carter were shooting at Bassett from the inside of the freight car and Danny and Johnny Reb were shooting at O'Brien and Johnson on the other side of the car. The four outlaws in the freight car were caught in a crossfire.

Then Caldwell, who was lying on top of a cattle car, got a clear shot at Tex who was kneeling on the ground next to the wagon, and drilled him with a direct hit to the neck. Tex died instantly.

When Tex fell to the ground, Frank stood up to shoot at Caldwell. That put Frank in a compromising position and Johnson, who was behind the fence on the backside of the stockyard, got a clear shot at Frank and hit him twice in the chest. Frank fell dead.

Jay began running east along the side of the train toward the engine. The engineer saw the outlaw running toward him and leaped off of the locomotive on the other side of the train. While Jay was running, both Caldwell and O'Brien got a clear shot at Jay and unloaded four slugs into Jay's back. Jay slammed forward to the ground.

There were still four outlaws in the freight car; Mick, Lance, Johnny Reb, and Danny.

Now, Bassett, Caldwell, O'Brien, and Johnson were all directing their shots toward the freight car. Johnny Reb was next to take a bullet to the gut and then Lance was shot through the heart.

Mick then shouted to Danny as bullets were whizzing by from both sides of the car, "There's no way out. I'm not dying in a dang railroad car. I'm giving up."

Danny said, "Me too."

So they both yelled out, "Stop shooting, stop shooting, we're throwing our guns out!" Then that's exactly what they did.

Marshal Bassett, who was hiding behind a water trough shouted, "Jump out of the car on this side and put your hands in the air." The outlaws followed the marshal's order. Then Bassett demanded "Lie on the ground with your faces down and put your hands behind your backs." So they did that too as the marshal, ever so carefully stepped toward them with his pistols drawn, and pointing toward Mick and Danny.

In the meantime, Caldwell, O'Brien, and Johnson came running between the cars of the train and saw the outlaws lying facedown in the dirt. Bassett was already handcuffing them. As

Mick and Danny stood up, Thomas O'Brien looked at Danny and said, "My word!"

Marshal Bassett asked, "You know this guy?"

"I'm afraid so," Thomas O'Brien conceded. "He's my brother, Danny O'Brien."

Danny O'Brien put his head down in shame and said nothing.

The marshal and Caldwell then went for the long walk escorting the two outlaws to the jailhouse while O'Brien and Johnson stayed with and guarded the gold until further instructions.

When Marshal Bassett and Caldwell reached the jailhouse and locked the two outlaws in separate cells, James Masterson walked in. The outlaws he was chasing from a saloon robbery made a clean getaway. "James, you will not believe what just happened while you were out galavantin around," the marshal said.

In the meantime, the telegraph operator came running into the jailhouse with a telegram from Secretary of Treasury John Sherman. The letter read:

Marshal Bassett

Inform me immediately of the outcome of the robbery. There were twenty-five boxes of gold bullion on that train in wood crates marked "Ranch Supplies". They must all be retrieved. What has happened to the soldiers and Colonel Jeffrey who is in charge of the mission?

Contact me immediately.

Secretary of Treasury John Sherman

Before sending a message back to Sherman, Bassett took Danny O'Brien aside to interrogate him.

"Look Danny, I'll see what I can do for you if you give us the information we want to know." Danny squealed like a stuck pig.

He laid out everything: Mick was the leader of the gang, there were seven outlaws plus Mick, they killed nine soldiers outside of town, and Colonel Jeffrey was Mick's cousin and the turncoat who gave the outlaws Sherman's whole plan. He also said that Whiskers and the colonel got away with thirteen boxes of gold and they were heading north to Wyoming. Danny O'Brien sang like a songbird and spilled his guts to the marshal hoping somehow that he would be granted some leniency.

The first thing that came out of Bassett's mouth was, "Dang, this will give Horace Greeley another reason to call us "Bloody Kansas."

Bassett then sent a message back to Sherman.

Secretary Sherman,

Two outlaws escaped with thirteen boxes of gold. We captured two and killed five. One of the bandits who got away was your own Colonel Jeffrey who gave the plans to the outlaws. Three men in town helped me to kill and capture the outlaws and save part of your gold shipment. They are Jesse Caldwell, Thomas O'Brien, and Scott Johnson. They should be commended for their courageous duty to their country.

Waiting for instructions from you.

Marshal Charlie Bassett

When Sherman received this message, he was horrified that all of the soldiers had been killed and devastated that Colonel Jeffrey was a no-good turncoat and outlaw. He thought about it awhile and then sent another urgent message back to the marshal.

Marshal Bassett,

You must retrieve the remaining gold at all cost. I want Colonel Jeffrey taken alive if possible. Deputize the three courageous men you talked about and send them after Jeffrey and the gold. You and your assistant marshal must guard the remaining gold.

When the three men recover the gold, we will then make arrangements to ship all the gold together on a special train to the Philadelphia Mint. Once again, keep me informed every step of the way.

Secretary of Treasury John Sherman

Sherman now had the unpleasant task of informing President Hayes of the catastrophic occurrence in Dodge City. President Hayes reminded Sherman that he questioned the discretion of the group to send the train to Dodge City although with an insider being an outlaw too, the holdup could have happened anywhere along the train route.

Sherman also informed the President of his recommendation to deputize the three men who helped Marshal Bassett.

"Can they be trusted?" President Hayes asked.

"I hope so," Sherman said with uncertainty in his voice.

In the meantime, Bassett had James Masterson gather some trusted townspeople to load the remaining gold and bring it to the jailhouse to be locked into a cell for safekeeping.

He then had the telegraph man ask Caldwell, O'Brien and Johnson to come back to the jailhouse for an important message. Caldwell and O'Brien had gone back to their hotel rooms while Johnson went back to the gunsmith shop. All three were drained from the stressful shootout.

After the message was delivered, all three men arrived at the jailhouse within minutes of each other. O'Brien's wife was obviously shaken from the event and now could not imagine why her husband was being summoned back to the jailhouse.

Bassett read the back and forth communications between himself and Secretary Sherman and pleaded with the courageous three to allow themselves to be deputized and go after the gold and the outlaws.

"My wife is not going to be happy with my decision but I deem it an honor to do this for my country and my President," O'Brien said with pride.

"I'm in," Caldwell added.

"You can count me in too," Johnson said. "I haven't had this kind of excitement since us Texas Rangers captured John Wesley Hardin in Florida."

Bassett then hired and officially deputized all three men and handed out extra ammo. They all carried a Henry rifle in addition to their revolvers.

O'Brien went back to his wife and children and told them what he had signed up to do. Elizabeth was visibly upset and angered that Thomas would do this without confiding in her first. She would eventually learn that Thomas' adventurous spirit trumped their family life and unfortunately, he would break his wife's heart more than once over the next several years.

The marshal had three horses saddled in thirty minutes with saddlebags stocked with food and full canteens.

The marshal said his goodbyes and the three courageous men rode eastward out of town riding into the wind at a full gallop. They followed the wagon wheel grooves in the dirt which ran parallel to the railroad tracks.

The outlaws had about a ninety minute head start but did not have extra horses. Since the wagon was loaded down with the weight of the gold bullion, their wheel tracks would be easy to follow.

About one mile out of town they discovered where the ramp was built by the outlaws to cross the tracks. Their trail seemed to head northwest. Jeffrey did not want to wait by the tracks for the second wagon so they rode up the road a piece.

After about two hours, Whiskers and Colonel Jeffrey thought they were home free. They had no idea of the outcome back in Dodge City and were not aware of the fate of the rest of their gang.

At about 5:00 p.m. Jeffrey told Whiskers that they needed to stop and rest the horses and wait for the remainder of the gang and the second wagon of gold. So they pulled up by a stream in a small valley. Little did they know that Caldwell, O'Brien and Johnson were right on their tails. While Jeffrey and Whiskers were watering the horses in the valley, the three deputies rode to the top of a hill and looked down into the valley and spotted the two outlaws. They wasted no time and rode hard and fast with a wide open gallop down the hill.

Whiskers saw the three charging at breakneck speed right at them and knew something had gone terribly wrong. He drew his pistols and shot several times but the three were out of pistol range. Jeffrey took cover behind the wagon but for some reason made a decision not to shoot. As Whiskers ran to the wagon for cover, Johnson came charging with his rifle aimed at Whiskers, and shot him dead on the spot.

Jeffrey threw his gun on the ground and put his hands up high in the air and surrendered as the three circled him on horseback while pointing their rifles directly at his head.

"It's all over you coward," Scott Johnson said. Johnson tied his horse to the back of the wagon after they hog-tied the colonel and threw him in back of the buckboard with the gold. They also threw Whiskers' dead body back there with Colonel Jeffrey, as well.

It was already dark when they finally arrived back in Dodge City. Nevertheless they were soon surrounded by onlookers and several people yelled at the top of their lungs, "They're back, they're back!"

O'Brien's wife heard the shouting and looked out the hotel window with relief as she saw her husband dismounting his horse. She knew it was all over and he was safe. That was the most important thing. O'Brien looked up and saw Elizabeth with her head out the window and he waved to her.

Most of the townspeople by now knew what happened. They had heard the barrage of gunfire earlier in the day and then later watched the train passengers, who were forced to exit the train a mile west of town, begin arriving in town. It was a long walk for those poor souls.

The marshal threw Colonel Jeffrey into the cell and had the undertaker come get Whiskers' body to be buried in Boot Hill with the rest of the criminals. There would be no burial ceremonies for those killers. Additional Army troops were sent in from the nearest fort to collect the dead bodies of the soldiers west of town and the three corporals who Colonel Jeffrey killed in and outside the freight car.

Many of the townspeople helped unload the gold from the wagon and stow it in the jail cell with the other gold.

It was too late to send a telegram to Secretary Sherman so Bassett decided to wait until the next morning. Caldwell and Johnson talked O'Brien into going over to the saloon for a drink even though Elizabeth was waiting with their children to greet O'Brien. The three had four drinks together and then staggered home in the dark of the night.

Their job was complete and now they could go back to their normal life, or could they?

The next morning Bassett sent a telegram to Secretary Sherman and told him that the gold was secured, and Colonel Jeffrey and two other outlaws were in jail. They were Danny O'Brien and Mick Stonehill. Bassett gave the total credit to Caldwell, O'Brien and Johnson.

Then a telegram came over the wire, which surprised the three heroes along with Bassett and Masterson. When Bassett received it, he immediately summoned Caldwell, O'Brien and Johnson. It read:

Jesse Caldwell, Thomas O'Brien and Scott Johnson,

Thank you for your brave service to your country. You are truly heroes. I now have another job for you and pray that you will accept it with open arms. We are sending a special train with one freight car and a passenger car to pick up the gold bullion and transport it to the mint in Philadelphia.

We are requesting your assistance to board this train and see it to its final destination. You will be paid handsomely for this duty in the amount of $10,000 per person.

The train will arrive the day after tomorrow.

After you reach your destination, I ask that you attend a meeting with me in my office regarding a future project. I promise that you will be well compensated.

> Sincerely,
> Rutherford B. Hayes
> President of the United States of America

All three were extremely excited to receive a personal telegram from the President of the United States. They talked amongst themselves and immediately accepted the job by replying to the President's telegram.

However, they all had loose ends to take care of before the train arrived for the trip to Philadelphia.

Caldwell had to load his cattle onto a train to Chicago and then pay off his drovers.

Johnson had to inform ole Pops that he was leaving and may not be back to buy the business.

And of course, O'Brien had his wife and children to talk to. Thomas convinced his wife to take a train back to Kentucky the next day with their children. He told her about the assignment he received from the President and about the money he had already earned and would earn in the future.

"Don't you see dear, in a year or two, we'll have enough money to buy our own ranch back home in Kentucky. We'll grow tobacco, hemp and even raise some cattle."

Although everything seemed to be happening so fast, Elizabeth started feeling good that their future would be more secure and that they were going back home to the bluegrass state. When the O'Briens arrived at the train station the next morning, Elizabeth asked Thomas, "When will you join us in Kentucky?"

"I can't answer that but I'm sure it will be soon," Thomas said as he gave Elizabeth and his children a big hug as they boarded their train.

Caldwell's cattle were loaded on the original train that was still located in town but passengers were not, because the passenger cars were not fit to be used as a result of the killings.

The new train arrived three days later to take the gold to Philadelphia.

As Johnson was leaving the hotel to board the train, Janice was waiting for him at the door and gave Scott a big hug and kiss. "When will I see you again, Scott?"

"I don't know Janice, but I will promise you this, I'll write you every chance I get," Scott said. "Please do," Janice insisted. They shared hugs and kisses one more time and Johnson was off to board the train with Caldwell and O'Brien.

There was no trouble along the way and the gold bullion arrived safely to the Philadelphia Mint without any further incidents.

Caldwell, O'Brien, and Johnson then caught the next train to Washington, D.C. where they had a scheduled meeting with President Hayes. Dressed in the best duds they had, they entered the White House as nervous as three cottontails being chased by a pack of coyotes with canine teeth the size of rusty railroad spikes.

The President asked them to sit down and he offered them a Cuban cigar. Hayes lit one up for himself as well.

"Gentlemen, it is indeed a pleasure to meet you," Hayes said. "I want to personally thank you for your heroic service to our country. You have successfully completed *Operation Last Spike* for us. As I stated in my telegram to you a week ago, I have another important job for you and I am hoping you see fit to see it through. It's a tough job so I need men who are smart, courageous and able to handle a gun with the best of them. You men fit that bill perfectly. Are you interested?"

They didn't have to think twice. All three said, "Yes sir" at the same time.

"Well good then," President Hayes said as he puffed on his cigar. "I'll consider you hired. In fact, from here on out, to me you'll be known as the

THREE FOR HIRE.

I still don't know why Sherman insisted we stop that dang blang train in Dodge City," President Hayes said underneath his breath as he leaned back in his leather chair puffing on his Cuban cigar.

THE END

Epilogue

Mick Stonehill was convicted and found guilty of murder on thirteen counts and found guilty of conspiracy to steal government property. He was sentenced to be hung on July 10, 1880.

Mick Stonehill's cousin was court marshaled and found guilty of murder on thirteen counts and guilty of conspiracy to steal government property. He was sentenced to death by a firing squad and was to be executed on June 3, 1880.

Danny O'Brien was found guilty of murder on one count and found guilty of conspiracy to steal government property. Because of his willingness to supply information to the Government, he received 20 years in prison with eligibility for parole in 10 years.

Before Mick Stonehill would be executed by hanging, he hinted to Danny O'Brien one day in the prison yard that he and his cousin belonged to a secret society. However, at the time, Danny thought nothing of it.

Watch for the Next Episode:

Three for Hire

THE SHADOW ASSASSINS

Bibliography

Rutherford B. Hayes and his Cabinet
http://en.wikipedia.org/w/index.php?title=Rutherford_B._Hayes
&oldid=527646985

Jesse James
http://en.wikipedia.org/w/index.php?title=Jesse_James&oldid=52
6010745

Wild Bill Hickok
http://en.wikipedia.org/w/index.php?title=Wild_Bill_Hickok&old
id=527412575

Butch Cassidy
http://en.wikipedia.org/w/index.php?title=Butch_Cassidy&oldid
=531201877

Bloody Bill Anderson
http://en.wikipedia.org/w/index.php?title=William_T._Anderson
&oldid=527392646

Wyatt Earp
http://en.wikipedia.org/w/index.php?title=Wyatt_Earp&oldid=52
7379061

James Earp
http://en.wikipedia.org/w/index.php?title=James_Earp&oldid=52
6831248

Bat Masterson
http://en.wikipedia.org/w/index.php?title=Bat_Masterson&oldid
=527966639

James Masterson
http://en.wikipedia.org/w/index.php?title=James_Masterson&oldi
d=520074932

Ed Masterson
http://en.wikipedia.org/w/index.php?title=Ed_Masterson&oldid=525715251

Sam Houston
http://en.wikipedia.org/w/index.php?title=Sam_Houston&oldid=528026136

Joseph McCoy
http://en.wikipedia.org/w/index.php?title=Joseph_McCoy&oldid=523492564

John Sherman
http://en.wikipedia.org/w/index.php?title=John_Sherman&oldid=523023526

John B. Armstrong
http://en.wikipedia.org/w/index.php?title=Special:Cite&page=John_Barclay_Armstrong&id=510466031

Leland Stanford
http://en.wikipedia.org/w/index.php?title=Leland_Stanford&oldid=527905684

John Wesley Hardin
http://en.wikipedia.org/w/index.php?title=John_Wesley_Hardin&oldid=523336127

Nathan Meeker
http://en.wikipedia.org/w/index.php?title=Nathan_Meeker&oldid=523497716

John B. Stetson
http://en.wikipedia.org/w/index.php?title=John_Batterson_Stetson&oldid=524908428

Major General Edward Canby
http://en.wikipedia.org/w/index.php?title=Edward_Canby&oldid=523790901

White River War
http://en.wikipedia.org/w/index.php?title=White_River_War&old
id=522726758

Battle of the Little Bighorn
http://en.wikipedia.org/w/index.php?title=Battle_of_the_Little_B
ighorn&oldid=527879674

Centennial Exposition of 1876
http://en.wikipedia.org/w/index.php?title=Centennial_Exposition
&oldid=524217279

San Francisco Mint
http://en.wikipedia.org/w/index.php?title=San_Francisco_Mint&
oldid=519585694

Philadelphia Mint
http://en.wikipedia.org/w/index.php?title=Philadelphia_Mint&ol
did=526252075

Smith & Wesson Model 3
http://en.wikipedia.org/w/index.php?title=Smith_%26_Wesson_
Model_3&oldid=526621044

Texas Ranger Division
http://en.wikipedia.org/w/index.php?title=Texas_Ranger_Divisio
n&oldid=526653498

Jayhawker
http://en.wikipedia.org/w/index.php?title=Jayhawker&oldid=527
836143

Battle of the Alamo
http://en.wikipedia.org/w/index.php?title=Battle_of_the_Alamo
&oldid=528107081

Little Dixie (Missouri)
http://en.wikipedia.org/w/index.php?title=Little_Dixie_(Missouri
)&oldid=502158959

Great Western Trail
http://en.wikipedia.org/w/index.php?title=Great_Western_Cattle
_Trail&oldid=527224900

Shawnee Trail
http://en.wikipedia.org/w/index.php?title=Texas_Road&oldid=5
10886215

Dodge City, Kansas
http://en.wikipedia.org/w/index.php?title=Dodge_City,_Kansas&
oldid=527741790

Santa Fe Trail
http://en.wikipedia.org/w/index.php?title=Santa_Fe_Trail&oldid
=526909929

Sod House
http://en.wikipedia.org/w/index.php?title=Sod_house&oldid=52
3204549

Palace Hotel, San Francisco
http://en.wikipedia.org/w/index.php?title=Palace_Hotel,_San_Fr
ancisco&oldid=523674775

Conquistador
http://en.wikipedia.org/w/index.php?title=Special:Cite&page=Co
nquistador&id=527428817

Battle of Shiloh
http://en.wikipedia.org/w/index.php?title=Battle_of_Shiloh&oldi
d=527863462

Derby hat
http://en.wikipedia.org/w/index.php?title=Bowler_hat&oldid=52
7317106

Boss of the Plains hat
http://en.wikipedia.org/w/index.php?title=Boss_of_the_Plains&o
ldid=527551858

The Yellow Rose of Texas (song)
http://en.wikipedia.org/w/index.php?title=The_Yellow_Rose_of_
Texas_(song)&oldid=520954167

Transcontinental railroad
http://en.wikipedia.org/w/index.php?title=Transcontinental_railr
oad&oldid=525580664

Hemp
http://en.wikipedia.org/w/index.php?title=Hemp&oldid=527982
191

Smith & Wesson Co.
http://en.wikipedia.org/w/index.php?title=Smith_%26_Wesson&
oldid=527016127

Dixie Land (song)
http://en.wikipedia.org/w/index.php?title=Dixie_(song)&oldid=5
26621905

Aura Lee (song)
http://en.wikipedia.org/w/index.php?title=Aura_Lea&oldid=522
603441

When Johnny Comes Marching Home (song)
http://en.wikipedia.org/w/index.php?title=When_Johnny_Comes
_Marching_Home&oldid=525970663

Gasconade Bridge train disaster
http://en.wikipedia.org/w/index.php?title=Gasconade_Bridge_tra
in_disaster&oldid=451100906

Eads Bridge
http://en.wikipedia.org/w/index.php?title=Eads_Bridge&oldid=5
28072183

Showboat
http://en.wikipedia.org/w/index.php?title=Showboat&oldid=514
232724

CPSIA information can be obtained
at www.ICGtesting.com
Printed in the USA
LVOW03s0922210717
542097LV00003B/6/P